STICK PLAY

CATHRYN FOX

COPYRIGHT

Stick Play
Copyright 2024 by Cathryn Fox
Published by Cathryn Fox

ISBN Ebook: 978-1-998943-71-5

ISBN Print: 978-1-998943-72-2

GINA

NHL Summer Break:

I stare at the big man crouched on the floor before me. A man the puck bunnies called Ash-hole—a playful combination of his name, Ash, and alpha-hole. His fellow hockey players, however, call him Mountain because of his size and the fact that he comes from Colorado. But as I stare at him, only one word comes to mind.

"Hot."

"What?" He lifts his head, and the second his astute, almost translucent blue eyes meet mine, I realize my mistake.

Oh God, did I say that out loud?

Acting quickly to cover my blunder, I wave my hand in front of my face. "It's so hot in here." Fortunately, it's not just my commercial fridge that's on the fritz today. My air conditioning decided to go on hiatus during Boston's worst heat wave as well, forcing me to close the café for the day and call in help. Really, it was my friends Dani and Conner who called their friend Ash Wheeler in to help, and can I really consider a broken air conditioner fortunate? Then again, when it helps cover the fact that I'd been staring at and drooling at the world's hottest hockey player, I guess I can.

Truthfully though, I really need to stop blurting things out—which I only ever seem to do around Ash—and I also really need to stop staring at the hot hunk of man on his knees before me, his mouth right freaking there. If I moved my hips just an inch...

Cut it out, girl!

He turns his attention back to the fridge, and once he gets it working again, I'm sure I'm going to have to climb inside to cool myself down. "I can look at your air conditioning for you too, if you'd like."

The deep tenor of his voice trickles down the length of my body, strumming certain parts like a fine-tuned instrument. "I don't want to ask too much of you."

If I *did* want to ask too much of him, I wouldn't waste his talents on my air conditioner. No, I'd ask him to take off his shirt, so I could admire his upper torso as he works. Eventually, probably, definitely most likely, I'd also ask him to take off the rest of his clothes too, so I can climb over his body and...*tell him what tool you need.*

My lord, what is happening to me?

Actually, I think I know. After Ash arrived with his toolbox, my friends Dani and Conner packed up my daughter Zoe for a fun sleepover at their place, but just before they left, Dani whispered those very playful and naughty words in my ear.

Tell him what tool you need.

Gawd.

"Gina?"

"Yeah."

"Screw." He holds his hand out and I stare at it for a moment. I suck in a breath as my mind goes in a direction I really shouldn't allow it to go, regardless of how much my body likes the visuals involved.

"I need to put the panel back in place," he explains, his words breaking the strange spell he seems to have over me.

"Screw. Right." I hold my hand out to present the screw in my palm. Judging by the indentation in my flesh, I must have been squeezing it hard.

Don't think about hard.

Dammit, I'm thinking about hard...

"Are you okay?" Intense blue eyes narrow in on me. "You seem out of sorts."

I wave my hand again. "The heat is really getting to me."

"Maybe you should go take a cold shower."

"That's probably a good idea."

He picks up the screw from my palm and the rough pads of his fingers scrape over my soft flesh. I try not to react, I really do. The last thing I want is for this man to know what his presence, his touch does to my body.

I pull my hand back quickly, and shove it behind my back. He eyes me for another second before turning his attention back to the panel and I'm grateful for the reprieve. Honestly, I know what my problem is. I haven't been with a man in five long years. Sad, I know.

But I can't be ogling this man like the bunnies who hang around after a game, wanting a piece of him. It's wrong. He's a professional hockey player, not some boy toy here in my café for my personal pleasure. Unfortunately.

No. No. No. Not *unfortunately*.

I'm not interested in anything from Ash and he's here helping me out because his buddy Conner asked him to. Ash is a good guy like that, always there for his friends when they need him. I'm not really his friend, I'm a friend of a friend, and while I don't know what that makes me to him, I seriously appreciate him helping.

A niggling bit of guilt crawls into my stomach. Ash is supposed to be on his way to Noah's resort in Sparrow Springs. It's Noah's turn with the cup and he's planned a big celebration with friends and family. My heart tightens with joy as I recall my luck in meeting Melanie and Brady on the beach last summer. It was the beginning of a great friendship, when I had no friends at all after moving here from California. I love the closeness between the guys and the WAGs. I'm a little bit of an outsider with the WAGs. Not that they ever make me feel that way. It's simply that I'm not dating or married to one of the players.

"Ash," I begin, about to tell him to leave it, that he should head to the resort.

"Yeah?" He jumps up to his full height and tears off his T-shirt. He exposes his very big, muscular body as he waits for a response, and I try very hard not to swallow my tongue as I stare at the delicious lumber-snack before me. He shakes his head as he glances around the empty café. "Oh, wait is this not okay?" he asks, obviously misunderstanding my stupefied reaction.

Sure, I'm taken aback, and I'm probably turning a thousand shades of red, but it's not because he shouldn't be shirtless in my café. He should be. Oh yes, he really, really should be. "With the café closed, I thought it'd be okay to take this off." He wipes his brow with his forearm. "It must be a hundred degrees in this kitchen."

No shoes. No shirt. No service.

Dammit, I really want to service this guy.

Oh Lord.

"I..." Why are words so hard today?

He holds up his damp shirt. "I'm sorry. I wasn't thinking." He makes a move to tug it back on, and I snatch it from him.

"No," I answer quickly, probably too quickly because now it looks like I want him shirtless, and of course I do. Why wouldn't I? It's only like my secret fantasy come true. "I...it's not that. It's just...you should go to the party. This is taking longer than it should and I don't want to keep you from celebrating with friends."

He shrugs. "We all get a turn with the cup. I'll have it soon enough." Once again, I try to form a coherent sentence. He pauses, a haunted look passing over his face. "I'll leave if you want me to."

"No," I say again, once again too quickly, especially when my stupid, traitorous eyes are leisurely strolling down his rock-hard body.

Don't go there, Gina.

But there's a small part of me that's asking why I shouldn't go there, and that small part might just be centered between my legs. It's telling me it's been ages since I've been touched, and if I know what I'm getting into with Ash, why shouldn't I have a good time for once in my life? It's not like I want a commitment, and with his revolving door, not to mention his no commitment attitude, he's clearly living his best life with the bunnies.

What could possibly go wrong?

Unlike my ex, a well-known psychiatric doctor who turned out to be something he wasn't, I know exactly who Ash is, and what to expect from him. A hot, hard time between the sheets, and an adios afterward. His muscles flex as he puts his tools back in the box, and I can't help but think...

Maybe he could put his tool in my box.

Ohmigod, what is happening to me?

Ash...Ash Wheeler...

That is what's happening to me.

You know what else is happening? My brain and body are telling me that an Ash-hole is exactly what I need in my life today. As a former nurse, and now single mom, who owns her own café, I go from morning to night doing everything for others.

Why can't I hand my body over to Ash, let him take control of me. Allowing him to remove all decisions from my brain as he takes what he wants. As he uses and abuses my body in the most delicious ways? Sure, as an Ash-hole, he might be out to take what he wants, but there's no denying I'm going to get something out of it too.

A buzzing sound reaches my ear, and he pulls the refrigerator doors open and puts his big hand inside. "Starting to cool already."

"Thank you so much. How much do I owe you?"

He closes the door, and when his intense gaze lands on me again, a burst of heat arcs between us. "You don't owe me anything." He glances around and clears his throat. "Where's your air conditioner?" I'm about to protest, but he moves around me, his arm brushing mine as he steps into the dining area. My body quivers, begging me to seduce him. I'm just not sure how to go about it. "A wall-mounted unit," he mutters under his breath. "I can fix that."

"You're a man of many talents." He turns my way. Is that a smirk on his face? Is he taking what I said the wrong way...or maybe it's the right way. Damn, I'm really out of practice with this seduction stuff. His gaze drops and that's when I realize I'm toying with the top button on my shirt, exposing a bit of cleavage as I open and close it.

He clears his throat again and turns from me. "Why don't you go cool off in the shower?" With a curt nod, he gestures to the stairs that lead to my upstairs apartment, abruptly dismissing me. "I'll get this fixed for you and lock up on my way out."

"Oh, okay." Jeez, here I just set my mind on seducing this man, and he's making it clear that he's here to fix my appliance and a fast hook-up isn't on the table.

Sex on the table...ooh.

I redo my top button, and with my proverbial tail between my legs, I dart upstairs. I go straight to my shower, needing something to cool my body down. I glance at myself in the mirror and see a streak of grease on my face. Oh, that's attractive.

I strip and climb into the cool spray. I guess at the end of the day, not having sex with Ash is for the best. In my desperation to be touched I must have been imagining the sexual tension between us.

Honestly, he's an ash-hole and I'm an asshole magnet. I guess I thought one little hook-up couldn't hurt. It's not like anything would develop. Not only do I know better than to fall for a guy like Ash, one who is admired by every woman on the planet and makes those women feel special—much like my ex—I have a daughter to consider. I don't bring men in and out of her life. Besides, Ash is terrified of her. That brings a laugh to my throat. How can a big guy like Ash be so afraid of a little girl?

I stay under the spray until I'm cool, and then climb out and wrap myself in a big fluffy towel. I work on knotting it as I open the bathroom door, and come face to face, or rather face to chest with the man I've been fantasizing about for far too long. My fingers lose all ability to work and my towel drops to the floor.

A loud, tortured groan crawls out of Ash's throat. "Jesus, Gina." I'm about to grab the towel. This man made it clear he doesn't want me, right? But then he takes a step toward me, and just like my air conditioning, my brain goes on hiatus. "You're so fucking beautiful."

His warm scent curls around me and my body reacts. "Ash..." He stares at me with hungry blue eyes and I go up on my toes, my lips parting as I put my hand on his chest. He hesitates for a second as his muscles tighten under my palm and just when I think I've read him wrong again, he puts a hand around my back and roughly tugs me to him.

A little gasp of pleasure catches in my throat as he lowers his head and claims my mouth like a hungry man on a mission to devour everything before him.

Yes, please.

He picks me up and I put my legs around him, kissing him deeply as he heads down the hall. I'm about to tell him the bedroom is the other way, but can't bear to tear my mouth from his as his tongue explores and tastes the depths of me. God, I want his tongue in so many other places.

He breaks the kiss for a brief second when he reaches the end of the hall, his gaze going to my kitchen. "Hurry," I whisper, my voice full of need and desperation.

He gives a curt nod, his steps hurried, determined as he walks into my kitchen, and glances at my table.

Table...yes.

My God, I must have done something right in a past life because everything I secretly wanted is happening. Go me.

With the utmost gentleness, which takes me by surprise, he sets me on the hard wooden tabletop, and grips my legs and widens them. He unzips his pants and as I offer myself up to him, I prepare for him to pull his hard cock out and thrust into me, but what he does instead surprises the hell out of me.

"This," he growls and reaches between my legs to lightly stroke my sex, the rough pad of his thumb doing delicious things to my clit. His eyes briefly close. "I've wanted this—you—for so damn long."

What the heck?

Okay, so I guess I wasn't imagining the tension between us.

He wets his bottom lip and I nearly orgasm.

"Babe, I've been dying to taste you."

I grip his head and widen my legs even more. "I've been dying for that too," I admit shamelessly, which is so unlike me, and it pulls another groan from his mouth.

He sinks to his knees, wetting both of his lips this time as he goes, and now it's my turn to moan. His big fingers bite into my thighs, and I actually hope they leave tiny love bruises so I can relive this hook-up tomorrow, next week, well into the new year. Truthfully, this isn't like me, and I can't say for sure what it is about him that brings out a different side of me.

His warm breath falls over my sex and a hard quiver goes through me. I grip the table and hang on for what I know is going to be the ride of my life. That first sweet touch of his tongue to my clit sends me skyrocketing to the moon, and I begin to breathe harder. God, why does that feel so good? I know it's been a long time, but come on, it's never felt quite this intense before.

His deft tongue slides over my sex, and I grow wetter, wanting more...wanting everything he has to offer—tonight. Just tonight. I close my eyes as he eats at me, takes charge of my pleasure, giving me nothing more to think about than how sexy and delicious this is. But the second he inserts a big thick finger, my eyes spring open.

Oh God, no. I'm going to come. It's too fast, too soon. I grip his hair, run my fingers through it, and work to hang on. My body, however, has other ideas and as he pushes in deep, delicately rubbing the bundle of nerves inside me as his mouth devours my clit. I let go and ripple around his finger. I bite my bottom lip and pray he doesn't register my climax. My desperation is nothing short of embarrassing.

His finger slows inside me and it's then I realize he knows. I wait for him to say something, call me out but he doesn't. He displays thoughtfulness, sensitivity and simply keeps his finger inside me, allowing me to ride out each glorious pulse. As tremors run through my body, a weird little wave of gratitude curls around my heart.

When my body finally stops spasming, he stands, and there's a new kind of intensity about him that arouses me all over again. Like a man desperate to be touched, he takes my hand, and puts it on his chest, and I hold it there, loving the feel of his strong heartbeat beneath my palm.

"I'm going to fuck you now, Gina." He pulls out a condom, and as he tugs his pants to his knees, his eyes lock with mine, checking in with me. That thoughtfulness, sensitivity, once again does something weirdly delightful to my insides. "Tell me you want that."

"I want that."

He bites into the foil and quickly sheathes himself. "Even though it's not a good idea?" he asks.

He's right. It's not. At least I know why it's not a good idea for me. Why it's not a good idea for him, I'm not sure. Not that I can consider it right now. Not when he's pressing his crown against my opening and gripping my hips for leverage.

"Ash..."

"Still want it."

"Tonight, Ash. Us. Just tonight."

He gives a tight nod, understanding and agreeing with what I'm saying. I move my body and he pushes into me, filling me with his thick cock, and when his crown hits my cervix, my hard tremble practically moves the table across the floor. He stills for a moment, giving me time to get used to the fullness and when I put my arms around him, he tugs me to the edge of the table and begins to properly fuck me. I can only assume it's properly, as it's never felt this incredible before. Was I even having sex before Ash?

I hold on for dear life as he slicks in and out of me. His mouth finds mine, and he kisses me hard. I kiss him back with a hunger I've never before experienced. He growls deeply as I slide my hands down to cup his ass, and when he in turn slides a hand between our bodies to toy with my clit, I gasp for breath and burst around him.

"Jesus," he growls, staying deep inside to give my sex something to clench around. I claw at his back as I concentrate on the points of pleasure and when I can breathe again, he presses his forehead to mine and whispers, "You good, babe?"

"Yes."

He pulls out, only to power in again, and I hold him tight as he chases his own orgasm. I love how uninhibited he is, grunting and growling as he takes what he needs. Giving him full access to my body, I move with him, wanting his orgasm to be as powerful as mine.

"So good," I murmur and my words must do something to him. He powers in once, twice, and then grabs my hips to hold on as he depletes himself inside me. "Ash." I cry out his name as my body absorbs his hard pulses. He puts his head on my shoulder, his breath hot on my neck as he curses quietly. I can't help but smile, loving that he seems to be as wrecked by this as me.

Ash backs up, removes the condom and pulls his pants up. "Stay put," he commands, and walks back down the hall, his muscular body and tight backside holding all my attention. I take a few deep breaths, never having been so sated in my entire life. He comes back with a damp cloth and the second he steps between my legs to wash me, one word comes to mind.

Ash-hole.

Honestly, he knew what he wanted and took it, but he didn't cross into alpha-hole territory at all, doing what he wanted without regard as to how his actions affected me. I mean yes, he took charge of my body, which I loved, but he also cherished me with his mouth, his fingers, his cock. He cared about my pleasure, and every fiber in my body reveled in that —maybe a little too much. Maybe Ash Wheeler isn't an alpha-hole at all—maybe he's a guy a girl like me could actually fall for.

Then again, I've been wrong before.

2

ASH

February, All Star Weekend.

"To think you could have flown to the Caribbean with your friends on a private plane yesterday and missed last night's snowstorm," Dad grunts out with a laugh as he steps outside to help me clear his driveway.

I shrug, slide my shovel across the path, and toss the heavy wet snow over my shoulder. "I don't like the heat."

I glance at him as he pulls on his gloves. "That's news to me." His breath turns to fog in the cool morning air. "When you were a kid, all you wanted to do was go to the community pool."

"That's because I don't like the heat and wanted to cool off."

"If you say so."

Clearly, he doesn't believe me and why would he? I loved playing outdoors shirtless in the summer. Swimming, biking, running under the sprinklers. In fact, I like being shirtless most of the time. But it's really only acceptable in summer.

"I do say so." He grunts again, and as I wipe my face with my gloved hand, he reaches for a shovel. I put my hand on his to stop him. "Don't. I got this. It's almost done."

His gaze jumps to mine. "You think your old man can't shovel his own walkway?" Mumbling curses under his breath, he cocks his head and I avert my gaze because the man can read me like an open book. "Is that why you stayed home, so you could keep an eye on me?" he challenges.

Partly.

I don't tell him that, though. He's a proud man, and after his heart attack two years ago, I was finally able to convince him to come live in Boston near me. I've been worried about him. He assures me the stent they put in has made him feel twenty years younger, but he's the only family I have, and I'm not taking any chances. At least I convinced him he didn't have to work anymore. I have enough money for the both of us, but he does take odd jobs just to keep busy.

"No, Dad. I know you can do your own driveway. I'm home because I don't like the heat."

"That's the third time you told me that and now I'm wondering who it is you're trying to convince." I scoop more snow, scraping my shovel along the cement to clear it all. I don't want to leave any traces behind. I'm not sure I trust the local meteorologist, but the temperature is supposed to drop tonight, and I don't want Dad slipping on ice when he goes out for his daily walk. Not even the frigid weather can keep him inside, and honestly, I'm happy that he's exercising and eating better.

"I don't need to convince anyone of anything." Jesus, I sound grumpy.

Dad waves to his neighbor as he drives down the street. "You realize you've been in a slump now for about six months."

"Been playing my ass off, and I'm just tired. You know what the NHL season is like?"

He throws his arms up in the air. "All the more reason you should have gone to the Caribbean with your friends."

Exasperated with the way he's pushing my buttons, I drive the shovel into the snow, and lean against the handle. "What's really on your mind, Dad?" I huff out.

He adjusts his wool hat and shrugs. "Just saying, lots of pretty girls on the beach."

"You know I'm not into that."

A smirk plays at the corner of his mouth. "Oh, is there something else you want to tell me?" He puts a gloved hand on my shoulder. "I love you for who you are, son and—"

I shake my head. I love my father with every fiber of my being. He's a hard-working handyman, who taught me everything he knows. After Mom left us both, he worked day and night to pay for my hockey, but today, he's pressing, trying to get me to admit something...

I know what that something is.

"I need to keep a low profile." I soften my voice. I'm not mad at him. "You know that. We've talked about it." Christ, after my ex-girlfriend, a well-known influencer—correction, she only became *well-known* after she threw me under the bus—went on social media and accused me of horrible things, like drinking and driving and banging numerous bunnies at the same time, she went viral and I... Well, as the world sympathized with her, I was hauled into Coach Sanders' office and torn a new one.

Clean up your act, Ash. We don't need this negative publicity.

He wanted to get me a publicist. I thought that would only draw more attention to a situation that was nothing but lies and embarrassing enough. I assured my teammates it wasn't true, and they believed me, never bringing it up again. But now I have to keep my head down, my stick on the ice, my focus on hockey. There's no room for bunnies, drama, or accusations.

Is there room for Gina?

Gina Martin.

I'd fought so damn hard to ignore her over the last couple of years, but when I went to help with her fridge last summer and she had that adorable smudge of grease on her face, it was all I could do not to tear her clothes off and take her right in her café. Then when she came out of the bathroom in nothing but a towel, not even Portland's strong defense team could have kept me away.

Afterward, she ignored me.

Completely and utterly pretending I didn't exist.

Like we didn't have the best sex of my life on her dining room table.

Even at group events, she acted like nothing happened—like she didn't come apart with my fingers, my mouth...my cock.

My dick twitches at the memories.

"You're a man in your prime, Ash." Dad's voice pulls me back and I start shoveling again. "You should be in the Caribbean having fun."

"I don't want to have fun." The truth is, I never was much into the bunnies, even though everyone thinks the opposite. I'm kind of a one-woman man, and that one woman I currently can't stop thinking about is a mother of a small girl, and she wants nothing more to do with me—and the fact that she has a small girl should be enough for me to run the other way.

Having grown up with no mother of my own, with zero female influences in my life, what do I know about girls? If she had a boy, I could at least take him to the rink, teach him to play hockey, but when it comes to sugar and spice, I'd just fuck that up.

What am I even saying?

I'm not going down that winding road with her or anyone. I need to stay on the straight and narrow, head in the game.

"Well, I'm not getting any younger, you know. Maybe you would have found a nice girl in the Caribbean. Someday I'd like grandkids. That would give me something to do with my day." He snorts. "Maybe I'll just go back to work full time."

"Dad, you're not...I'm not..." Dammit, he loves to hold that over me. Maybe grandkids are exactly what he needs. If only I had a sibling, but I don't because dear old Mom ran off. "What do I know about raising kids?"

When he looks like he's about to protest, I pull myself up to my full height and fold my arms. "I just want to play hockey,

Dad, and make my team proud. I was never going to find a nice girl in the Caribbean."

Oh, is that because Gina opted to stay home, Ash?

"I am not looking for any sort of a relationship or commitment, short or long term," I continue, and shake my head. "If Coach hears one more negative word..."

While I'm trying to do what's best for the team, Dad is astute enough to know that Coach reaming me out is not why I've been grumpy for the last six months.

But you know that staying away from Gina really is for the best, dude. You basically told her it was a bad idea before you put your cock inside her.

Yeah, so. Shut the fuck up.

You have a reputation to keep clean. Messing around with a single mom isn't going to help.

Fuck you.

That summer day, while it was fucking awesome, had to be a one-time thing. It's not like either of us were looking for a deeper relationship. Lessons learned early on taught me all women leave. Thanks, Mom. Or that women want something from me. Thanks, Liza. But still, staying away from Gina is for the best, and I know it.

After that internal debate, I exhale and do one last pass over the driveway and set my shovel against the side of the house.

"I should get going."

Dad starts up the three steps leading to his front door. "You're not coming in for breakfast? I thought you were hungry."

"I'm just going to grab something on the way home. I have a lot to do today."

He turns and holds the wooden rail that will need a fresh coat of paint come spring. He smirks and says, "Say hello to her for me."

Jesus. My body stiffens even though I'm trying for casual. "There is no her," I grouch, and he just waves his hand and laughs.

"Call me later."

He steps inside and closes the door and I just shake my head. I don't know how he knows, but he knows. I turn and walk back to my truck, and while everything in me urges me to drive home, I don't. I head toward the Nook, Gina's café. It's not that I want to see her. I'm just worried about her getting her walkway cleared. She's home with her daughter, and is also babysitting Brighton and Noah's kids, Camryn and Tate. Three kids and running a café. There's no way she can get out to clear her walkway. I'd do it for any of the guys, their wives or girlfriends, if they needed the help. This has nothing to do with me wanting her.

Yeah, you just keep telling yourself that, dude.

I drive slowly through the streets and find parking close to the Nook. It's Monday morning, and I'm sure Gina, being run off her feet with the work week crowd, could use a hand.

With hurried steps, I make my way to the Nook, and find the snow in Gina's walkway trampled down with footprints. It's a good thing I came. This could easily turn into ice and someone could get hurt.

I open the door and the warmth of the place, along with the fresh scent of coffee, curls around me. Gina's head lifts as the bell overhead jingles, and honest to God, for the first time in a long time, she seems relieved to see me. Okay, I'm going to be honest with you here. It's not the first time I've been lurking around her place, offering to help her out with this or that. She never lets me, and yet here I am again skulking around like a ridiculous hormonal teen with a crush.

"Ash." The panic in her tone grips my gut and squeezes tight.

"Gina," I say and tug off my gloves and hat. "Everything okay?"

A fork drops near me, and she winces as she looks around my body. "Just a second." She hurries to the kitchen to get the customer a new fork, and after handing it over, comes back to me. "I'm short-staffed. Sherry has been out sick for days. Carla called in this morning. She's not feeling well either, and my backup Andre couldn't make it in with the road closures, and Margo my sitter was late getting here from next door because she was snowed in, and waiting for someone to clear her steps, and I was late opening, and there was a crowd waiting outside."

As the list goes on, I ask, "What can I do?" Somewhat breathlessly, she blinks up at me and I unzip my coat as the warmth of the place heats me up. At least I think it's the warmth of the place. I guess it could be her close proximity that's messing with my body temperature. "Wait tables, cook, or clear the walkway first?"

Her hand lands on my arm, and I swear to God, it's like a bolt of electricity right to my balls.

"Ash, no, it's okay."

"It's fine. I didn't have anything to do today, and I wanted to check on your walkway anyway."

Warmth and appreciation move into her face. "That's really nice of you. But cooking? Waiting tables?"

"I'm a man of many talents, remember?"

Heat rushes into her face, and my heart leaps. Okay, so maybe she's not as unaffected by me as she lets on. I have no idea why that gives me pleasure. I know I need to stay away from her.

Yet here I am.

She looks to the left and then to the right when someone raises their hand to signal. When her gaze zeroes back in on me, it's like a shot of adrenaline to the heart. "You can cook, for real?"

"Yes, I can. For real. I had a lot of responsibility as a child." Now why the hell did I tell her that?

A wave of something that looks like sympathy moves over her eyes, before she frowns in worry again.

"It's café cooking, Gina. Not a Michelin star restaurant. I got this."

She gives a curt nod. "Okay, I'm backed up in the kitchen." She takes my hand in hers and pulls me into the kitchen. "The orders are here." She shows me the tickets lined up. "Once an order is ready, just ring this bell."

"Got it." She hesitates for a second. I put my hands on her shoulders and turn her. "I got it, Gina."

"Okay," she breathes out and steps toward the swinging door. Before she leaves, she looks at me over her shoulder. "Thank you. I owe you."

"You don't owe me anything."

"We'll see."

With that, she leaves and I pick up the oldest order and start on it right away. Breakfast foods are easy. If I had to make gourmet meals, I might not be such a great help. I work methodically and start putting the orders up fast, and each time I ring the bell and Gina shows up with a grateful smile on her face, it makes me want to do even more for her. But I know she's never going to let me. She's damn independent, and while I hate that, I also love that about her.

She's definitely not the kind of girl to use others to get ahead in this world. She relies only on herself and again, while I hate that, I also love that.

We work long and hard through the morning rush, and when it slows before the lunch crowd, I tug on my coat, hat and mitts, and go out to clear her walkway. Every once in a while, I glance into the café to find her eyes on me, and yeah, okay, I kind of like her looking. Jesus, I really am a ridiculous hormonal teenager with a crush.

As soon as I finish clearing the snow, I head back in, shrug out of my wet coat, hat and mitts and slip my apron back on. Gina gives me a quick rundown on how to make the lunch food and goes back to take orders.

It's late afternoon by the time she turns the sign on the window from open to closed. As I put the last dish in the dishwasher, she comes into the kitchen, a tired but happy look on her face. She's a giver, likes what she does and I'm happy about that.

"Done." She unties her apron and hangs it onto the hook. I wipe my hands on the dish towel to keep them occupied as she tugs the elastic from her hair and lets it splay over her shoulders.

"I should go."

"No."

That one word, spoken so fast and abruptly stops me in my tracks. "What?"

"Stay for dinner. Let me cook for you. It's the least I can do for all your help today. I don't know what I would have done without you."

I roll one shoulder. "You're tough and would have been just fine, but I'm glad I could lighten your load."

"Okay let me…" Her voice falls off. "Wait, maybe you already have plans tonight. You are on break this weekend."

"I don't have plans."

She crinkles up her nose, and pushes her dark hair from her face. "Okay, let me do something to thank you for today, and I still owe you for fixing my fridge and air conditioning last summer."

As I consider last summer, heat zings through my body and strokes my dick. "You don't owe me anything."

Her grin is mischievous and holds a measure of playfulness that arouses the fuck out of me. "And well, what we did afterward…"

I gulp as she alludes to what we did on her kitchen table. My body tightens and I tug off the apron and set it on the counter. "What are you getting at, Gina?"

She glances around the clean kitchen and smiles. "Just that you've done a lot for me last summer. In both of my kitchens."

I clear my throat as my dick jumps, anxious to visit her upstairs kitchen again. "You weren't the only one who benefitted."

"No, I guess not." She turns the light off and pulls the bottom of my shirt, guiding me to the stairs that lead up to her upstairs apartment. "So, I guess in a way, I did pay you back."

"Are you saying sex was payback for my repair work?"

She thinks about it for a second. "Payback, no. Not really. I guess it can't be when we both got something out of it, right?"

"What exactly are you saying, then?"

"That I want to cook for you and if you don't consider that payback, maybe there's something else I can do to thank you." She lets go of my shirt and starts up the stairs. My gaze zeroes in on her perfect heart-shaped ass, and as I watch her climb, I'm pretty sure I know what she's talking about.

"I'm going to need clarification." *Why the hell are you even asking that, dude.* Just fucking go for it. "I mean, you just said it's not payback when it's mutually beneficial."

"Mutually beneficial," she mumbles. She stops, glances at me over her shoulder and gives me a grin full of promise. "That's what I'm hoping."

What the ever-loving hell is happening? I'm not sure, but I should leave, turn around and never come back because I know this is a bad idea.

Why then am I hurrying up the steps two at a fucking time?

GINA

o you have any idea what you're doing, Gina?

No, I really don't. All I know is that I'm tired. Tired of being alone, of doing things alone—in and out of the bedroom—and when it comes to Ash, I don't think I've been that fair to him. After that one glorious night last summer, I put distance between us. While I think he's a good guy, he does have a reputation, and everything about him is larger than life. I once fell for a man who was admired by all, and he hurt me badly. I don't want to get hurt again, and I have my daughter to protect. I can't make another mistake.

While I might have brought Ash into my bed—or rather, my kitchen—I can't bring him into my life, or my daughter's. What if she grew attached? He's not a man to settle down, not that I'm looking for anything like that, but still, I don't need anything to complicate my simple life.

When it comes right down to it, I'm happy with the way things are going now. I have my daughter and my café, and I don't want to ruin what I have by bringing a man every woman wants a piece of into it. I simply want to keep low profile, but dammit, I'm lonely. I glance at him over my shoulder as I climb the stairs, and can't help but think we could at least be friends.

Friends with benefits...ooh.

I'm about to shut that inner voice down, only to stop because didn't I just suggest sex where we both got something out of it? Honestly that was so out of character for me. This man, combined with my body which is aching to be touched, is clearly messing with my decision-making skills.

Go for it, Gina.

I consider that for a second. We're both consenting adults, and if I'm only bringing him into my bed, not my life or my daughter's life, and if we keep it a secret, maybe we can have a little fun and I can poke a hole into the bubble of loneliness engulfing me.

Poke.

I laugh. Jeez, I sound like Melanie telling the story of when Brady nearly poked her with the fireplace poker. I never would have guessed that those two would have married and had kids. But they did and are so happy. It's not like a little fun between Ash and me will lead to happily ever after. It was different for Brady and Melanie. For as long as I've known them, Brady was in love with her. Ash is not in love with me, and vice versa. We simply had a hook-up. And unlike Melanie, my life is unconventional. I'm a nurse who's running a café, and raising a little girl alone—a little girl whose needs will always come first.

Who's taking care of your needs, Gina?

A little groan crawls out of my throat, because dammit, I want Ash to be that guy. For a little while, anyway. Or at least until I feel less lonely—and a whole lot sated. Just then, his hand lands on my hip and the heat from his big palm trickles through my body and settles deep between my legs.

"Hey, are you okay?"

Hell no, I'm not okay. If he keeps touching me like this, I might not ever be okay again.

His mouth is near my ear, and the warmth of his breath, combined with the deep tenor of his voice, sends shivers through me. I clear my throat. "Yeah, I was just thinking I haven't been to the grocery store in a while and I don't even have a beer to offer you. I have wine."

"Wine is good, but I can run to the store if you need anything. I'm sure it's hard to get anything done with three kids in the house."

Honestly, he's always so helpful, always going out of his way to make sure I'm okay. A girl could fall for a guy like that, and that's something I can't do. Nope. Not going down that road again. Not getting involved with a man who has a harem of women.

"Wait, why aren't they in school?"

"Tate is only two and Zoe and Camryn are off for February break this week. Brighton was reluctant to leave without them this weekend, but she really needed a break so I insisted."

"When do you get a break?" he asks.

"I started taking weekends off a bit ago. I do have to cover when we're short-staffed like now, but I'm sure Brighton and

Noah will take Zoe overnight when they get back from the Caribbean, likely more than once. Speaking of the Caribbean." I stop at the door. "Why didn't you go?" I turn to face him.

He gives an easy roll of his shoulder. "Not a fan of the heat," he responds.

My mind suddenly goes back to last summer. Hell, who am I kidding. My mind is always on last summer. "Yeah, I remember you having to take your shirt off when you were helping me in the kitchen." Warmth centers between my legs at the memory. "My place was stifling."

"Yeah." I wait for him to say more. He doesn't, he just stands there looking at me with his intense blue eyes. I turn from him, and push open the door. The noise of three kids playing some board game that clicks and clacks reaches our ears and Ash stiffens, his eyes going wide like he's about to encounter the monster under the bed. I cover my mouth to stifle a laugh. It's insanely funny that this big defenseman is afraid of my little girl.

I put my hand on his shoulder. "They don't bite." When he doesn't look convinced, I joke, "Not that hard, anyway."

He swallows. "I don't know much about kids."

I step into my upstairs hallway, and close the door behind Ash when he joins me. Zoe bursts out laughing and comes running to me when she sees me. "Mom, I popped a six," she screams. "Six is what you need to play."

"Indoor voice, sweetie." I glance around the corner to see my babysitter Margot watching the kids from her favorite wing-back chair. Zoe loves the old-fashioned games Margot brings over and it helps limit her screen time.

"Ash, come on." She reaches for him and when his big mitt tightens around her tiny little hand, my ovaries nearly burst. God, that has to be the most adorable thing I've ever seen. As I watch them, my heart hurts. I know her own father wants nothing to do with her, and while she's resilient, smart and easygoing, I have no doubt that she could use a little more male influence in her life. Am I doing her wrong by not trying to find her a father?

Ash takes a couple of steps. "I uh, don't know how to play."

"I'll teach you. Come play and see if you can get a six."

Once again, that horrified look crosses his face as Zoe, completely oblivious that he's terrified of her, drags him into the living room. Margo, who is always willing to help me out in the winter when I can't hire a summer student, pushes to her feet and smiles at Ash.

"My granddaughter is a big fan," she tells him. "When she called today, I told her you were helping out in the café." Margot glances at me when I arch a curious brow. "I saw him out front shoveling." I nod and she looks back at Ash. "If it's not too much trouble, would you mind signing something for her? I'm sure she'd love for you to sign her jersey with your lucky number seven on it."

"Wow, she really is a big fan," I mumble.

"You'll be around at some point this weekend?" she asks.

His gaze goes to me, like he's checking in, and I give a nod, letting him know it's okay. "Yeah, I'll probably be around." Zoe drags him down to the floor, and he casts a fast glance my way as he sits cross-legged beside her.

"Great, I'll send her over next time I see your vehicle out front."

"Is it okay with you, Gina?"

I do love how he always seems to check in with me. Just like he did when we were having sex. Okay, mind off sex. Now is not the time for my cheeks to go red. "Of course." I pull Margot's coat from the hanger and help her into it, and something strange tightens in my stomach when I think about her granddaughter's crush.

"I didn't know Pippa was a fan." I've met Pippa a few times. Like me, she was raised by her grandparents. She's a sophomore at Boston College, and mostly keeps to herself. I wouldn't have taken her for a hockey fan.

"Not Pippa, Callie."

"Oh, right." I've heard her talk about Callie before. She lives in California and is a senior at Berkley.

"She's on spring break and is coming tonight to stay the week. She loves Ash." Margot chuckles and gives me a wink. "But who doesn't?"

Yeah, who doesn't? All the more reason, not to get into anything more than a friends with benefits relationship with him. Then again, I'm not even sure he's going to agree to that. Although he does seem to want to help me out with different things. I'm sure it's because our mutual friends put him up to it. As a jack of all trades, he's the guy they all call when they need something fixed, and he's always there for them. That's admirable.

"I told her you knew him and a bunch of the Bucks. She was hoping to meet him." She leans in. "I think they'd make a cute couple and maybe he could show her around Boston this weekend. She doesn't have friends here, and I hate to see her all alone." She stops abruptly and hikes her purse over her shoulder. "Unless of course, you two…"

"No," I blurt out quickly. "Friends. If even that," I add in with a snort that seems to intrigue Margot. Her brow lifts like she knows something I don't, and I straighten myself out. "Friend through friends type thing, you know."

She cocks her head, a gleam in her eyes. "Yes, I think I do know."

"Same time tomorrow?" I ask, changing the subject.

Her eyes go wide, and she puts her hand on her forehead. "Oh dear. Did I not tell you?"

My stomach cramps as worry races through me. "Tell me what?"

She shakes her head. "I don't know what is wrong with me. I've been so forgetful lately." She blinks at me. "My daughter Sarah is coming with Callie too, and you know how rarely she comes home. I thought I booked the week off from babysitting so I could spend time with her. Oh dear, I'm so sorry. You don't mind, do you?"

I fight off a burst of panic. How could I mind? She rarely gets to see her daughter and granddaughter, as they live in California, but I have to work and I have three kids to look after. What the hell am I going to do? My mind starts racing, wondering if any of the sitters I've used in the past are available. Some must be home from college but they're not going to want to babysit for the weekend.

"Maybe Ash could help out?" Margot suggests kindly.

"Help out with what?" Ash asks, stepping into the hall.

"Nothing." I nibble my bottom lip and try to fight down the unease. "I just have to figure out..." I let my words fall off. When I offered to take Brighton and Noah's kids for the weekend, I had no idea I'd be losing my sitter, or that my staff would all be home sick, and a huge snowstorm would hit. Talk about a triple whammy.

"Oh, I'm so sorry, Gina." Eyes full of worry, Margot puts her hand on my shoulder. "I'll just tell Sarah and Callie I'm busy."

I give a quick shake of my head and Ash's curious gaze goes back and forth between Margot and me. "No, I don't want you to do that."

"What's going on?" he asks.

"My daughter Sarah and granddaughter Callie are coming for a visit and I thought I'd cleared the week with Gina, but I didn't. I thought maybe you could help out with the kids."

"Margot," I begin as Ash's body stiffens. "It's okay. I'll figure something out."

I open the door for Margot and a big gust of wind rushes in. I cross my arms to warm myself.

Margot peers out. "Looks like that cold front is coming through. The roads are going to be icy tonight. You be careful driving home, Ash. In fact, you might not even want to be on them."

She turns worried grandmotherly eyes on me, and my heart squeezes tight. I love that she's getting to spend time with her family, even though it makes me miss my grandmother and grandfather terribly. They did right by me, and by my mother, but she went spiraling down the wrong path anyway, falling for one asshole after another, and always choosing them over me.

"Thanks, Margot. You have a great week with your family. We'll be just fine."

"Okay, dear." She steps onto the stoop and Ash hurries into his boots to help her down the long flight of stairs. Margot beams at him. "Such a gentleman." She gives a little wink. "No wonder Callie is smitten."

He walks her home and when he comes back, the cold air radiating off him, I automatically put my hands on his arms and create heat with friction. "You shouldn't be out without a coat on."

"Okay, Mom."

I grin at him and realize what I'm doing. "Sorry. Once a mom. I'm sure yours would have scolded you too."

"Wouldn't know." I stiffen at that and sense I hit a sore spot, so I leave it.

"I should get started on dinner." I turn to walk to the kitchen, and he follows me. With his big body behind mine, and my gaze on the kitchen table, a hard quiver goes through me.

"I can help."

I turn and he's right there, his entire presence eating up the small kitchen. He dips his head and if I wanted to kiss him, all I'd have to do is go up on my toes.

"Ash, no." I glance down, before I do just that. I can't risk kissing this man with my daughter and my friend's kids in the next room.

"Hey," he whispers, his thumb under my chin, lifting my gaze to his. "I'm not going to leave you high and dry."

Dry?

Nope not leaving me dry at all.

"Kids are smart. They can smell fear," I joke. "I'd probably find you tied up at the end of the day getting beaten with pool noodles." Is he serious? He'd really step up for me like this? Why, though? Why would he do this? I mean I know he'd do anything for his friends—I've seen it with my own eyes how he's there for everyone, even helping me when they ask—but babysitting kids he's afraid of goes above and beyond.

His gaze settles on my lips. "Gina..."

My heart thumps hard as he continues to move closer. "I can't ask you to be my manny."

"Manny?"

"Male nanny," I explain and the corner of his mouth turns up.

"You're not asking." He lowers his head even more, his warm breath on my face.

"We're not even really friends."

"Yeah, Gina, we're friends." His big hand lands on my hip again. "We slept together last summer, remember? Right here on this kitchen table. I think that kind of makes us friends."

"Friends with benefits," I mumble, testing that out on my lips as I watch for a reaction.

"Yeah."

There's always something so sexy, almost devilish and mischievous in the way he says that one word, and it really gets to me. God, I really am in bad shape here. "Actually, I don't remember us doing any sleeping on this table," I tease as a warm front nestles between my legs. So much for a cold front going through.

"What do you remember?"

"Everything," I blurt out, breathless and aroused and wanting. "It was...so good."

"Yeah." I melt a little more as his grin widens. "Just so you know, you can ask me anything you want."

I swallow. Hard. "Yeah?"

He nods. "Is there anything you want?"

"Yes," I say quickly. "Lots of things, but this..." I nod toward the living room as the kids giggle about something. "This, though...it's too much."

"I'm sure you'll find a way to pay me back."

His body brushes mine, and that's when I feel his arousal. Oh God, he's thick and hard and if I didn't have a houseful of kids I'd push him down on the table and climb on board.

"I could never pay you back for something this *big*."

Clever boy that he is, he grins, knowing full well I'm half talking about the favor he's offering and half talking about his lovely erection. But who am I to tease? My nipples are so hard, they could score glass.

His grip on my hips tightens. "I'm sure we can find a way, and make it...mutually beneficial."

"Mom..."

Damn.

4

ASH

I can't believe I'm going to be babysitting three small kids—who all scare the crap out of me—for the next few days. How did I get myself into this, anyway? Oh right, Gina needed help and I'm not a guy to turn his back on anyone in need—especially a friend. Yeah, we're friends now. Plus, there was something about payback being mutually beneficial. Let's be real here, I'm not one hundred percent altruistic.

But now here I am, sleeping in Gina's spare room alone after I helped her cook dinner and feed three hungry kids, because the Department of Transportation warned everyone to stay off the roads due to ice.

After the dishes were done, Gina gave me the rundown on meals, snacks and naps, then took the three to Zoe's room to read them a bedtime story, only to fall asleep in her daughter's bed. I called Dad to let him know where I was in case he needed me. Then I waited for Gina to meet me in the living room—before I knew she'd passed out.

When I told Dad I was simply helping out a friend, he wanted to know all the details. I love the man, I really do, but he needs to stay out of my private life. I know he wants what's best for me, and he also knows the promise I made to Coach. So, what's best for me right now is not getting into a relationship—I never should have driven to Gina's earlier, I know.

Gina...

God, what am I even doing? I don't know but I do know this is all crazy and risky. I should have left, would have left if I could have. Maybe I wouldn't have. Fuck. All I know is before she took the kids to their room, we'd talked about watching a movie, and of course I had other things on my mind, and when she didn't come back, I went searching for her. When I saw her sleeping, so tired and run off her feet, I didn't dare wake her. She's always taking care of everyone else, and dammit, I want to take care of her. She just doesn't usually let me. But she let me help today when she was in a jam, and she finally caved when I insisted I could babysit. Why again was I so persistent?

Right, not altruistic.

How the hell am I going to entertain three kids, two of them being girls? I roll over in the small single bed made for a child, and nearly fall out of it. Jesus. I fluff my pillow as wind whips around the house, twisting the siding, and beating at the shingles. Swallowing against a dry throat, I toss my legs over the side of the bed and push to my feet. Two small steps take me to the window and I glance out into the dark night, to see the quiet street below.

I sleep naked, so I tug on my jeans and quietly open the bedroom door. When my ears meet with silence, I tiptoe down the hall and make my way to the kitchen, where I once took Gina on the table. A beam of light trickles along the floor. I was sure I'd turned off all the lights before bed. Did I miss one in the kitchen?

I walk quietly and the second I enter the small space and see her sweet ass in the air as she pulls something from the fridge, I grip the back of the wooden chair to stabilize myself. The chair scrapes the floor and Gina darts upright, and turns to me, her hand on her chest.

"Ash," she says, breathlessly. "You scared me."

"Sorry. I didn't mean to. I came down for a drink. I thought you were asleep."

She closes the fridge and plunges us into darkness. "I'm the one who's sorry." Her feet shuffle on the floor and a second later, the light above the stove illuminates the small space. With her long dark hair a mess around her shoulders, and dressed in big flannel pajama pants and a T-shirt, she frowns at me. "I can't believe I fell asleep on you. Did you watch the movie without me?"

"You were exhausted." I let go of the chair and take a step toward her. Jesus, how can she make big flannel pajama pants so sexy? "I'm glad you had a time out." I close the distance, and run the back of my hands over her cheek.

She laughs quietly. "A time out is for misbehaving. I haven't done any misbehaving in a long time."

"Maybe we should rectify that," I tease.

Her eyes light with desire. "Maybe we should."

I take the water bottle from her, crack it open and hand it

back. She takes a big gulping drink. Once she's done, I take the bottle and practically finish it.

She blinks up at me, color moving into her cheeks. "We were both pretty thirsty."

"Yeah."

She gulps at that one word and sways slightly. "I don't think I'm quite sated yet."

"Oh. I'll get another bottle." She makes a move to go back to the fridge and I pin her against the counter with my body. "It's not water that's going to sate me, babe."

"No?"

I slide my hand along her hip, and when she quivers, it's all the answer I need. I dip my hand between her legs and lightly stroke her sex through her pajamas. "I'm going to need my mouth here. That's the only thing that's going to quench my thirst tonight."

"Oh, God, Ash. I...I need that too."

With that, I pick her up and carry her across the room. I move a chair away from the table, giving me space to ravish her, and set her on the tabletop. I dip my head and moan as her lips part for me. Her arms circle my neck and she drags me to her, as desperate for me as I am for her, and that sort of fucks with my heart in a strange way. I've had women want me, sure, and that's not ego speaking. But there's something different in her hunger for me. Or maybe I'm imagining it. I don't have a whole lot of blood left in my brain.

She runs her palms over my back and my muscles quake as she reacquaints herself with my nakedness. Time for my mouth to reacquaint itself too. I slide my hands under her ass. "I need you naked."

"Yes please," she murmurs and a rough chuckle crawls out of my throat as she lays back. Gaze locked on hers, I untie the string holding her pants up, and tug on them just enough to expose her pussy. "I've wanted back in here for a very long time now." I part her lips, and lightly brush my thumb over her damp, swollen clit.

Her muscles tighten, and she tries to widen her legs, but I hold them together with mine, wanting to tease and torment her, just a little bit. "But you totally shut me out."

"Ash," she moans, her body aching for so much more, and I plan to give it to her, but maybe a little payback is in order. "You knew it was a bad idea too. You even said so."

"Yeah, I did. We both have our own reasons. I realize that." Fuck, I'm supposed to be on the straight and narrow, head down and only on the game, no complications, no women. Any kind of relationship, with a single mom at that, is a side road I'm not supposed to be on. "It doesn't mean I didn't want to fuck you again, though."

"You've been thinking about me? Thinking about this…"

I slide my hand down and circle her entrance, grazing her ever so lightly. "Yeah." Another hard quiver goes through her. "Have you been thinking about me?"

She goes up on her elbows, her gaze on my fingers between her legs. "If I say yes, will you touch me?"

I chuckle. "I don't know, babe. I'm not sure I should make this so easy on you after the hard time you've given me."

"Hard, yes...Ash please."

Hard is right. Ever since we fucked on this table, I couldn't be around her without getting hard and I'm pretty sure it has nothing to do with the fact that I hadn't had a hook-up with anyone since.

"Please," she begs again.

Answering her demands, I slide a finger into her and her muscles clench around my finger. Fuck, she's so damn tight. Has she not been touched, not been with anyone since me, either? I don't know why I like the thought of that.

Her mouth opens and closes and she finally murmurs, "That is so good."

I fuck her with my finger a few times, but goddammit, I need to taste her. "Lay back," I command in a soft voice and she obliges. With her body flat on the table, I tug her pants off and lift her legs, putting them around me as I move her body to give me better access to her hot little pussy. I breathe in her aroused scent and moan as I bury my face between her thighs.

Her legs tighten around me as I eat at her, wanting her juices all over my face.

"Ash...ohmigod, yes."

Her voice is barely a whisper as she lets me take charge, doing whatever I want to her body, and there are so many things I want. My cock hardens even more, and I'm in fucking agony as it presses against my zipper. I slide one hand down and unhook my button and tug my cock free, giving it a long tug as I slip another finger inside her hot, tight channel.

Her hips come off the table, her pussy banging against my face as I lick her clit and finger fuck her. I love this needy desperation about her, love how much she wants me right now—even though this is all kinds of wrong. But I can't think about that, not when she's quietly chanting my name and spasming around my probing fingers.

I lift my head, wanting to see her face as she lets go, and the sight is one of beauty. Her eyes lock on mine, and the pleasure I see there wraps around me and holds tight. Jesus, this woman needs to take a time out more often. It looks good on her.

"Ash."

"I know, babe, I know." I still my fingers deep inside her, giving her something to clench around. "Come all over my fingers. Take everything you need, and when you think you're done, I'm going to give you more." She ripples harder, her chest rising and falling erratically as she pants. Soon enough her muscles settle and I pull my fingers out, bringing them to my mouth. She watches in amazement as I lick my fingers, and moan around the sweet taste.

"Now I'm going to fuck you. You want that, Gina?"

"I do." Her voice is hoarse, and I have no doubt her throat is dry.

"Don't move."

"I don't think I can even if I want to."

I laugh quietly, and grab the bottle from the counter. Two steps later I'm back with her, and I help her sit up and give her a drink. Before she can lay back down, I grip the bottom of her T-shirt, and she automatically lifts her arms. I love how she's letting me take care of her tonight. She's not one to hand over control, but goddammit, she needs the break.

"These..." I lightly brush the sides and bottom of her breasts. "I didn't get to spend any time here the last time I had you on this table."

She arches forward. "We should rectify that."

I chuckle at her enthusiasm. "You're not wrong." I bend, and her sweet moan wraps around my dick as I take one pert nipple into my mouth and suck. "Fuck," I mumble around her hard bud. Her hands wrap around my head, her fingers knotting my hair as she holds me to her, and I brush my thumb over her other nipple, giving it the attention it deserves.

One hand slides down my back and around to the front, to touch my cock, and it jumps as a new kind of desperation takes hold of me. She dips into my pre-cum and slides it around my crown and I nearly fucking shoot off in her hand. Her nipple pops from my mouth as I inch back, her hand no longer able to reach my dick.

I'm seconds from grabbing a condom and sheathing up when she slides from the table. A measure of panic hits. Is she having second thoughts, or worse, are we about to get caught? This is fucking risky, I know that, but I'd lost all control the second I got close to her. I'm about to back off, only to stop when she sinks to her knees, and takes my cock into her hands.

Sweet Jesus.

"Gina..." I run one hand through my hair. "Fuck, Gina."

"Soon," she teases. She takes my cock into her warm palms. "The last time I had you in this kitchen, I didn't get to spend any time here." With that, she leans forward and takes my cock to the back of her throat. I've wanted her for so long, had whacked off to the memory of what we'd done so many times, I fear I'm going to shoot down her throat, ending this before it even gets started.

Math.

I start thinking about math, a trick I learned back in junior high when I wanted to get my dick under control. What the fuck is two plus two again? Jesus, that's not even working.

"Gina," I mumble as she grips my balls and works her sweet mouth along my throbbing cock. With barely any blood left in my brain, I back up and she pouts as I pull my dick from her mouth.

"On the table."

She grins, knowing the state she's put me in and climbs back on the table, spreading her legs for me. "Fuck me, Ash."

Jesus Christ.

I fish a condom from my pocket and put it on in record time. I grip her hips, put my cock at her entrance and her mouth opens as I drive into her. With little finesse and much enthusiasm, I fuck her hard on the kitchen table. She moans, her head going from side to side as my manners walk out the door. But judging from her moans, the way her sweet pussy is tightening around my pistoning cock, this is exactly what she needs tonight.

My fingers bite into her soft hips as I hold her down, and the table practically slides across the floor as I pound into her soft flesh. I bite down on my cheek as pleasure gathers in my dick. I take one of her hands and press her finger against her clit and her eyes go wide. At first she doesn't do anything, but as I keep my gaze locked on hers, she reads me, and begins to move her finger over her wet nub.

I grin. "Yeah." Her finger moves faster, matching the rhythm of my fucking and when her cheeks flush, and her eyes briefly close, I know she's right there, hovering on the edge. "I need you to come all over my cock, babe."

"Oh God."

Her body lets go, and I grunt as I fill her and stretch her with my girth. She lifts up a bit, and I slide my hands around her back and pull her to me, chest to chest. Her hands go around my back and she hugs tight, like she needs the connection, the intimacy as she continues to come around my cock. Everything in the way she's holding me breaks my control and she puts her face on my shoulder as I let loose a grunt and climax inside her beautiful, welcoming body.

She gasps. "Ash, I feel you."

I put my arms under her sweet ass and lift her clear from the table as I pump seed into the condom, wishing there were no barriers between us, which is crazy. I always use a condom. I hold her to me and she clings as I deplete myself inside her. Once I'm sated, I set her on the table, cup her cheeks and press my lips to hers. I kiss her deeply, and our lips linger, touching, tasting, savoring...

Have I ever savored a woman before?

She exhales a contented sigh and murmurs, "We have to stop meeting like this."

I know she's kidding, but I say, "I don't think we do." In fact, I want to keep meeting like this and when it comes right down to it, I want to know more about this woman. Other than she has a child, runs a café and we have friends in common, I don't know much.

"Me neither. But there are kids in the house and if we're going to keep doing this, we need to be careful."

"Are we going to keep doing this, Gina?"

5

GINA

"Friends with benefits for the weekend?" I ask as he pulls out of me with a groan, and removes the condom.

He nods, grabs a tissue from the box on the counter and disposes of the condom. "I'm into it."

He steps back to me and I put my palm on his face. "I like being with you, Ash. This is...incredible. I just want you to know, I'm not into relationships and I have a child to consider."

He snorts out a laugh and it seems a bit forced. "I'm not looking for anything more, Gina. Besides, your daughter scares me."

I laugh at that. "You know I find that adorable, right?" Too adorable, actually. Seeing him around the little ones does the craziest things to me. He helps me from the table and hands me my clothes. As I tug them back on, he zips up and fixes his jeans.

My stomach tightens. "I just think we should keep this…" I wave my finger back and forth between the two of us. "…under wraps. A secret."

"It's just sex, Gina. I'm not looking for any complications in my life, either, and no one has to know about this. It's for the best that way."

"Okay." While I'm wondering what complications he's talking about, I don't ask.

Once we're both decent again, I grab another bottle of water from the fridge and some strawberries that I'd washed earlier. I set the bowl on the counter, pick up a berry and hold it out to him. His eyes are narrowed, full of questions as he lets me feed him.

"Something on your mind?"

He shrugs. "I guess I was just wondering if Zoe's father is in her life…or in yours." I take a deep breath at that loaded question. He must read the pain in my eyes because he hurries out with, "We don't have to talk about that if you don't want to."

"She doesn't know him." This time I snort out a laugh, and it's not forced. "I didn't even know him."

"You did in-vitro or something?" he asks, real curiosity in his eyes.

I snatch up a strawberry and bite into it. As the flavor explodes on my tongue, I consider my answer. "No, what I mean is…" I pause for a second. I don't talk about this at all. It's actually embarrassing to be such a cliché. "Sometimes people turn out to be something they're not, and sometimes people find out they're not as special as they thought they were."

His face goes hard. "Did he hurt you?"

"Yeah, actually he did." I guess if I'm telling him this story, I might as well tell him everything.

He straightens to his full height, his eyes dark and murderous as they search my body for any kind of evidence. "Where does he live?"

I put my hand on his arm, and his thick muscles tighten beneath my palm. "He didn't physically hurt me. He just tried to pay me off when I got pregnant, and that really hurt."

Shock moves over his face, and his jaw clenches. "What the fuck, Gina?"

"I wasn't a very good judge of character, just like dear old Mom," I admit, a little ashamed of that. I glance down as my hand falls from his arm. "I don't want to get serious, only to get hurt again."

"Gina, I know we're not going to get serious, but if we were, I would never hurt you. I know they call me Ash-hole, but—"

"Would an Ash-hole help me out the way you did today, and the way you're going to help with the kids tomorrow?" Honestly, it was easier when I thought he was an Ash-hole. I thought I knew what I was getting into, yet I didn't know anything at all. "Would an Ash-hole take his time to pleasure my body the way you did, and give me the most incredible orgasms?"

"That's what friends do." The softness in his voice wraps around me, and when he steps into me, pulling me against his body, I hold him tight and the sudden need to share more overcomes me.

"It's crazy, Mom wasn't really in my life, and yet I went on to make the same bad choices."

"I grew up without a mom too," he says quietly. "I mean, she wasn't in my life much. She's not dead. I just have no idea where she is."

I don't miss the ache of loss in his voice. I work to swallow the lump punching in my throat, hating that he's been so deeply hurt. "My grandparents raised me," I whisper. "They were good people and they did right by me and by Mom, but, just like Zoe, I never even knew who my father was, and I'm not sure my mom knew either. My grandparents are both gone now." My voice cracks, the pain of their loss still hurts my heart.

"I'm sorry, Gina. They sound like great people and I know it's not easy growing up without a mom. Mine left when I was quite young, and I don't know if she's dead or alive. I was lucky to have a great dad who worked hard to fill all the roles. I try to take care of him now, but he's a stubborn bastard who's too proud to let me, and I swear to God if he asks me about grandkids one more time, I'm shipping him back to Colorado."

There's so much love and respect in his voice as he talks about his father, it curls around my heart and squeezes tight. To know my daughter will never have that kind of bond with a male figure guts me. I don't want to do wrong by her, but I'm just scared. "He taught you a lot of things, I hear."

A warm smile moves over his face. "Yeah, he's all I have. He lives here in Boston now. I finally got him to leave Colorado. I wanted him to move in with me, but no, he insisted I needed my own space, because you know...girls." He does air quotes around the word girls.

"He's probably not wrong."

He grumbles something. "My house over on Beacon Hill is far too big for one person. I bought it as an investment. Dad and I could live there and never run into each other for a week." A beat of silence as he grins about something. "You'd like him."

"I'm sure I would." Not that I think I'll ever meet him. This is a friends with benefits for a weekend kind of relationship and getting to know family is out of the question. After a long stretch of silence, I continue, "I didn't mean to get pregnant. I wasn't trying to trap him. It was an accident. I was on the pill, but it's not always one hundred percent."

"He wanted to pay you off to keep you quiet? He didn't want the child, or for anyone to know?"

As he stares at me with a mixture of anger and disbelief, I nod, open the water and take a drink. "I'm such a fool."

"I don't think you're a fool." Once again his eyes turn murderous. "He didn't deserve you. The man doesn't deserve anyone and as much as it hurts I'm glad you found out who he really was. You should be with a guy who knows how special you really are."

"I don't think I'm anything special, but Lucian sure made me feel like I was." I give a fast shake of my head. "I'm not going down that road again."

He nods. "Right. Well anyway, that guy is an asshole."

"Actually, he's a lot of things." He arches a questioning brow, and I go back and forth on whether to tell him everything. As he waits for an explanation, I blurt out, "The biggest thing he was, or rather is...is married. His family was in Texas. His wife stayed with his kids, who I believe were around six and seven at the time, to finish the school year. I knew his house was pretty empty. I just thought, bachelor life, you know. It turns out the furniture, and the family, were coming later."

He gives a low slow whistle. "Jesus."

"He was also a narcissist and a player. He had lots of women that I knew nothing about. I thought I was special. I thought he was the one. I thought wrong. About so many things. I honestly feel sorry for his wife, but one of these days she's going to find out. I just couldn't be the one to get in between them. I had a baby to protect from the whole situation."

"Are you sure I can't pay this asshole a visit?"

I shake my head no, wanting to leave that part of my life behind. "He is an admired psychiatrist. He moved to California, and I met him at the hospital."

"You were a patient."

"No, actually, a nurse."

His head rears back. "You're a nurse, and you used to live in California?"

I nod. "After I got pregnant and found out who Lucian really was, and that my uncle left me this café, I ran away with Zoe."

"You just let him get away with it?" He shakes his head. "I'm sorry, I'm not judging, I'm just mad that this fucking asshole did this to you, and his unborn child. You both deserve better."

I shrug. "I got away with Zoe, and that's all that mattered."

His voice softens as he brushes my hair from my shoulder. "You're a good mom."

"The thing is, Ash, I don't really have anything against assholes who come right out and own it, you know. I'm not a homewrecker and never would have fallen for his charming ways if I'd known he was married. But if he wasn't, and he slept around, and I knew about it, okay. At least let me make my choices on whether I want to be with you or not, based on truth."

He goes quiet for a second, reflective, and I sense he's struggling with his own demons. "I get it," he finally says. "You don't care if a guy sleeps around, you just want to know where you stand."

"Exactly." Ash has a reputation, we both know that, and that's why I wanted to clarify that we could be nothing but friends with benefits for a weekend. "At the end of the day, I'm glad I found out who he was and got out with my daughter. I don't want her knowing him, and even though I swore I wouldn't, I found myself following in my mother's footsteps. Believing the best of an asshole who didn't deserve my respect, and he certainly doesn't deserve to be part of Zoe's life. That's why I was quick to leave my nursing job and move here when I found out I'd inherited this café."

He nods and goes quiet again, like he's trying to take it all in and really, it's a lot to take in. "You know Josie, my buddy Jesse's wife is a nurse too, right? Does she know any of this?"

"No one other than Melanie knows that I'm a nurse." I brush his hair back. "She doesn't know much about my background. I don't talk about my past with anyone."

"You just talked about it with me."

I shake my head, perplexed. "I don't know why I'm telling you all this."

"You're telling me because it's heavy and sometimes you just need a friend to talk to, and probably because you're tired, and you just need a damn time out."

I laugh at that. He's right, and I think I'm also a little chatty because the sex was intense and now I'm feeling a little bit vulnerable, and that's not something I like to feel. "You and your time outs. Did your dad put you in a lot of time outs or something?"

"Actually, no. I was a good kid. Never got into trouble."

I eye him. "Why do I have a feeling your dad would tell a different story?"

He grins. "Beats me."

"Not that I'll ever meet him."

"Right." He inches back, his demeanor changing. Was it something I said? "We should probably get to bed. If I'm going to get myself untied from that chair before the kids can beat me with pool noodles," he gestures toward the chair pulled out from the table. "I'm going to need rest."

I touch his face, oddly needing the contact again. "I really appreciate this."

"No problem." He jerks his head toward the hall. "Come on, you need rest too."

With that he takes my hand, and it's the strangest thing holding hands with him. He guides me down the hall and stops outside my bedroom door. I glance up at him and my stupid heart wobbles. I am not the kind of girl who can have sex and not feel something. Dammit, why did I think I was? I don't know but I need to pull myself together. I can't let sex muddy the waters here, and mess with my emotions. Maybe I just need sleep. Yeah, sleep will help clear my thoughts and get me back on track.

"Night," he murmurs and bends to kiss me on the forehead. With that, he walks away and I stare at his muscular back until he disappears into the small spare room. I cross the hall and check on the kids, my heart squeezing tight when I see Zoe in her bunk bed, Camryn and Tate sharing the other, which is beside it. Zoe didn't like them stacked when we first got them. The kids all insisted they be in the same room and that worked out well, considering I needed a bed for Ash.

At least they won't be surprised to find him here in the morning and they know he'll be watching them tomorrow. I head to my bed, and climb in, my body sated and sore in the best possible ways. When I open my eyes again, it's to the sound of laughter in the kitchen, and the second I hear Ash's grumbling voice, I jackknife up and check the time.

I don't usually sleep so soundly. It's crazy that I didn't hear them all get up. I guess the sex completely knocked me out. While that is great, the knot tightening in my stomach is making me question all this and thinking that maybe sex again isn't such a great idea. I bite my lower lip and throw my legs over the side of the bed. Yes, we said we'd be doing it again, but I didn't expect to feel so emotional. Maybe I can't do this anymore.

I hurry from my room, make a fast trip to the bathroom to wash up and brush my teeth, and follow the voices to the kitchen. When I get there, I find three little ones on stools, all stirring batter in their own bowls. My gaze meets Ash's and he looks frazzled and terrified, and a whole lot out of his element, but everything about this, about the way he's trying, and doing a great job is…adorable.

Calm down ovaries.

"What's going on?" I ask as I step up to the island and glance into the bowls.

"Mommy, Ash is letting us all make our own pancakes."

He raises his brow, checking in with me. "Isn't that nice of him."

He relaxes a bit as I reassure him. "Coffee?"

I nod and he puts a cup under the coffee machine and tosses in a pod. "I didn't even hear you guys get up."

"I heard them and got them all rounded up and quiet so you could get some sleep." He steals a fast glance at the clock on the microwave. "You're not late, are you?"

"Nope. I have time for pancakes too." His phone pings, and he pulls it from his back pocket and quickly reads a message. I note that he doesn't message back as I reach into the batter, and dab Zoe's nose.

"Mommy," she bellows, and then I do the same to Camryn and Tate.

"Gina," Camryn shrieks as Tate laughs. Camryn grabs the paper towel and wipes her little brother's nose first. The two of them are so cute together. Camryn is seven and Tate is only two, and she's like a mother to him. Would Zoe be like that if I had another child? Wait, where the heck did that thought come from?

"Don't even think about it," Ash says, pulling my attention back. He holds his big hands up, palms out.

I laugh and grab for the milk in the fridge. "Mommy," Zoe begins, her voice questioning.

"What's up, buttercup?"

"Camryn and Tate have a daddy. How come I don't have a daddy?"

6

ASH

Well, at least there's nothing awkward about that question...

"I...uh..." Gina stumbles, her brow punching together as she searches for an answer.

Zoe continues to stir. "Camryn told me she used to only have a daddy, but then he married Brighton and now she has a mommy too. Do you have to get married for me to have a daddy?"

I can practically hear Gina's brain spinning when she sputters, "I...uh..."

"What is getting married?" Tate asks.

"I told you," Camryn pipes in. "It's when a boy puts a ring on a girl's finger, and then they sleep in the same bed, and they *kiss*."

She slaps her hands to her face as she draws that one word out. Tate crinkles up his nose. "I don't want to kiss a girl."

All right then…Time to shut this down.

I grab the pan I found under the cupboard earlier. "Okay, who's ready to cook their pancake first?"

"Me, me, me," they all shout in unison.

Gina briefly closes her eyes and when they open again, she gives me a grateful look. I guess she hadn't prepared herself for Zoe's question. I don't know anything about kids, but I do remember asking my father why I didn't have a mother. I'm sure Gina asked her grandparents a few questions of her own as well.

"How about we go youngest to oldest? Tate, you're up first."

I hold on to him as I slide his chair around to the counter, setting him a good distance away from the stove. "Do you kiss girls?" he asks me and scrunches up his face like he just ate something sour. "I don't want to do that."

Oh yeah, buddy. That'll change one day.

"I'm not married," is all I say. "Gina, do you still have straw-berries in the fridge?"

She heads to the fridge. "Strawberries, yes."

"Zoe," Camryn says and grabs her wooden spoon. "Stop stirring."

"But I have lumps."

"You want lumps." Camryn looks into Zoe's bowl. "Right there. They're wish lumps."

Zoe checks out the lumps. "Wish lumps? What are wish lumps?"

"My dad told me about them when I was little. I wished for a mommy and got one, and then I wished for a baby brother."

"I'm your baby brother," Tate beams.

"I should wish for a daddy?" Zoe asks.

Camryn shrugs. "If you want one."

"Do you like having a daddy?"

She folds her hands and puts them to her heart. "I love my daddy."

"I should wish for a daddy," she states.

What the fuck is happening in my life? Are kids always this chatty, and do they always talk about important things, and what the hell was Noah thinking, telling Camryn there were wish lumps. Jesus. I'm about two seconds from telling them there is no such thing as wish lumps, but I don't want to burst anyone's bubble.

"Whipped cream," Gina yells, as she draws all the attention to herself. "Open up." Zoe opens her mouth and Gina sprays some in.

"Me, me," Tate yells, and she does the same to him and then Camryn.

Wanting to change the subject, again, I spray the pan with oil and pour Tate's batter in, as I ask, "What do you guys want to do today?" I really have no idea how I'm going to entertain these three.

"I want to go sledding," Zoe squeals.

I nod. "That could be fun. Do you all have sleds?"

Tate shifts on his chair. "I want to swim."

"A bit too chilly for that, bud."

"Uncle Ash, you're silly. He means at the indoor pool at White Sands," Camryn explains.

Oh right, I forgot that Noah and Brighton's resort has an indoor pool. "The roads aren't great and it's a bit of a drive, so let's just do something in the city today." I flip his pancake, and he breathes in the aroma. "First we're going to clear the walkway and driveway, okay?"

"Thank you," Gina says.

"Are you fully staffed today?"

"Sherry is still off sick." She picks up her phone and checks it. "Nothing from Carla or Andre, so hopefully they're both coming in today, and with you taking care of these three, I can make it work."

She glances at the clock. "Go on and get ready. I've got this under control, for now." She smiles at me. "I just have to keep them away from the pool for the rest of the weekend." She arches a brow. "Noodles," I explain. "I know what Tate is up to."

Her laugh curls around me as her hand lands on my back. For the briefest of seconds, as she leans forward, I think she's going to kiss me. We can't kiss in front of the kids. No way am I about to give them anything to talk about. I don't want Zoe to think I'm going to be her daddy or anything crazy like that. This is a friends with benefits relationship, and come the end of the weekend, when everyone returns home from the Caribbean, and Gina's sitter is back, I'm sure this will all end, and that's for the best.

"You better flip it."

"Flip what?" I ask, my brain no longer working as Gina continues to stand close.

"My pancake," Tate yells.

"Oh right." I slide the spatula under it and flip it over. "It's perfect."

"You sure you got this?" Gina asks.

No, I'm not sure. "Yeah, it's all good. Go get dressed. I'll have a pancake ready for you when you get back."

"Do you want lumps in yours, Mommy?" Zoe asks.

She kisses her daughter on the forehead. "I have you and that's all I ever wished for."

With that she heads down the hall and I put Tate's pancake on a plate and slide him back to the table. "You're up next, Zoe."

I slide her over, and repeat the process, but this time I don't let my mind wander and nearly burn it. Up next is Camryn, who insists she's old enough to flip her own pancake, and pouts when I refuse. What was I doing at seven years old? Probably flipping pancakes, because I learned independence very early on. It was only Dad and me and we were a team. Camryn might be old enough, but I don't really know how things are done in her house, so I'm not going to let her close to the stove.

"How about this," I say, lowering my voice. "We can make cupcakes later when Tate takes a nap, and surprise him with them. You can help fill the muffin pan." She beams, loving the idea of responsibility.

Maybe I'm not so bad at this.

I make a fist and she bumps it with me. "It's a deal, Uncle Ash."

A hissing sound reaches my ears, and I turn to see Tate pretty much empty the can of whip cream on his pancake. "Tate," I yell, and turn to snatch it from him. Zoe giggles, as Tate dips his face and starts eating the whip cream.

I turn back to the stove to see black smoke and hurry back to flip the pancake, only to find it black on the other side. "You burnt it," Camryn says, and puts her hands on her hip. "I could have flipped it."

"Let's whip you up some more."

She side eyes me. "I'm going to use my wish lumps to wish for a pancake that's not burnt."

"Good idea."

I toss the burnt pancake into the garbage and put the pan in the sink to wash it, as Camryn goes for the box to put more mix into her bowl. She takes it to the sink and adds the perfect amount of water. Once she's done, I clean the frying pan, and spray it with oil.

I get Camryn's pancake back on, and pay close attention to it this time. Once it's done, she sits at the table with the others, and I head down the hall to check on Gina. She's walking from the bathroom to her room, wrapped in a towel, and I instantly have to tame my dick.

I clear my throat outside her bedroom door, and she turns to see me. "Hey," I say for lack of anything else.

She frowns. "Everything okay? Did something burn?"

"Yes, I burnt a pancake and no, not everything is okay." A

worried look comes over her face. "The kids are fine." I let my gaze race over her body. "It's me who's not fine."

She laughs at that and I glance over my shoulder to make sure the coast is clear. "I'm not going to get this image out of my brain all day."

"Oh, let me give you a different one then." She opens the towel and exposes herself to me.

I grip my hair and tug. "Jesus, Gina. Are you trying to kill me?"

"Kill you no. Give you something to look forward to, yes." She wraps herself back up again, and goes to her closet to pull out clothes. "You better not leave them alone too long."

"Right." With that I head back down the hall, happy to find them all still at the table. "When you're done, go brush your teeth and get dressed. We'll clear the driveway and walkway and then go sledding."

A round of cheers erupt from the table, as I work on making a pancake for Gina. The kids jump up. "Plates on the counter."

They do as I ask and all run down the hall. I turn around as Gina enters, looking warm and inviting, dressed in jeans and a blouse that I hope to take off her later.

She sits and I put the pancake in front of her. "A girl could get used to this kind of service."

"Oh, I plan to service you."

She laughs at that. "Funny, I had that thought about you when you were fixing my fridge last year."

"You didn't just have that thought, you followed through with it." I glance up. No kids. I bend quickly and press my lips to hers. I only mean for it to be a fast kiss, but the second I taste her sweet mouth, I linger a moment longer.

Footsteps sound on the wooden floor, and I jolt upright before we get caught. "This looks delicious," Gina says, recovering quickly as Tate runs back to grab his little toy car from the table.

He disappears as fast as he appears, and I exhale. "Sorry about that."

I take in her half-lidded eyes. Okay, maybe she didn't recover as fast as I thought. "Now I'm going to be thinking about that all day."

"Good, you deserve it after you just flashed me."

Her warm chuckle curls around me as she pours syrup onto her pancake and slides the fork into her mouth, and for the first time in my life, I'm jealous of a fork.

"Where should I take them sledding?" I ask, working to get my focus on something else.

"Boston Common. My car has all the booster seats so you should take that. Also, there's a spare house key for you. It's in that drawer."

I open the drawer and fish out a key with a dolphin keychain. "I didn't know you were into dolphins."

"There's a lot you don't know about me." As I examine it, she explains. "A friend at the hospital where I worked gave it to me. She knew I liked dolphins. Someday I'd like to swim with them in the wild."

I never stopped to think about her life back in California. "Do you miss nursing, and your friends?"

She shrugs. "Sometimes, but I have a new life here." I'm about to ask if she ever considered going back, when there's a knock at the door. "Who the heck could be here so early in the morning?"

"Want me to get it?" She nods, and I set my coffee cup down and walk to the door just off the kitchen. A pretty girl, who looks to be in her early twenties, is standing there, a Boston Bucks jersey in her hands. That's when I realize she must be Margot's granddaughter.

I open the door. "You must be Callie." She nods quickly. "Your grandmother said she'd send you over when she saw my vehicle. I had to stay the night because of the weather," I say, not wanting to give her the wrong idea—or rather the right idea. Gina wants to keep what's happening between us a secret and I don't need anyone starting rumors.

"Getting here from the airport last night was scary." She holds her hand out to me. "It's so nice to meet you, Ash. I'm a huge fan." I shake her hand. "Grandma said that was your truck on the road, and I wanted to come over early and catch you before you left."

"I'll be here this weekend. I'm helping Gina with the kids so Margot can spend time with you and your mom."

"Nice of you." She steps a bit closer to me. "My mother and grandmother will be doing old lady mother things. I'm not much into that."

Old lady mother things?

She must read the question in my eyes as she goes on to explain, "You know, like bingo, shuffleboard. Cards. I'm so not into that, and I'm sure you're not either so what I'm suggesting is, in the evenings, if you're free, maybe you could show me some not old lady mother things." She laughs and I turn at the sound of footsteps to find Gina coming up behind me.

"Gina, this is Callie, Margot's granddaughter."

"It's great to meet you, Callie. Your grandmother is really looking forward to spending the week with you."

"I'm thinking that might not happen." She grins at me, before turning her attention to Gina. "Oh, it's nice to meet you too. I heard all about you and your daughter Zoe."

There's a strange almost astounded look on Gina's face, and I don't get what's going through her head until she speaks.

"You must be freezing."

I quickly realize Callie's dressed only in a tight, long-sleeved T-shirt and equally tight jeans, with sneakers. "I plan to put the jersey on after Ash signs it." She tugs on her T-shirt, the one she's wearing, exposing quite a bit of cleavage and I pray to fucking God she doesn't want me to sign her breasts. Yes, we're often asked, and no, I no longer do that. Even if I did, I think it would be highly inappropriate under the circum-stance and I'm not just talking about Zoe coming down the hall to see who's at the door.

"Hi," Zoe says.

Callie forces a smile and steps back a bit, sort of the same way I greeted Zoe the first time she bombarded me with questions. I guess she must be afraid of kids too. "You must be Zoe."

Zoe nods and Gina pulls her close, telling her exactly who Callie is as Callie produces a marker. I'm about to take it from her when she reaches for my arm and puts her phone number on it. "Uh, thanks," I say for lack of anything else. She hands me the marker and I quickly sign my name to the back of her jersey.

"What are you doing, Ash?" Zoe asks.

"I'm signing my jersey for Callie."

Just then Camryn and Tate come down the hall. "We wear our dad's jersey to the games," Camryn tells everyone.

Zoe glances up at Gina with hopeful eyes. "Mommy, can I get a jersey and wear it to a game?"

Camryn, being helpful, suggests, "I can probably get you one of Dad's. Or maybe Uncle Ash can give you one of his."

"Can I, Mommy?" She starts hopping from one foot to the other and I note Gina's unease. I've only ever seen Gina at the rink once, when she came with Melanie. I'm pretty sure hockey isn't her thing, but I'm sensing her unease is about something else entirely. "Can I?"

She pulls her daughter against her body. "We'll see, honey."

"Well, I'm an Ash fan," Callie pipes in, and everything about this situation suddenly makes me uncomfortable. "I'm going to your home game on Thursday."

"I'm an Ash fan too. I want to go on Thursday, too," Zoe says, and lifts her eyes to me. "Ash, will you sign a jersey for me?"

My gaze flies to Gina's, and I spot worry there. "Ah, we'll see. I'm not sure they make them in your size."

"Oh, they do," Camryn so helpfully provides. "They even make them in Tate's size. Right, Tate?" Tate nods emphatically.

I hand everything back to Callie and she pulls on the jersey. "Give me a call and…" Her voice falls off, her gaze going back and forth between Gina and me. "Wait, you two aren't—"

"No," I answer quickly, as Gina grabs a hat from the closet beside her.

"I didn't think so. I'll see you soon, Ash."

Being the mother that Gina is, she quickly hands her a hat. "At least put this on. It's freezing out there."

"I'm only going next door."

"I know…I just can't…"

"Stop being a mom?" Callie provides.

"Yeah."

"Well, when Mom and Grandma get together for bingo, I'll have them call you."

She laughs and pulls the hat on as she heads back out into the cold. As she gives me a little finger wave and a come-hither look, I can't stop thinking about why she didn't think Gina and I could be a couple. Sure, I have a reputation as a player —who likes to drink and drive and bang numerous bunnies at the time, all thanks to my ex—and I'm not much of a parental figure, but is it so outside the realm of possibility in people's minds that I could be with a woman like Gina?

I guess it is, and I guess I can understand why. But it does leave me wondering, does anyone out there besides my teammates believe the truth?

GINA

I spent the better part of the morning letting Callie live in my head rent free which is insanely ridiculous. Sure, I took what she said personally. How could I not? She was basically saying any woman with a child should be doing old lady mother things like playing bingo with her mother and grandmother. There is nothing wrong with bingo, and yes, I've been known to play shuffleboard and cards a time or two.

God, am I an old lady who does old lady things?

I don't know, but I do know Callie is the type of girl I'd seen Ash hanging out with in the past. Come to think of it, I haven't seen him out much lately and I'm not sure why he bailed on the Caribbean. Hating the heat seems like a poor excuse, if you ask me. But no one is asking. What I'm asking myself, however, is what's going on with Ash. Why isn't he out with the bunnies, lately? Maybe it's because it's regular season and he's trying to concentrate.

But will he take Margot up on her suggestion and show Callie around town? My stomach cramps. When she asked if we were a couple, he quickly shut that down. Then again, so did I when Margot asked. When it comes right down to it, we do not have claims on each other, and he can do whatever he wants. I have no right to feel jealous.

Then why do you?

Ugh.

I shut that down and focus on what's going on here and that once this weekend is over, we're over. I guess a part of me thinks that if we're going to be sleeping together until everyone gets back from the Caribbean, then maybe I'd like for us to be exclusive. Is that too much to ask? Jeez, I just don't know the rules of dating. Not that we're dating. We're hooking up. And believe you and me, I'm out of my comfort zone and have no idea how any of that works anymore.

A fork clangs on the floor, and pulls my thoughts back to the present. I glance around to take in the last couple of customers, lingering over coffee. With the lunch crowd dying down, I put Callie out of my brain and begin to clear tables. As I do, I check my phone for the hundredth time. Ash might be afraid of kids, and might not think he's good with them—there really is no one-fits-all manual, and I too had to learn through trial and error—but he totally stepped up this morning, and did a great job. Of course, they're all great kids, happy and easy to be around. My heart tightens a little in my chest at the way he ushered them all into the kitchen so I could get some extra sleep.

The man really isn't what I thought he was, and I'm not sure if that's a good or bad thing. But he was right about me needing the sleep. After the delicious, and somewhat risky, sex on the kitchen table, I really wanted the extra time in bed. I just wish he'd been in it with me. If we're going to do that again, we're going to have to be careful. We can't, under any circumstances, get caught kissing. With Camryn planting the idea of marriage and kissing in Zoe's head, I don't want her getting the wrong idea.

The bell over the door jingles and I glance up, half expecting it to be Ash and the kids. They've been gone for hours now, and he did text me earlier, letting me know he wanted to stop at his father's place to check on him. I might never meet the man who raised the Mountain, but the three kids are going to have the pleasure. My stomach takes that moment to tighten. I just don't want Zoe getting attached to Ash. But I guess if he's only watching her for a weekend, that's not likely to happen.

Heck, I don't want to get attached, either. But sex before bed, and pancakes and coffee upon awakening—while he tended to the kids. Yeah, I could get used to that.

My gaze goes to the gentleman searching for a seat. "Hello there," I greet as I scoop up a menu. "Table for one?"

He nods and blue eyes that seem a bit familiar light up as they land on me. "Just one."

"How about right here?" I guide him to the small table with a view of the outside, even though it's a miserable cold day. This way he can people watch as he eats, and maybe that won't feel so lonely for him. I'm not saying that he's lonely. I don't know the man. Maybe he likes being alone. Nevertheless, I care about my customers, and this way he has a choice between solitude and people watching.

He turns his coffee cup over and offers me a big smile. "Are you the owner of this lovely place now?"

"I am, for a couple of years now. I inherited it from my uncle. Did you know him?" I turn and look at the quaint café from his point of view. My life has changed so much in the last couple of years, and for the first time in a long time, I'm content. Happy? Well, I'm happy with my business and daughter, and I have great friends. That's enough for now. I don't know if it will be enough later on, and even if it's not, that's okay. I am keeping life status-quo.

"Heard it changed hands, but I've never been here before." He takes his coat and hat off and sets them on the other chair. "Only been living in Boston for a couple years now, though."

"Well…" I spread my arms. "Welcome to the Nook. I hope you become a regular." I fix his placemat. "What made you try it today?"

"Heard good things."

"Excellent. You go ahead and look over the menu." I hand him one. "And I'll be right back with the coffee."

I walk to the coffee pot behind the counter, just as the gentleman's cell phone rings and I glance back to see him fish it from his coat pocket. I reach for the carafe, and try not to eavesdrop on his conversation as I pour. He laughs and shakes his head as he catches my eye.

"I just thought I'd go out for lunch today." He covers the phone. "It's my son. He worries about me." That warms my heart. Ash takes care of his dad, too. Or rather, from the sounds of things, he'd like to, but his father is a proud man, or rather a stubborn bastard. That thought makes me want to laugh. For some reason, I find the thoughts of anyone giving the Mountain a hard time rather amusing.

You gave him a hard *time, Gina.*

I gulp at that, and work to maintain professionalism as my customer covers the phone. "My son. Needs to know where I am every damn minute of every damn day." I laugh, thinking about Ash's father and how he gives him a hard time.

"I think that's nice," I tell him. "It's nice to have someone in the family worry about you."

"I guess you have a loved one who worries over you too, huh?" My stomach clenches, because actually I don't have a loved one who worries over me. "I hope your husband or boyfriend or whoever your loved one is, isn't as big of a pain as my son."

I chuckle at that because while he's being a curmudgeon, his voice and eyes are full of love, and it fills me with an equal measure of joy and sadness. Joy for what this man has, and sadness for what I don't—family members who worry about me.

My mind goes to my late grandparents and my throat squeezes tight. They left everything to me when they passed, but it wasn't the material things that mattered. It was the love, kindness and forgiveness they always showed me. I want to be the same kind of parent to Zoe. It's not always easy doing it by myself and at times I'm just barely doing my best.

You can only do your best, Grandma used to say to me when I struggled in nursing school. They truly were good people, and Grandma always said they didn't make them like Grandpa anymore. I don't think she was wrong. It's funny, because back in their generation, the woman never asked the man out. But Grandma did. She saw what she wanted and went after it. I love that about her. She was so unconventional, and it paid off. They had a lifelong love affair. One day, she took me aside and told me they were leaving me something special in a safety deposit box and what she left me came with special instructions. When I fled California, I left the contents of the box behind.

"Are you kidding me?" the man seated before me says into the phone. I step back and he continues to talk to his son for a second. He laughs into the phone, and asks, "Do you think it's broken?" My ears perk up. I hope everything is okay. "Okay, son. I'll see you later." With that he hangs up. "Kids," he grouches and throws his hands up. "Do you have children?" he glances at my nametag. "Gina," he says. "I'm Grant."

"Well, Grant, I do have a child. One daughter. Six going on sixteen."

"Oh yes, my son was the same. He was hardheaded at times and stubborn as hell. Although," he begins sadly. "He had to grow up fast." I don't press, and he continues. "Just the two of us."

Is Zoe growing up too fast? Do I give her too many responsibilities?

"He's a fine young man, though." He jabs his thumb into his chest. "Takes after his father, I'm happy to say."

I laugh at that. "From what I can tell, I'd say that's a good thing."

"I like you," he says with a wink and under his breath murmurs, "I can see why he does too."

My head rears back. "I'm sorry, what was that?"

"What do you recommend?" He turns his attention to the menu, and I let go whatever it was he was talking about. Perhaps he has some memory issues.

I point to the special on the menu. "I have to say the chicken pot pie is pretty delicious."

"Chicken pot pie...the last time I had chicken pot pie was..." He goes quiet, thoughtful, then a laugh bursts out of his throat. "...I can't remember the last time. It sounds just about right for today, though."

"Chicken pot pie it is, then. Perfect to warm you up on this chilly day."

He takes a big drink of his coffee as I head to the back to put in his ticket. Once his meal is prepared and I see that there's not much left in the dish, I scoop some up into a take-away container for him. Come late afternoon, we mostly sell pastries and coffee, and I don't want this to go to waste.

I bring him his steaming bowl of chicken pot pie, and he picks up his fork as he breathes in the delicious scents.

"Lovely."

I wink at him. "I had a bit extra. Not enough for a meal, but definitely an evening snack." I set the bag on the table. "It's on the house."

"That is awfully kind of you. You'll have to let me thank you somehow."

I grin, his words reminding me of how I'm always trying to thank Ash for all he does for me.

"Just knowing you'll enjoy it is thanks enough."

I leave him to his meal and check my phone as I head to the kitchen to help Carla clean up. We get only a few stragglers in the next half hour, so I head back out to clear the gentleman's dishes. Worry gnaws at me, but I didn't tell Ash he had to check in. I don't want to call and have him think I don't trust him to handle all three kids.

A loud noise on the front window, right where Grant is sitting reverberates through the café. I swivel and the second I see Ash there, tissues stuck into both nostrils as he points an accusatory finger at Grant my heart nearly stops.

What the heck is going on?

8

ASH

What the ever-loving fuck is my dad doing at Gina's café. I tear off my glove, tap on the window, hard, and his head lifts. "What are you doing?" I ask even though I'm sure he can't hear me through the glass.

He gives me a wide, innocent look—but I know him well enough to know he's up to something and that something is no good. I shake my head, and swear to God if he's messing around in my life, and of course he is, I'm going to strangle him.

My gaze leaves his and meets Gina's as she walks toward him. Her steps slow, and when her eyes go wide with worry, I remember I have two tissues shoved up my damn nose. Dad just shakes his head at me, barely worried, because it's nothing he hasn't seen before.

Gina comes running to the door as the kids press their lips to the window and blow. They're laughing and joking and Tate is practically falling over from exhaustion, as the door flings open and Gina stares at me in shock.

"Ash. What the heck? Are you okay?" She rubs her arms as a gust of cold wind rolls down the street.

"Yeah." The only thing hurt is my pride. Okay, and my nose. It fucking hurts too, but I'm too embarrassed to admit it. That's what I get for acting like a big kid, but dammit, the sledding looked fun.

She steps closer, her head bobbing around as she examines me. "Is it broken?"

"No. Yes. I don't know." I'd broken my nose before, numerous times, and it always hurt like hell. Probably more than it hurts right now. I touch it and wince. "I don't think so."

"Come in, come in." She ushers us all in, and the kids kick the snow off their boots before they trudge inside, bringing a burst of cold air with them. The delicious scent of coffee reaches my nose and I guess that's a good sign that I can still smell...and breathe.

"I want hot chocolate." Tate's eyes are drooping in their sockets and I'm a little worried he's going to faceplant on the floor any second.

Gina points to the corner. "Yes, you three grab a booth and get out of your wet coats."

They all collapse at a table, and Gina calls for Carla, asking her to bring three hot chocolates and a glass of water with ice.

She examines me again going up on her toes, and her breath is so warm on my face, it makes me sleepy, and aroused. "What happened?"

"A bump happened," I grumble, more focused on my grinning father than Gina's concern. He's going to hear about this from me when we're alone. What does he think he's doing anyway? When I went to his place and he wasn't there, I should have known he was up to his meddling ways. I never should have called him last night to let him know I had to stay over at Gina's.

He wipes his mouth with his napkin and stretches his arms over his head, like he's not in a hurry to go anywhere. Seeing me with a nice woman and a handful of kids is all he's ever wanted.

"What are you doing here?" I ask.

"Ash," Gina scolds. "He's a customer. Can you remove those tissues so I can have a look." She takes my arm. "Actually here. Sit down." She guides me to the table beside my father's and starts lightly pressing my nose.

I try to jerk away. "It's fine."

"Stubborn." Dad chuckles. "Told you so." He leans toward me, to examine my nose.

"What's that?" Gina asks, her eyes narrowed in on me, as she picks up a napkin, and dabs it in the water Carla just set down.

Dad taps his head. "Hardheaded." He laughs. "Must get it from his old man."

As soon as the words leave his mouth, Gina's head lifts. I stare at her, and the moment her eyes go wide, I realize she's put two and two together. "Yeah, that's my dad."

"You're...Ash's dad?"

"The one and only. Who knew I'd run into him here today." He narrows his eyes. "I don't think it's broken. Not like when you were playing street hockey and ran into that street sign."

I refuse to let him change the subject. He knew damn well he'd run into me here today, and I'm not letting him off so easy. "Give it up, Dad."

"Give what up, son? I simply went out for a walk. You know I love my walks, and saw this café. I thought I remembered you once told me it had great food. Thought I'd check it out for myself, and I'm happy to say you were right." He winks at Gina and I grumble at his blatant nosiness. "Great company too."

"Out for a walk?" I arch a brow but the movement hurts my nose. "Is that why your truck is parked down the road?"

He gives a sheepish look. "Saw that did you?" He taps his head. "Getting senile. Must have forgotten I drove."

There's not a damn senile thing about him. "Yeah, and since when do you walk ten miles?"

"I drove for a bit and then jumped out and walked the rest of the way. Slipped my mind."

"Wait, wait, wait," Gina says, hands up, palms out and all eyes turn to her. "Grant is your father?" Her gaze goes back and forth between the two of us. "I thought there was something familiar. I should have guessed."

"He's my father and he's here sticking his nose into my business—where it doesn't belong."

"If I remember correctly, you called him earlier wanting to know where he was. Doesn't that mean you were sticking your nose into his business too?" She winks at my dad. She actually fucking winks at my dad, like they're co-conspirators. What the hell is happening in my life?

"That's right," Dad bursts in. "Right mad that I wasn't home where he left me. All up in my business, wasn't he, Gina?"

"That's the way I saw it." She leans into my dad. "But that's a good thing because it's nice when family worries, right Grant?"

"Yeah, you're right." He turns his attention to the corner table. "Those your kids?" he asks and stands. "I thought you only had one."

"I do, the one in the corner." Gina gestures with a nod to Zoe, who is tugging on the braid I'd put in her hair this morning. I did a damn fine job of it too. I'm a man of many talents. *Okay, no time to be thinking of talents Gina appreciates when your dad is watching, dude.* A boner is the last thing I fucking need.

"I'm babysitting the other two for a friend," Gina explains.

I grumble under my breath, and I'm about to tell him it's time for him to go home, when he crosses to the kids, and drops down next to Tate.

"Gina," I begin.

"Let's just get this nose taken care of and then we'll deal with your dad, okay?"

"Fine."

"Do you want to tell me what happened?" She carefully washes my nose, and I wince as she runs her finger along the bone. "I don't think it's broken. We can go get an x-ray to make sure, though."

"No, I'm good, and don't worry, the kids weren't hurt."

She inches back and her eyes meet mine. "I wasn't worried about that. They look completely exhausted and happy. It's you I'm worried about."

My stupid heart pounds a little harder in my chest. It's crazy that I like that, right? Didn't I say I wanted to take care of her and now here she is, worrying about me, and taking care of my stupid fucking nose.

She fills a napkin with ice, and gently holds it to my nose. "Are you going to tell me what happened?"

"No," I grouch.

"Mommy," Zoe burst out as she comes running over, bending to try to look up my nose. "He went on my sled, and he didn't fit, and he hit a bump and he punched himself in the face with his knees."

Gina stifles a laugh and I glare at her. "It's not funny."

"No, not funny at all."

"You're visualizing it, aren't you? Me on a small kids sled with my knees at my chin and then 'punching' myself in the face."

"No, but I guess technically it's kneeing yourself in the face."

"I'm going to get you a cinnamon roll. They always make me feel better." Zoe darts into the kitchen and when she's out of ear shot, I reach for Gina's arm.

"You're fucking laughing," I say my voice low, for her ears only as I pull her toward me. Her hair falls forward, framing her beautiful face, her eyes bright with laughter as she bites her lips to keep them from curling upward. Jesus Christ, it's all I can do not to kiss her. But with everyone watching, that would send the wrong message and forget about the kids getting the wrong idea, my dad would cling to that like dryer lint to cotton.

"How about we get the kids upstairs. I actually think they could all use a nap."

Zoe comes running back with a plate of cinnamon rolls. "Here you go Ash, this will make you feel better."

"Thanks," I grumble and accept it. I carefully bite into one. "You're right, Zoe. I do feel better."

Gina waves her hands. "Okay, kids, time to head upstairs."

"Why don't you go ahead, too?" Carla suggests. "Andre and I can finish up here, and lock up."

"Are you sure?" she asks, already going for the ties on her apron.

Carla leans in. "I think you have your hands full." She gives a playful wink full of mischief. "And if they aren't, they should be."

"I'm right here," I say, and Carla lets loose a laugh and throws a tea towel over her shoulder as she walks away.

I catch Gina's eye. "I thought this was supposed to be a secret."

"It is, she's only speculating." I look around her.

"She's not the only one," I grouch.

Gina follows my gaze, and grins as my dad plays some game where he holds his thumb up and index finger out on one hand, doing the opposite on the other and switching. The kids keep trying, only to fail, cause it's damn hard and took me forever to get it.

"I like your dad. He's really nice."

"Yeah, well, be careful or the next thing you know he'll be wanting to walk you down the aisle. He likes to meddle in my life."

She laughs. "Nope, not going to happen." She crinkles her cute nose.

"I should have left him in Colorado."

"You don't mean that."

"I know."

She laughs. "Come on, let's finish these upstairs." She picks up the plate of cinnamon rolls. "Come on kids. Time for a nap." They all grumble about not wanting a nap as Gina ushers them toward the stairs. She stops and glances back as I walk toward Dad, who's tugging on his coat and hat. "Grant, would you like to come up for a cinnamon roll?"

I groan under my breath, and Dad smiles at her. "That's a lovely offer, Gina, but I must get going, though. I have an errand to run."

Gina makes her way up with the kids, and Dad grins at me. "I can see why you like her."

"Dad, I'm helping out a friend. She was stuck in a bind."

"A bind? Like with ropes?"

"Oh, my fucking God." His playful grin tells me exactly where his mind has gone and no I'm not going there with my dad. Sometimes I wonder who the adult is in this relationship.

Dad puts his hand on my shoulder. "No need to cuss, son. I get it, you were helping her out with the kids. Lovely kids they are, too."

"Yeah, lovely. Why don't you head home, and I'll come have dinner with you tonight. I'll grab us something. How about Italian from that little café you like?"

"I think this is my new favorite café. Gina packed me chicken pot pie to go. Besides I don't want to take you away. Seems like you're needed here."

"You're not taking me away from anything. I help out during the day while Gina is working and now she's not working. I'm free to do whatever I want."

He snorts out a laugh and pokes my forehead. "If you're choosing to spend that free time with me, maybe you might want to check to see if you have a concussion. You did take a hard hit in your last game."

"Dad, you know—"

He waves his hand and cuts me off. "Yeah, yeah, I know. Head in the game, no complications." He takes a step toward the door. "Although it might be a little too late for that." Whistling like the damn cat who ate the canary, he walks out the door with a little more pep in his step.

As I watch him go, my heart pinches. Honestly, all the man wants is to see me happy, with a family and kids of my own. After his heart attack, I promised him I'd give him what he wanted. Those words were spoken in the heat of the moment, when I thought I might lose him. Now, after the stunt my ex pulled, and with my coach down my neck, I reneged on that promise. Who can blame me, and again, even if I wanted something more with Gina, she made it perfectly clear she wasn't going down that path again.

Before I head upstairs, I follow my dad out. One, to make

sure he makes it to his truck okay, and two, to make sure he actually goes to his truck and doesn't go snooping around.

"You don't think I can find my way to my truck?" he accuses.

"I don't think that at all. I just forgot something in Gina's car."

He grumbles, knowing the truth and once he's safe in the cab of his truck, I walk to Gina's car, and fuss around in the back seat, pulling out some random toy. My father rolls his eyes at me as I head back to the café. I understand he likes his independence, and I knows he loves the relationship we have, and he realizes that I simply care about his well-being. He just likes to grump about it.

On the sidewalk, I run into Callie. Or rather she runs into me, literally. I slide my hand around her waist to keep her upright when she slips and nearly lands on her ass. "Whoa, are you okay?"

"I was hoping to run into you."

"Looks like that happened."

She laughs, and I note she's still not wearing a coat. Does she realize she's no longer in California? "My grandmother told me about a local Scottish pub, Kilting Around. Want to join me for a drink?"

"Oh, I can't." I glance over my shoulder as Dad pulls from the curb. "Having dinner with my dad tonight."

She pouts. "Be careful, Ash..." her gaze goes to the café and I follow it, and spot movement in the upstairs window. Was that Gina? "...or you're going to be old before your time and tied down playing bingo." She laughs, turns, and gives a little shake to her ass as she heads back to her grandmother's. "Another time then."

Once she's gone, I head inside the cafe and go upstairs. It's quiet when I enter the apartment. I walk to the kitchen and find it empty. Whispered voices from down the hall reach my ears, and I tip toe, stopping outside Zoe's bedroom door. I find Tate fast asleep in one bed, and Gina reading to the girls in the other, both of them desperately trying to keep their eyes open. I guess I really did wear them out on the hill. I stifle a yawn. I could probably use a nap too.

I'm about to step away when Gina's eyes lift and meet mine, and as I take in the warm, cozy image before me, it triggers something deep inside, awakens something long ago buried. What the hell is going on with me?

It's wrong of me to get involved with a single mom. Getting tied down with her when I'm supposed to be staying away from women? Out of the question. Let's face it. Lessons learned have taught me women don't stay, and if they do, it's only until they get what they want from you.

Why then do I suddenly feel like playing bingo?

Maybe Dad was right. Maybe I did take a hard hit to the head last game.

9

GINA

It's so odd. The place feels so incredibly lonely without Ash here, and he only stayed the one night. Well, that's not good, considering emotions aren't supposed to play any part in this friends with benefits scenario.

He didn't have dinner with us, even though the kids begged him to stay and play games. He had to go visit with his father. I love the way they are together, even though Ash was mad that his dad came here to check me out. Does that mean Ash had been talking about me?

I shouldn't care about that. I really shouldn't. Yet, here I am a little amused by the idea of it. Ash might be big, rough and gruff at times, but I'm beginning to believe that underneath it all he's a cinnamon roll, like his father. I really liked Grant and the pride and love in his eyes as he stared at his son did the craziest things to my heart and my head. That look was also returned by Ash, and it hurts my soul to know my daughter will never have that.

The popping of the dice game the kids are playing, followed by Tate's laughter, pulls me back to reality, and for some reason, I don't feel like sitting around the house tonight. Melanie didn't go to the Caribbean, either. She and Brady are home with their baby. If she's feeling as cooped up as me, maybe she'd like some company.

I push to my feet and search for my phone. I spot it on the kitchen counter and as I walk toward it, it rings. Brighton had checked on the kids earlier, so I have no idea who would be calling. I pick it up and my heart does a weird little happy dance when I see that it's Ash. Jeez, I really wish I wasn't so happy to hear from him.

I slide my finger across the screen, and try to sound casual. "Ash."

"Yeah."

God what is it about his one-word answers that mess with me. Maybe it's the deep tenor, the way he breathes it out, that has the ability to tease the needy juncture between my legs. I really don't know. All I know is I'm melting a little inside as I sink into a kitchen chair.

"What's up?"

"How are the kids?"

My heart wobbles. I like that he's asking about them, even though they scare him. Although, maybe after today's sledding adventures, he's come to realize they're not so frightening. "They're good. Playing a game. How's your dad?"

"Stubborn bastard."

"Takes one to know one," Grant responds in the background.

"Jesus, Dad, are you twelve?"

I stifle a laugh at their banter, and hear a horn honk. Is he driving? "What's going on?"

"Dad said he's not feeling well. His stomach hurts. I want to take him to a clinic, but he won't go. I at least convinced him to come to my place. We're on our way there now."

"How is his temperature?"

"I don't know. He doesn't own a thermometer. Not that he'd let me take it anyway."

Grant's voice is a little closer to the phone when he responds with, "Gina can take my temperature."

A frustrated sigh escapes Ash's lips. "He said—"

"I heard."

"We're almost at my place now. I can turn around."

"No, if he's not feeling well, it's best to get him settled. I can pack up the kids and come over."

"Gina, I don't know."

"It's okay, really. It's still early and I'm feeling a little cooped up anyway. I was thinking of giving Melanie a call to see if she wanted some company, so I was planning on heading out your way anyway."

A moment of quiet, and then, "If it's not too much trouble. I worry about him."

"Ash, it's the least I can do." I stand and walk to the window to look out at the backyard. It's dark after dinner, and dreary. I could really use the adult company. "Look at everything you've been doing for me."

"We're here now." His voice is low, tired. Did the kids wear him out today? Am I asking too much of him, or is he just really worried about his father? I know how much the man means to him. "I'll share my location."

"Okay." My phone pings as he shares his location and I don't admit that I already know where he lives. Melanie pointed it out to me ages ago. I think she was trying to get a reaction, so she could see if there was anything going on between Ash and me. My friends do know I'm lonely, and how long it's been for me. I sort of made that clear when I told Dani and the others that I wouldn't be opposed to casual sex, but if they knew it was with Ash, it could complicate things when we end it. I don't want anyone to be uncomfortable around us.

"Ash?"

"Yeah?"

"Did you guys eat? I have some leftovers." I walk to the fridge and pull it open. "I could easily pack them."

"Don't go through the trouble. I'll just order in. I'm not sure Dad can eat anything anyway."

"I am going through the trouble. Fast food is awful for you, and I want you to be healthy when you play this week. You are not getting clogged arteries and having a heart attack on my watch. You're a professional hockey player and need to be in your best shape."

I hear a car door slam and his voice is soft, amused, when he whispers, "Thanks, babe."

Thanks, babe.

Gawd, why does that sound so nice, so deliciously intimate... like we're partners in this thing called life. I'm not going to lie. I've always wanted that. A man to share the good times with, the bad times with, to be together at night to wind down with after a long day, to...

Get it together, Gina.

I close the fridge and walk into the living room. My heart warms as I take in the sight of the three kids playing. Am I wrong to take them to Ash's place? I'm sure Camryn and Tate must have been there before, as their father and Ash are best friends and play on the same team. Will Zoe start getting attached if she sees Ash as more than a temporary babysitter? Do I really have a choice, though? Ash needs me, and he's always been there for me whenever I needed him, and even when I didn't.

"Who wants to go to Ash's place tonight?" I ask.

"Me, me, me," Tate bursts out. "He has a pool table."

"Oh, you play pool, do you, Tate?" I ask and he starts jumping up and down.

He throws his arms out. "I am the bestest pool player ever."

"Do you know how to play pool?" Camryn asks Zoe, who shakes her head no. "I can teach you."

My heart squeezes tight. They really are great kids. Brighton and Noah are doing a fantastic job raising them and that thought tightens my stomach. I hate that Zoe is missing a father, but hers wanted nothing to do with her and that can only damage her more in the end.

"Okay, go get your coats and boots on. It's cold out there."

As they get ready, I pull the lasagna from the fridge and pack up enough for Ash and Grant, although with a bad stomach, I doubt his father will be eating. It's flu season, and it's probably nothing more than that. I'll just be sure to keep the kids in another room. Although they did sit with him this afternoon while having hot chocolate. Damn, I hope none of them get sick. Once the food is packed, I go find my mom bag, which contains medication, a thermometer, and everything else a nurse could need.

I find the kids at the closet, and I pull out my coat and slip into my boots. We used the upstairs door, and make our way down the long set of steps to the ground.

The night air is cool and there's a few flakes of snow falling as I usher them to the car. I know better than to try to buckle any of them in. They're all too independent for such foolishness. I pop the trunk, carefully place the food and mom bag in it, and hurry to my door. In the driver's seat I adjust the mirror, and pull out onto the street, which is rather quiet this Saturday night.

I drive carefully through the light layer of snow on the ground, and I'm grateful I don't have that far to go. I finally reach the elite Beacon Hill area, and slow as I drive by Melanie's place. I'm going to have to plan a girls' night soon, when everyone is back from the Caribbean and the guys are all back to playing. I've only gone to one game this year, to be honest. I'm usually too tired at the end of the night. Fortunately, I don't usually work weekends anymore, and only fill in when I'm short-staffed.

Camryn points out the window as I turn the heat down. "That's where Melanie and Brady live." She hugs herself. "She has a new baby and he's so cute."

"Mom, can we get a baby?"

Oh, dear God.

"That comes after you get a daddy," Camryn so helpfully supplies. "Let's ask Uncle Ash to make more pancakes tomorrow, and I'll give you one of my wishes."

In the rearview mirror, I catch my daughter's smile and my heart jumps into my throat. Now she wants a daddy and a baby. I'm afraid neither of those things are going to happen, and I just don't have the heart to sit her down and tell her. Perhaps after the weekend is over and Camryn goes back home she'll forget all about daddies, and babies and wish lumps.

I ease my car in behind Ash's and take in his big mansion. Oddly enough, my thoughts go back to Lucian, and his monstrous home. I used to think it was crazy for him to have such a big place for one person. I snort out a laugh. Little did I know how wrong I was.

"Mommy, what's funny?"

"Oh, I was just remembering a joke."

Or rather, that I was the joke. Yeah, that's me, a big stupid joke. But in the end I got Zoe and she's the best thing that ever happened to me.

While Ash's house is big too, I realize it's an investment and a lot of the guys live nearby. He does not have a secret family hidden in another state, of that I'm sure.

"Okay, everyone unbuckle."

There's rusting in the back, and Camryn is out first. My heart warms as she helps her brother, who wants no help at all. I usher them up the long walkway as wind whips around us, and I glance back, looking at the way the streetlamps light up the falling snow, which is getting heavier. Damn, was it a mistake to bring the kids out in this? I'd better make this a fast trip before the roads get bad.

I stop for a quick moment, just to enjoy the view, and the strange peacefulness of it all. Unlike the center of the city where I live, it's quiet here, and it gives me a very weird, almost nostalgic feeling. Not that I ever grew up in such a luxurious neighborhood. I think it has more to do with the families that live in the homes. I'm picturing warmth, Sunday dinners, laughter, movie nights…

All the things you secretly want, huh, Gina?

The door swings open and the second I set eyes on Ash, standing tall, as a warm smile curves his lips at the sight of us, my heart misses a beat.

"Uncle Ash, can we play pool?" Camryn asks.

"Of course, you can. You know where it is."

"Hi Ash," Zoe says. "I like your house."

She brushes past him and he grins at me. "She likes my house."

"It is a nice house." He glances over his shoulder, like he's checking to see if the coast is clear and when it is, he pulls me to him. I slam against his hard body, and he dips his head. God, I feel like I'm back in high school, sneaking kisses in the hall with my boyfriend.

"Thanks for coming."

"Of course." His lips brush over mine, soft and tender at first. When I moan, and grip the front of his shirt, needing the contact with his body, he groans and drags me closer. A car goes by and someone honks, and it pulls us from our stupor. Ash lifts his head and waves.

"Who was that?"

"I don't know. Let's just hope it's not a reporter or we'll be all over the news."

God, I don't want that. "Do you think they saw me?" I turn and scan the street, as the car slows and pulls into a driveway.

"Looks like it's one of my neighbors. Just being friendly, I guess." He pulls me inside and shuts the door behind us, locking the world out and us in.

"How's your dad?"

"Ornery as ever."

I hold up my bag. "I brought my mom bag."

"Mom bag?" He looks at the black bag in my hand and I laugh.

"When you're a mom, you rarely go anywhere without all the meds and thermometers. When you're also a nurse, it's a big mom bag."

He laughs and takes it from me. "Jesus, this is heavy. I'm guessing you can cure whatever's ailing him."

I give him a hopeful smile. "I'm going to try." I hold up another bag. "This is dinner."

"That was really sweet of you. I owe you."

I grin. "Maybe you do."

"Hang on." He hurries down the hall with the dinner bag, and when he comes back, he puts his hand on the small of my back and leads me to the stairs. In the distance, I can hear balls clanging. "Are they okay playing pool on your table?" I can just imagine them driving the stick into the felt and tearing it.

"They're fine. Camryn knows her way around this place, and there's nothing they can get into." We head up the long staircase and I note there's no pictures on the walls, or anything that really makes the place homey. Does he ever get lonely in this big old place? Or does he fill it with bunnies when his father isn't here, and when he's not helping out a friend—with benefits?

"He's in here." I step into the big bedroom and find Grant lying in bed, watching TV on a huge TV over the dresser. The minute he sees me, he moans and puts his hand on his stomach.

"How are you feeling?" I ask.

"Horrible."

I take in his pallor, which is no different from earlier today, and step up to him and put my hand on his forehead. "You don't feel hot. Is it okay if I take your temperature?" He nods and Ash brings my bag to me. I fish out the thermometer and put it to his ear. I click the button and check. "No fever. That's a good sign. Can you tell me about the stomach pain you're experiencing?"

Just then the news comes on and he turns it up. "Look at that," Grant says, sitting up like he doesn't have any kind of distress. "More snow coming tonight." He clicks his lips. "Probably best if you and the kids stay here tonight. No need to be on the roads if you don't have to be. Amiright or amiright?" He fakes a cough and I angle my head to study him. I thought I was here because he had a bad stomach and possibly the flu. I'm about to ask about this new symptom when he takes my hand and pats it. "Also, with me not feeling well, it would be good to have a nurse close by."

"Dad," Ash says in a low, warning voice. "What are you up to?"

"Dad?" I ask again when he lays back down, turns the TV off, and moans like he's in total agony.

"I need to try and get some sleep. Don't go far, Gina." Suddenly his voice is feeble, and I flashback to the time he had his heart attack. My gut tightens. Dammit, I really hope he is playing matchmaker here. If he's not, I can't risk his heart failing on him again. Maybe Gina should stay. Would that be asking too much? She's busy enough as it is, and my father isn't her problem.

Dad points to her bag. "I might need something in that bag. Something to help me relax."

"Do you feel like you're going to vomit?" she asks, everything in her words and demeanor so damn sweet and caring, my heart could be at risk.

He coughs again. "It's possible."

She reaches into her bag and pulls out something for nausea. "This will help and it will also help you sleep."

"Oh, yes, I'd better take one. I could use a good night's sleep."

She pushes a pill through the foil package. "What about your cough? Is your throat sore?"

"Just a tickle. I probably just need a glass of water. Son, why don't you run and get that." As he waves me away, he smiles at Gina. "I'm in good hands with Gina."

Jesus Christ.

Not really wanting to leave them alone—Lord knows what the man is going to say to her—I stand there for a moment.

"He could use some water," Gina says. "That's one thing I don't have in the mom bag."

"Mom bag." Dad laughs, like a man who is faking sick. But I can't accuse him of that, or come right out and say he's trying to trick Gina into staying overnight. What if he really is sick, and something happens? I'd never forgive myself.

"Do you think he needs to go to a clinic or the hospital?" I ask.

"No," Gina assures me. "I think he might just have a stomach virus, and his throat isn't sore. The air inside can get dry in the winter, and that's probably the cough." She glances back at Dad. "Maybe we should set up a humidifier in here."

"Oh, great idea. Do you have one of those, Ash?" His bushy brows bunch together as he focuses in on me.

I fold my arms. "No."

"We can order one online, and it will likely be here tomorrow," Gina provides.

"Let me get the water first." I glance out the big window and take in the fat flakes falling. "Gina, if you have to go before the snow gets heavy, I totally get it."

Dad moans and holds his stomach. Gina frowns and takes his hand. "If you need me to stay Grant, I can stay. I have the kids, though."

"This is a great house for kids. Look at Ash, he's like a big kid himself, getting on a sled today." He laughs as Gina looks at my nose, and then as if remembering he's sick, he puts his hand on his stomach and wipes the smile from his face. As if that's not enough to convince Gina to stay, he adds, "Big TV's, games room. Lots to do. I'm sure they'll love to have a sleepover."

She frowns, and runs her hands over her yoga pants. "We don't have any clothes or even our toothbrushes."

Dad snuggles into his blankets, looking so damn pleased with himself. "I'm sure Ash can round up some things. Isn't that right, Ash?"

"Gina, I don't want you to stay if you don't want to. If you do, there are plenty of bedrooms and I can probably find clothes, though they'll be too big for you all, especially Tate."

"Can we stay, Mom?" Zoe asks from the doorway. "This place is the best. There's a whole games room." She opens her arms wide. "The TV is this big."

I turn, not realizing Zoe had been standing there listening in. She gives me a big smile. "Your house is one hundred times bigger than ours. I love it here."

A strange noise crawls out of Gina's throat and when I glance at her, there's a hint of concern in her eyes. "Gina?"

Dad moans again and she stands. "Why don't you get him some water so he can take his pill?" She pauses for a moment, and glances at the window. "And maybe you can find us all some clothes to sleep in."

"Yay." Zoe jumps up and down before rushing back to the games room, to tell Camryn and Tate, I assume.

I nod at Gina, and head to the kitchen. I grab a bottle of water from the fridge and by the time I get back upstairs, Gina is leaning in, and listening to Dad who's talking quietly. I have no idea what they're talking about and maybe I don't want to know. Clearing my throat to make my presence known, I step into the room, uncap the bottle and hand it to Dad.

"Thanks, son." Gina hands him the pill and he takes a sip of water to swallow it down. "Can you stay in the bedroom right beside me?"

"That's my room, Dad."

"Oh right."

"She can stay across the hall." I glance at Gina. "Is that okay? It's a king-sized bed. We can put the kids all together in the room beside yours. It also has a king-sized bed. Plenty of room for all three."

She gives me a warm smile, a bit of worry from earlier dissipating from her eyes. "They'd like that."

I jerk my thumb out, toward the hall. "How about you give me a hand to find some clothes? Dad, are you okay for now?"

He can't seem to hide his big smile, and while that convinces me more and more that he might be faking, it also gives me a measure of relief.

Gina tucks Dad in, then follows me into the hall and I point to my room. "I'm right here." We walk into my bedroom, and I note the way her steps slow to take it all in. Not that there is much to take in. I have a bed and a dresser. It lacks the warmth of her house, but I don't have anyone to impress.

"Such a big room," she finally says.

I pull open my closet. "I have some old sweats and shirts. We can cut them down for the kids."

She laughs. "I don't want to ruin your clothes."

I pull out a gray pair of sweats and hold them up. "These might work for you." I toss them to her, and she examines them.

"I can work with these."

I pull more sweats out, and throw them on the bed. "I don't wear these anymore. The kids might have fun cutting them up."

She grins. "They'd probably like that."

"I also have some very old jerseys from when I was younger." I pull out the smallest ones I can find. "These could work."

Gina frowns and folds the sweats. "Are you sure? They don't have value to you?"

"This was before the NHL. Earlier in my career. I just never toss anything. I should probably go through this closet and donate things."

"You could probably do a raffle and make money." She sits on the edge of my bed, and as she makes herself comfortable, my damn dick twitches. Fuck, I suddenly can't stop thinking about what it would be like to see her between my sheets, with me between her legs. Fuck. "It'd be a great donation for peewee hockey. I know you give a lot of your time to that."

I cock my head and eye her, working to get my mind off sex, although that's a difficult task with her in my room, the memories of what we did in her kitchen, twice, racing around my lust-rattled brain. "How do you know about peewee hockey? You've been checking up on me."

"How can I?" She throws her hands up in defeat. "You don't have any social media."

My throat tightens. She's right. I don't. I got rid of all my personal accounts after my ex dragged my name through the mud. So many horrific comments on my posts. I couldn't fucking take that, so I deleted everything.

"Ash?"

"Yeah."

"Everything okay?"

"I'm good. Just uh, I hate social media."

"Honestly, I do too. I have accounts for the café, but don't post on my personal ones anymore. I don't want people knowing my business."

"But you did try to check mine?" I tease.

"A girl can be curious."

I push all thoughts of my ex to the back of my mind as I laugh and reach into the closet to pull out a sweatshirt for Gina. "How is this for you?"

She walks over to me, and takes it. "It's perfect for right now, but it might be too warm to sleep in. Do you have a T-shirt I could borrow?"

"Right." I go to my dresser, tug it open and find a T-shirt for her.

"Thanks." She holds the clothes in her hands, and glances toward the door. "We should probably go check on the kids. It's quiet. When it gets too quiet, I get worried."

I laugh at that. "This house is well insulated. I made sure of it because I need to sleep during the day sometimes. You can't hear much from up here. They're probably still in the games room having fun."

We walk into the hall, and I open the bedroom door, showing her where she'll be sleeping. It's pretty much the same as my room. A bed and dresser. Kids are in there," I tell her with a nod.

As we walk by Dad's room, she peeks in and he's on his side, facing away from us. I quietly pull his door closed, but not all the way.

"Looks like he's resting nicely now," she whispers.

We head downstairs to the games room, and the kids are having a blast with the pool table, and my old pinball machine.

"Hey guys, looks like we're going to have a sleepover," Gina says.

Camryn beams with happiness. "I know, Zoe told us."

Gina cocks her brow. "You're all okay with that?"

"Yes, I love it here," Camryn says and Tate nods in agreement.

"I have some clothes for you guys. We're going to cut the legs off these pants and make shorts. Doesn't that sound fun? I also have some of Ash's old jerseys for you to wear."

That gains Zoe's attention and she comes running over. I hand her the jersey and she pulls it on. It's huge on her and I start to roll up the sleeves.

Her eyes light up as she glances up at me. "I love my new jersey. Camryn and Tate get to wear their dad's number and now I get to wear yours, Ash."

The excitement in her voice makes me laugh. "You can have it. You can take it home."

"Mommy, Mommy, I get to keep Ash's jersey." She throws her arms around my waist. "Thank you, Ash. I'm never going to take it off." Once again, I see that worried look on Gina's face, but she turns from me and walks to my pinball machine. She runs her hands over it.

"I love this, Ash." She looks back at me, and the haunted look is gone from her face. "Where did you get it?"

"Dad got it when I was a kid. He was doing some electrical work for an old arcade and they were tossing the old machine out. Dad asked if he could have it, and when they agreed, he brought it home and fixed it for me." He's such a good dad and maybe I'm being an asshole, thinking he's trying to matchmake here. "I can beat you at it later, if you like?"

She laughs. "You think you can beat me."

"I don't know. Did you have a misguided childhood?"

Her smile is a mixture of warmth and pain. Nothing about our upbringings were traditional, that's for sure and I really hate that she thinks she's an asshole magnet. Gina just hasn't found the right guy for her, that's all.

"No, I was a saint, Ash. Just like you." She grins. "Oh, I guess now I can ask your dad all about your childhood."

I laugh. "Maybe don't do that."

She grins and focuses in on the kids. "Okay, kiddos. You have fifteen more minutes in here, and then you're going to wash up, help me cut up these clothes and I'll put on a movie before bed."

As I watch her put the clothes on the sofa, I can't help but grin. In the span of an hour, my house went from one person sleeping here, to six. I'm used to the quiet and solitude, but I can't really say as I hate any of this.

And that's probably not a good thing, for numerous reasons.

GINA

With three kids sitting between us, I glance over their heads at Ash. He's as enthralled with the movie as the little ones and it brings a smile to my face. I've watched this show numerous times, but without kids of his own, I'm guessing it's his first time.

As if feeling my eyes on him, he turns my way and a small smile touches his mouth. He puts his hand on the back of the sofa, where mine is and lightly—secretly—runs the rough pad of his thumb over my hand. Warm shivers go through me, and as I take a fast breath, I look away.

My God, I can't believe I'm staying at his place—in my own bedroom, of course—but I have to say, I didn't see this coming. But under the circumstances, with his dad unwell and the snow outside, I made the decision based on everyone's safety.

The fact that we both might get up for a drink, meet in the kitchen again and corrupt his table much in the same way we corrupted mine did not play into my decision.

Much.

I glance at my daughter, who looks quite sleepy, and I check the time. They're all up past their bedtime, but they did rest today after sledding. Still, I think it's time for them to get to sleep. Unfortunately, I don't have a book to read them and it's clear there are none in this house, so I guess I'll have to make up a story.

I lightly rustle my daughter's hair. "I think it's time I put you all to bed."

They groan and complain, but all jump from the sofa when I grab the remote and turn the movie off. "Mommy, are you going to read to us?" Zoe asks.

"I don't think Ash has any kids' books." A cute, almost sheepish look comes over Ash's face. "You do?"

"I'm a bit of a pack rat." He shrugs. "Actually, Dad is the pack rat, and when he moved here he brought all my childhood things with him. His place is too small to store them, so I have them. Like Dad, I have a hard time throwing things away."

"When I saw the jerseys and the old pinball machine, I should have figured."

He pushes to his feet and heads out of the room. "Come on."

The kids are about to hurry behind him as he walks to the stairs, and I put my fingers to my lips.

"I need you all to be quiet, okay?" I point upward. "Ash's dad isn't feeling well, remember, and he's sleeping."

They all tip toe up the stairs, and Ash leads us into the spare room the kids are using. I lag behind for a second and put my ear to Grant's door. When it's met with silence, I step into the kids' bedroom. Ash pulls open the closet to reveal numerous boxes.

"My childhood right here in these boxes."

I laugh, and the kids all jump onto the bed. "I want Ash to read to us," Zoe announces.

"Me too," Tate agrees and Camryn nods her head.

Ash scratches his head. "Uh, I don't know."

"You don't have to," I tell him as I check the scratches on the boxes. One says toys, another says games, and I spot the one that says books.

"Please, Ash," Zoe begs, her tired eyes pleading with him.

As she wins him over his shoulders drop, the fight going out of him. "I guess I could."

I clap my hands. "Okay, why don't you guys all go brush your teeth and I'll find a good book." Ash had opened a pack of toothbrushes for us all earlier, and set them in the bathroom.

They all hurry to the bathroom and I smile up at him. "You're good with them."

"I don't know about that." He bends and picks up the box of books, carrying it to the bed. "I hope there's something age appropriate."

He peels open the box and I stand close to him, the warmth radiating from his body curls around me, and I put my hand on his back, needing the contact. His gaze jerks to mine, and the want I see there sucks the air from my lungs. Damn, I really want this man again.

He glances at the door, and then quickly presses his lips to mine. "I've been dying to do that all night."

I chuckle. "Same."

His voice is low, and gravelly when he whispers, "Not being able to have my way with you whenever I want is torture."

"Absence makes the heart grow fonder." As soon as the words leave my mouth, I realize what I've said. His demeanor doesn't change—heck, maybe he has no blood left in his brain—which is good. I don't want him thinking I want any hearts involved here.

"All done," Tate announces coming into the room and we quickly break apart.

"Now let's see what we have here." I start pulling out books and examining them. It's fun to get a glimpse into Ash's childhood, to see what he liked. There are a lot of novels that he likely read in high school, along with some younger books. "Do you still read a lot?"

"There's just not a lot of time for it anymore."

"True." I laugh when I pull out the monkey book I loved as a child. I turn it over, and grin. "Looks like we have something in common."

"Was that your favorite too?"

"Oh, yes, my grandmother read it to me many, many times."

"Monkeys. Monkeys." Tate starts chanting and jumping on the bed. "I love monkeys."

"You're a monkey," Camryn teases as she comes back into the room and jumps on the bed with her brother.

I put my fingers to my lips again. "Indoor voices, remember?"

They both drop, and when Zoe comes back, I pull the blankets back and they all snuggle in. The bed is so big, I'm sure all five of us could fit.

"Right here, Ash," Zoe says and pats the bed beside her. "Come sit by me."

His eyes narrow, as he circles the bed and drops down next to her. Seeing them all in the bed, messes with my head and heart. Unable to watch this, as my ovaries might explode—oh yeah, the scene is messing with them too—I start to back up.

"I'm going to go check on your father."

Fear moves over his face. "You're leaving me."

I grin. "You had them all morning," I remind him.

"But I've never..." He holds the book up and I get it. He's never read to kids before. I know he goes to the hospitals, and coaches the peewee team, and it's clear he's more comfortable around Tate than the girls.

"I can stay," I tell him, and walk around the other side of the bed, and sit next to Camryn. I pull her close and she rests against me.

"Ash, we don't bite," Zoe huffs and I can't help but laugh. Did she hear me say that the other day? Ohmigod, I need to remember there are always little ears listening.

"I know," he says with much more confidence than he's exuding. "It's the pool noodle I'm worried about."

Zoe crinkles up her nose. "What pool noodle?"

"Nothing, never mind. Okay, everyone ready?" They all nod and he begins the story about monkeys and bicycles. I smile the whole way through and absolutely love how much energy he puts into it, even using different voices for the different monkeys. The children are supposed to be winding down, but he's so animated, they're laughing and getting excited.

Once he finishes he closes the book, and is about to get up. Zoe touches his arm to stop him. "One more time."

"Nope," I say and push to my feet. "You are all up far past your bedtimes and we have to get up early and go home."

"I want to stay here tomorrow. Home is boring," Zoe whines with a pout.

"Home is boring," Tate mimics.

"I guess..." Ash begins and then stops himself. I meet Ash's eyes. "We'll see."

"Yay," They all shout in unison.

I hold my finger up in warning. "But we'll only see if you all go straight to sleep."

They all snuggle down and I tuck them in and give them kisses.

"Ash, are you going to give us kisses too?"

My heart misses a beat as he stands there not knowing what to do. But more importantly, it's clear the kids all adore him, and getting close was the last thing I wanted Zoe to do.

"How about he blows you all a kiss?"

He nods and does just that, and it's so adorable, my ovaries start doing the Macarena. Good Lord. They throw kisses back and I flick the light off. We step into the hall, leaving the door open an inch.

"Thanks for reading. They seemed to enjoy it."

He nods, puts his hand on the small of my back and leads me down the hall. I peek in on his father, who is still sleeping, and give Ash a satisfied nod.

"Glass of wine to wind down before bed?"

I should probably just go to bed. I'm tired after very little sleep last night, plus I worked all day, but my brain is stimulated…and well, let's face it. Other parts of my body are stimulated too. I just can't let anything happen between us, not with a house full of people.

Downstairs, we head to the kitchen and he grabs a bottle of wine from a shelf. "You keep wine on hand?" I ask and instantly wish I hadn't. Of course, he does. He entertains bunnies all the time.

But you haven't seen that lately, Gina.

He shrugs and I take in the way his muscles flex and relax again. My body warms, recalling the way those muscles did the same thing from my touch. "Yeah, lots of the WAGs like wine. I like to make sure I have their favorite kinds on hand when they visit." He glances at the bottle. "I've seen you drink merlot a few times, so that's what I grabbed for you."

Observant.

Considerate.

God, people who call him an Ash-hole got it all wrong. Am I the only one who sees this other side of him? If he treated other women the way he treated me, no way would they call him anything but sweet.

"Oh, right. WAGs." He pours me a generous amount and hands it to me. "That's nice of you."

He eyes me. "What, you thought I kept it on hand for all my bunnies?"

Busted.

"I'm sorry. That was presumptuous, and maybe not that nice of me. But you're a single guy and can have as many bunnies as you want. There's nothing wrong with that, Ash. It's when you're attached or married and having all the bunnies, that's wrong."

"For the record, I don't want or have all the bunnies, and don't believe everything you read."

Everything I read? I'm not sure what he means by that, and instead of pressing, I ask, "You haven't ever been serious with anyone?"

He glances down and a moment of heavy silence fills the kitchen as well as my lungs. His head slowly lifts, and I'm guessing whatever he's about to tell me comes from a dark, painful place. "Yeah, once. But like your ex, she turned out to be something different too."

I wince, truly gutted that he's gone through some kind of tragedy, as well. "I'm sorry."

Putting an end to the conversation—he clearly doesn't want to talk about his ex—he grabs a beer from the fridge. He takes a long pull from the bottle, and as I watch him, I can't help but want to kiss him and taste it on his tongue.

Alrighty then.

"Question," is all he murmurs as he continues to hold his bottle.

I sip my wine and take in the seriousness in his features. "What?"

He tips the bottle toward the stairs leading up to the bedroom. "That's how we handle it when they want something, by saying 'we'll see'?"

My heart squeezes at the way he says 'we'. It's only ever been me and for some reason what we're doing here feels like a team effort, and I don't hate it. Nope, I don't hate it at all, and that's really not a good thing under the circumstances. "It's the way I like to handle it. It's not a yes or no, and it seems to satisfy them."

"Got it." He grins. "You're good at this mom stuff."

"It's trial and error, to be honest. There is no manual. Well, there is, but there shouldn't be. Every child is different and just so you know, you're good with them too, Ash."

"I spent a lot of time with my dad. I think I get the 'guy' stuff. When it comes to girls, that's a whole different story. I didn't have any sisters, or a mom, and I think without that female influence, I'm just not sure about how to give a little girl what she might need. I don't want to mess them up."

"I do know." Zoe isn't getting the male influence she needs, and I can't help but think that could affect future adult relationships. Wanting to lighten the heavy mood, I bump him. "When it comes to grown women. You got it going on."

He steps into me and catching me by surprise, slides his hand around my body to pull me close and bends to kiss me. I moan and wrap my arms around his shoulders, going up on my toes as he deepens the kiss. When we finally break away, I'm breathless, panting, and...aroused.

I wiggle against him. "Didn't we say we had to stop meeting this way?"

"You said it, I didn't agree with it. But tonight, maybe I do."

"Oh." Here I am saying we shouldn't have sex in the kitchen again, and now, when he agrees, my feelings are suddenly hurt. Good God, I'm all over the place lately.

He tips my chin up, and I stare into his gorgeous blue eyes that are filled with lust and hunger. "I think it's time I put you to bed."

My God, that is the best thing I've heard all day, but... "Ash, we can't."

"Oh, but we can, Gina. I think it's a question of whether we should."

He leans into me, presses his soft lips to mine again, and one hand slides under my backside to pick me up. I wrap my arms and legs around him and groan as I grow wet and needy. He moans and I revel in the taste of beer on his exploring tongue as it tangles with mine. I slide a bit lower on his body, and as his hard cock presses against my center, the world closes in on me. I try to think, but lust overshadows all reasonable thought.

He slowly breaks the kiss, his forehead to mine. "What's the answer, babe?"

12

ASH

I hold her hand, keeping her close to me, and I guide her up the stairs. We walk quietly, and it reminds me of my high school days, sneaking girls into my room when Dad was asleep. We stop outside Dad's door, and when snoring sounds reach our ears, we check on the kids.

With everyone asleep, I take her into my bedroom, gently closing and locking the door behind us. She stands there, glancing around, an excited kind of nervousness about her. She steps up to the window and glances out. "It's so quiet and peaceful here."

"You like what you see?" I ask and with her back to me, she nods.

"I like what I see too." She turns, a grin on her face as she sits on my window ledge. "The view is great." I walk toward her. "The only thing that could make it better is having you out of these clothes."

"You don't like me in your sweatshirt?"

"No, I love you in it, but I love what's underneath it more." I slide my hands under the big sweater and run my fingers up her sides, brushing the outer edges of her breasts. By rights, we shouldn't be doing this—heck, we never should have started anything last summer, but for some reason we just can't seem to keep our hands off each other. I can only hope that by the end of the weekend, we'll have gotten this—whatever this is—out of our systems.

"I love the way you touch me," she moans softly.

"Look at that, our hobbies match perfectly, because I love touching you."

"That's what this is, a hobby?"

"Something you pursue for enjoyment. I'd say so."

She grins at me and lifts her arms over her head, wanting her sweatshirt off. I grip the hem and peel it over her head, and she's in her blouse and bra. "So many layers," I complain with a tsk. I try to work the small buttons, but it's not easy with my big clumsy fingers. I fumble and she backs up, out of my reach. My heart stalls. Is she putting a stop to this? If so, I'd commend her for her actions, and for having brain cells that currently work.

"How about I help you out?"

I groan, and drop down onto the bed to watch the show. She sways slightly as her small fingers work the buttons, slowly, tortuously.

"Are you trying to do damage?" I shift and tug on my pants as they tighten around my thickening cock.

"Oh no, that's not good." She finishes the last button, and with her blouse swaying open she drops to her knees and releases the button on my jeans, giving me a measure of relief. The hiss of the zipper is music to my ears, and once she has my cock free, she doesn't go back to stripping. Nope, she bends her head and takes me into her mouth.

"Sweet fuck."

I angle my head, watching the way she takes me to the back of her throat, and when she moves to the tip, the way my cock glistens in the light nearly pushes me over the edge. "Babe, that is so good."

I grip her hair and tug it to the side as pleasure wracks my entire body. She moans in delight, loving what she's doing to me, and I slide her shirt from her shoulders to expose her creamy flesh. Leaning forward, I unhook her bra with a flick and she doesn't take her mouth off my dick as she shimmies out of her clothes.

Her breasts sway beautifully as she pleasures me, and all I want to do is take them into my mouth and suck until she's crying out my name. "Babe," I groan, working to keep my voice low. The last thing we need is to wake anyone in the house.

I put my hands on her shoulders as she takes me deep and I try to tug her off. She moans in protest, and a tortured chuckle rumbles in my throat. "If you keep it up, this will be over before it gets started."

She inches back, and there's a gleam in her eyes. Well, isn't she proud of herself, loving that she can turn me inside out in seconds. I stand and pull her up with me, shaping her gorgeous breasts with my hands.

"You are so perfect."

"I'm not," she murmurs, and when I lift my head, her eyes latch on mine.

"You are to me."

Her lashes fall slowly and I lower my head to take a nipple into my mouth. She moans, and around her nipple, I mumble, "Perfect."

Her hands grip my hair. "You make me feel...perfect," she admits quietly, and it tugs at something inside me. One working brain cell takes me back to a previous conversation. Her ex made her feel special, only to tear her heart from her chest. Goddammit, she *is* special, and I plan to spend the rest of this weekend proving it to her.

I pull back and her nipple pops from my mouth. I cup both breasts with my hands and lightly rub her nipples with my thumbs. "Perfect in my mouth, and perfect in my hands..." She arches into my touch. "You know what else is perfect?"

"What?" she asks, her eyes fifty percent closed, and one hundred percent full of need.

I slide one hand down her body, and center it between her legs. "This is perfect." I rub her sex through her pants. "Perfect for my mouth." She makes a little gasping noise. "Perfect for my fingers." Sexy little needy noises that tease my aching dick crawl out of her throat. "And absolutely perfect for my hard cock."

"Show me," she manages to get out as her body weakens, and I chuckle as I scoop her up and set her on the bed, letting her legs dangle over the edge. My mouth waters for a taste of her as I slide her pants off, followed by her panties. Once I have her bare, exactly how I want her, I spread her legs and bury my mouth in her sweet, hot center.

"Yes," she cries out and I glance up at her as she clamps her hand over her mouth. I laugh lightly.

"This room is soundproofed. I think you're okay."

I put her feet on the edge of the bed, and her thighs tighten around my head as I go back to pleasuring and tasting. Fuck, man, I could stay here for the rest of the night, but my cock has other ideas, and I think Gina would like that too, but first, as promised.

I slide one thick finger into her. "Look at that, babe. So perfect."

"Yes, so perfect," she moans, moving her hips back and forth as I hold my hand still so she can fuck me. With each downward thrust, I brush my thumb over her swollen clit, giving her everything she needs to come.

"That's it. Take what you need from me, babe."

She begins to pant, and I slowly slide a second finger in and out and her mouth opens as she grows snug around me. I begin to match her movements, pushing as she rises and pulling back when she falls. As we create the perfect rhythm, her muscles clench tight, and her body bursts around my fingers.

"Fuck, yes, so perfect."

"Ash, oh yes, Ash." Her muscles continue to spasm, and I inch back a bit, keeping my fingers inside her as I take my aching dick into my palm. I stroke myself and glance at my nightstand. Do I have any condoms in there? It's been such a long fucking time, and I used up the ones I had in my jeans the other day.

The tightness around my fingers lessens, and I slowly inch out of her. I tear into my drawer. "Fuck," I murmur.

"What's wrong?"

I run agitated fingers through my hair. "I don't have any condoms." Fuck. I wasn't prepared for a woman in my bed, and not just any woman, this is sweet Gina who I've been crazy about for a while now.

"Oh." She glances down, deep in thought. Her hair veils her face, and I can't tell what's going through her mind.

I jerk my thumb toward the door. "I can run out."

"You can't go out on these roads, Ash." She bites her lips and eyes me, and I can tell she wants to say something but isn't sure how.

"What?"

She plucks at the bedding. "What if we didn't need to use one?"

"Are you on the pill?" As soon as the question leaves my lips, I remember the conversation where she told me she got pregnant when on the pill. She must read the panic on my face, and know exactly where my thoughts have gone, because she's suddenly jackknifing up. But I can't take the chance on her getting pregnant again. What would having a baby do to my life? Mess it up completely. Right? Especially when I'm supposed to be working on my reputation. Knocking up a single mom, yeah, that's going to clean it up big time.

"I...I can't have..."

She swallows. "I don't want that either, Ash." She puts her hand on my arm. "I'm not on the pill. It didn't work for me last time. I'm on Nexplanon. It's one of the best methods out there, except for abstinence." She glances at my still hard cock. "I don't think that's on the table tonight."

On the table.

Great, now I'm getting harder.

"Nor do I want it to be," she continues. "Nexplanon is even more effective than a condom. There's just something else we need to talk about."

"Trust—"

"Right, you're right," she blurts out quickly before I can finish. She looks away, but not before I see the pain in her eyes. "I totally get it, Ash. Why on earth would you trust me when—"

"Gina." I put my hands on her shoulders as she tries to slip past me. "Babe, what I was about to say is, trust me, I'm clean. I always use a condom, and I was tested after breaking up with my ex."

"Oh, okay." Her features soften and she settles back on the bed.

I look deep into her eyes as they narrow in on me. "Do you trust me?" Since I've met her I haven't given her any reason not to, but if she's looking at my track record and the things said about me, that could skew her views.

She nods. "I do."

My chest loosens, and believe me, I know that's not easy for her and I don't take that trust lightly.

"What about me?" The worry in her eyes fucks me over.

"I know you weren't trying to trap him, babe." In our profession, we see women trying to trap men all the time. I would never think that about her, and it bothers me a little that she saw me as that kind of cynical guy. Then again, I do have trust issues after Liza.

Her eyes glisten as she blinks dark lashes over them. "Does that mean you do—"

I kiss her lips, smothering her words as I gently push her to the bed, and fall over her. I spread her legs and answer her question by pushing deep inside her. I groan as she squeezes around me.

"Babe," I murmur as pleasure rockets through me.

She runs her nails along my back, her eyes conveying that this is as good for her as it is for me. I can't believe I'm inside her without a condom. Who knew skin on skin would be so fucking incredible? I revel in the warmth of her body, and she's so wet with arousal, it's amazing how easily I slick in and out of her.

Her hands slide to my butt, and she squeezes. Pleasure engulfs my entire groin area. We rock together, and I fuck her a few more times, only to pull all the way out when her groan curls around me.

"Ash, no," she moans in protest. I pull her up, and reposition on the bed, putting my back against the headboard.

"Come here, babe." I drag her to me and she spreads her legs to straddle me. "I want you just like this."

I put my hands on her hips and lift her, slowly guiding her down onto my steel hard cock. Her eyes roll back in her head as I fill her and I lean forward to take her nipple into my mouth.

"Ash, yes."

"So perfect, just like this." I hold onto her hips, not wanting her to have to do all the work with her legs, and control her movements and the depth of my penetration.

"Yes, perfect," she agrees as her head rolls to the side, exposing the long column of her throat. I lift her, and bring her back down and move her body, rotating her hot pussy on my cock. Jesus, she's so tight and wet, and squeezing my dick just right.

I try to slow the pace, to draw this out, because come tomorrow, she'll be working, and I'll be with the kids and our friends will all be coming home, and I won't be able to fuck her like this ever again. I don't think.

Or maybe we can, as long as it's in secret.

Maybe, if I make this so incredibly good for her, she'll want more. But what will that do to me in the long run? A guy could get used to being with a woman like her. Except I need to protect myself from being tossed away when she's done, and my coach will hand me my ass if anyone gets wind of this hook-up when I'm supposed to be cleaning up my image.

The best thing I can do is end this tonight.

"Gina," I begin as her body begins to quake and my brain is seconds from completely shutting down.

"Hmm."

I change my pace, lifting her and pulling her down a little harder to grind her clit against my pelvis. "Friends with benefits, for the weekend? This whole thing is a secret. Those were the rules we agreed on, right?" I grunt as she squeezes around me.

Her voice is labored and breathless when she answers, "Yes."

Stick to it, Ash. Nothing good can come from extending this relationship.

"I'm thinking friends with benefits, exclusive for the month. Still a secret."

Fuck.

As I drive down Ash's freshly plowed street, my phone pings, and I glance at it to see that it's from Melanie. I check the time, wishing I could pop by her place for a second. We don't get to chat much anymore, now that she's busy with a baby, and I miss her terribly.

I'll message her back when I reach the café and see if she has any free time this week. Right now, I need to concentrate on the road, and try to keep my mind off last night, and how we fell asleep together and I barely made it back to my room this morning before the kids got up.

Grant was miraculously better, and for that I'm grateful. I was glad I could stay the night and give both him and Ash a measure of comfort. Not that I did much, but I think my presence helped comfort them both.

Speaking of comfort. Having sex with Ash was incredible, as always. But actually sleeping with him and waking up with him, I'm not sure I've ever felt such warmth and comfort in my entire life. Which is probably why I agreed to extend this friends with benefits relationship until the end of the month.

After I left his bed, he got up and made coffee and as I got ready for work, he cleared the snow from my car. I'm so used to taking care of everyone else, when someone takes care of me, it messes with my brain and my emotions.

I still can't believe Ash and Grant are taking the kids for the day. I called Brighton to make sure she was okay with it, having explained what happened with Grant and she was perfectly fine. But she did want the deets on Ash and me. Since we're keeping this a secret to keep things uncomplicated among our friends, I told a little white lie—even though there was nothing little in that bed last night.

Nope, the Mountain, my big lumber-snack fulfilled me in ways no other man ever has. Yeah of course I was going to agree to more, even though it's probably not the brightest decision I've ever made. As long as I keep Zoe out of it, it should be all good, right?

I turn the radio up and hum as I drive, and I'm fully aware of the way my body is still tingling, craving a repeat of last night. Tonight, however, everyone will be arriving home late, and the guys start back to practice on Tuesday. I'll keep Camryn and Tate overnight, and hopefully I'm fully staffed on Monday so I can take the day off and drive them home. I want to hear all about their trip.

This time my phone rings, and my heart does a little jump when I see it's Ash. But then worry sets in. I just left, why is he calling? Are the kids okay? I press the button on my steering wheel and answer hands-free.

"Everything okay?" I ask, and hear laughter in the background.

"Yeah, everything is okay. Dad is playing a game with the kids and I wanted to check in with you. Actually, to be honest," he adds, his voice lower and a little bit playful. "Everything is not okay."

"Oh, why not?"

"Because you agreed to one month, and you're not here for me to have my way with you."

I laugh at that. "I know I agreed to it, but it's going to be hard this month."

"Babe, it's already hard."

He groans and I get it, he's not talking about finding time, he's talking about the movement between his legs. I warm all over thinking about how he felt inside me last night.

I flick on my signal and turn left. "What I mean is that you're back to practice, games and travel."

"Yeah."

His voice is low, almost distant. What is he thinking about?

I'm about to ask when he tells me, "Zoe wanted lumps in her pancakes this morning. I should have left lumps in mine too."

I laugh, despite the fact that I'm worried about Zoe and her wishing for a daddy. Damn, it hurts me to know she's missing out and while I'm trying to be both to her, it's impossible and she will be lacking certain things. I'm sure Grant understands what I'm going through. Although his son is proving to be one hell of a man who lacks nothing.

"What would you have wished for?"

"A longer month. Why does the All-Star Weekend have to be in February, the shortest damn month of the year?"

I take a few more turns, and Ash tells me what his plans are with the kids for the day. I left all the car seats with him, so they could leave the house. "Well, I'm sure Brighton wouldn't mind taking Zoe one of these weekends. Are you home or away these next couple weekends?" I don't actually know his schedule.

"I'm going to send you my schedule."

Something about that is oddly intimate and nice. "Okay, then we can plan around it."

"Next weekend I'm in Tampa."

"Nice, I've never been."

"After that, New York and Montreal."

"Maybe Dani can give you some French lessons."

"The only French lessons I want are French kissing and I want them from you."

My heart wobbles and I can't stop smiling. I really enjoy chatting with Ash like this. "You don't need any lessons, Ash."

We both laugh as I ease into my parking spot at home. "I'm here now. I should get going."

"Okay, I'll see you tonight."

"Can't wait."

"You guys can stay over again if you want. I never did get a chance to beat you at pinball."

While I love the idea of staying overnight, I say, "I should probably not let Zoe get used to being there and I'll be taking Camryn and Tate to the resort tomorrow."

He clears his throat. "Yeah, good call. I'll see you later."

With that we hang up, and I sit there a moment longer, just basking in the happiness curling around me, hugging like a well-loved blanket. A car horn beeps and pulls me back to reality. I quickly open the door, and a cold winter breeze curls around me. I unlock the door to the café and hurry inside to get the coffee and pastry going before customers start flooding in.

I double check my phone to make sure no one called in sick and I see a message from Sherry that she's feeling better and can make it today. That means, I'll be free tomorrow after I drop Zoe off at her school, to get Camryn and Tate home early enough that Camryn might not miss her morning classes.

Once I get the coffee going and the fresh pastry in the oven, I pick up my phone and pull up Melanie's message.

Mel: Did I just see you drive down my street?

Damn, it was so early I didn't expect anyone to see me but I guess with a baby she's up at odd hours. How do I answer this without raising suspicion? She is, after all, a trained psychologist, and is very good at her job. It's hard to hide anything from her.

Me: Yes, it was me. Ash's dad wasn't feeling well, and Ash asked me to stay the night to care for him. He's better this morning and they are both taking care of the three kids.

Mel: Ash is taking care of the kids?

Me: LOL, I know. He's not quite as scared as he used to be.

Mel: Is he taking care of you too? (eggplant, peach emoji)

Me: OMG

Mel: That is not an answer, my friend. Listen, why don't you guys all come by tonight for dinner. I am getting cabin fever. Invite Ash's dad too if he's feeling up to it.

I hesitate for a moment. If people actually see Ash and me together will they feel the tension, or possibly know what we've been up to.

Mel: I'm not taking no for an answer.

Me: At least let me check in with Ash.

Mel: Oh, you two check in with each other now, do you?

Me: Well, he is watching the kids, and he could have plans tonight with someone. Don't analyze this, Mel!

Mel: Fine, check in and let me know. Just FYI, I haven't seen Ash with a woman in a long time.

I don't know why that gives me little butterflies. I noticed the same thing, and he's not with anyone now because as friends with benefits, we're exclusive. I once thought I was exclusive and look how that turned out. Ash isn't hiding anything from me, though, and this arrangement is kind of nice, actually.

Nice enough that you want it to continue after the deadline, Gina?

Ignoring that thought because it really isn't an option, I finish texting Mel and shoot off a text to Ash, asking about tonight. He doesn't answer right away, probably because he's busy getting the kids ready. I'm sure he's happy to have his dad's help today, even though he calls him a stubborn bastard. I honestly love their relationship. I just don't want Zoe getting too invested in either of them.

My heart takes that moment to skip a beat. My grandfather would have loved Zoe. Would have given her all the male influence she needed. He was always my sounding board and maybe he would have seen through my ex and prevented me from getting caught in his web of lies. But, I have Zoe, and I will never regret that. Lucian doesn't even know where I am, and no one can ever take her away from me. Not that Lucian wants anything to do with her.

I set my phone down when Carla comes in through the front door, a cool breeze following her inside. "What I wouldn't do to be in the Caribbean," she says with a laugh. She still can't understand why I didn't go. I wanted my friends to have a good time and what fun is the Caribbean when you don't have anyone special to share the sunrises and sunsets with. Ash didn't go because he doesn't like the heat. I think there is a small part of him that was worried about his father, too.

Maybe he was worried about you too, Gina.

That's a silly thought, even though he did stop by to make sure I was shoveled out, and then stayed to help. Who does something like that? A guy who's helping a friend out, because yes, I'm sure Brighton and Noah asked him to take care of me, since I was taking care of their kids.

What about the other times he just showed up to check in on you, girl?

Okay, enough of those thoughts.

Carla takes off her coat, tugs on her apron and washes up. Andre follows in behind her, and then Sherry comes in, looking a lot better than she did last week when she was coming down with the flu. I have other part-time staff as well, but these three are my main crew.

We all get to work on prepping for the Sunday rush. It's not as bad in February as it is in the summer, when it's tourist season. Soon enough, we're lost in the flow of customers and pastries and sandwiches. When I finally make it back to my phone, there's a message from Ash saying he has no plans tonight and there's a picture of him and his dad with the kids at an outdoor skating rink. I blow up the picture to see all their smiling faces, and it occurs to me that Grant has the biggest smile of them all. The man definitely needs grandkids. Ash might not be looking for a relationship right now, or kids, but down the road that could change and I hope it does. Although, the tightness in my stomach when I think of him with another woman, isn't something I should be experiencing.

The rest of the day flies by and it's soon closing time, and I get a new burst of energy just thinking about heading back to Ash's. I'm excited to see him and hear about his day with the kids. I lock up behind everyone and head upstairs to shower and get into clean clothes. I opt for a pair of jeans and a soft blue blouse. I also grab clothes for the kids so they have something nice to wear to Mel's tonight.

Once I have everything packed, I grab the unsold pastries to take to Melanie's and hurry to my car. The sun is low on the horizon as I drive to Ash's place, and a little jolt of excitement curls through me when the front door opens and I find Ash standing there waiting for me. My grandparents always did the same for each other and I never knew what a nice feeling it was until now.

I hurry from the car, and meet him on the stoop. In the background I hear the kids playing with Grant. Ash leans in and kisses me and I love how he does that. "How was your day?" he asks, his voice deep and aroused.

"It was good. How about you? No noodle incidents?"

He shakes his head. "Why do kids have so much energy? I

tried to wear them out at the rink, but that only hyped them up. They're all pretty good skaters, even Tate."

"Maybe he'll grow up to be a hockey player like his daddy."

Something comes over Ash, some look I've never seen in his eyes before. Is it longing?

I tap his nose. "Maybe someday if you have a boy, he'll follow in your footsteps too."

An odd noise escapes his throat, as he drags me to him, and pulls me into the warmth of his home. His big house might not be decorated or homey, but with Ash and his dad in it, along with my daughter and her friends, it feels…right.

Feels like home.

I take a swig of my beer, watching from the sofa as the kids, along with Dad, play a board game on the coffee table, while Melanie and Brady's big chocolate lab Jersey beats everyone with her tail. Gina and Mel went upstairs to put Kayce down for a nap because he's been cranky all day and didn't sleep well last night.

Tate looks like he could use a nap too, but we're not going to fight over napping while we're visiting friends. Jesus. Look at me. Acting like Gina and I are co-parenting and making decisions together. I guess as the manny I do have obligations.

"I need to check on my sauce." Brady pushes to his feet and since everyone seems busy and happy, I follow him in. Delicious smells fill my nostrils, and my stomach takes that moment to grumble. When did I last eat? Oh right, the kids begged for macaroni and cheese for lunch, so that's what I served everyone. Not much protein in that to keep me going, and I have to get back on track for upcoming training and games. I haven't even been exercising like I should be.

Although what Gina and I have been doing...I bite back a moan.

Brady's words pull me back. Shit, what did he just say to me? "Ah, what?"

He glances at me over his shoulder as he makes his way to the stove. "How did you end up babysitting three kids? I'm exhausted with just one."

Thank God he didn't ask where my mind went for a second. I laugh and shake my head, wondering the same thing. "It just sort of happened. Gina's regular sitter Margot was tied up, and when she realized Gina was in a bind, and I just happened to be at her place, Margot kindly suggested I fill in."

"You just happened to be at her place."

I shrug like it's nothing. "After the bad storm, I did Dad's driveway and I figured Gina might need some help. Half the were in the Caribbean, and she was run off her feet."

"So, you thought you'd help her get off her feet?"

Okay, I see where he's going with this, and yes, I did help her get off her feet by wrapping her legs around my waist. "She's a good friend of Melanie's and Brighton's and a few of the other WAG's. Hell, she has Brighton and Noah's kids while they were in the Caribbean. How could I not help another player like that?"

"We all know we can count on you, Ash. It's just..." His words fall off as he looks at me with concern.

Fuck.

"I'm keeping my image clean, Coddy," I tell him. I can't even imagine how the paparazzi would spin it if they saw me with a single mom. "Just helping a friend."

"Although," he begins as if reading my mind. "Maybe this could help your image."

"Help? How's that?"

He stirs the sauce. "A wholesome family—found family, actually—it's straight out of those romance books the girls read at book club."

"Yeah, well this is real life, and the paparazzi aren't looking for a love story from me, they're looking for dirt. Especially after, well, I don't need to spell it out for you. You saw what went down."

He nods. "I get it, but this..." He glances toward the other room. "It looks good on you, Ash." Before I can respond, he holds up his empty bottle. "Want another?"

With my gut tightening, I shake my head no. He pulls a beer from the fridge. Ever since getting together with Melanie, he's a new man, and seems to carry less weight on his shoulders. It's a good look for him, although I will say he looks tired. But a baby will do that to you. At least I'm not up through the night with the three kids. My mind goes back to my conversation with Gina, and he lifts the lid off a big pot to check on his sauce.

"Maybe someday if you have a boy, he'll follow in your footsteps too."

Those words did the oddest things to me. I know Dad has been hounding me for grandkids, and I can see how much he adores the three he's been playing with today, but I can't have a kid because my dad wants grandchildren. Hell, can you imagine the shit my coach would give me if I fathered a child and caused more scandal?

He wouldn't if you were in a serious relationship, dude.

Ah, but I'm not.

Just then Gina walks into the room and the smile she gives me twists me up inside. With Melanie coming in behind her, and Brady looking right at me, I clear my throat and take a swig of beer, not wanting them to pick up on any of my emotions. Of course, all they'd pick up on is lust, because that's what's between us and I'm taking care of her kids because it's what Noah and Brighton would have wanted.

You keep telling yourself that, dude.

"Smells good," I say to Melanie. "Looks like you went through a lot of trouble."

"Not me." She walks up to Brady and puts her arms around him. "This is all Brady. I was busy with Kayce, so he made pasta sauce and meatballs."

"Kid friendly," he tells me with a shrug.

"No jiggs dinner?" I tease. Brady is from Newfoundland, and they have this tradition where you have to kiss a cod. Gina once had a graduation party for Mel at the café, and Mel actually kissed the cod. It was a hard no for me. But in Newfoundland on Sundays, it's tradition to cook jiggs dinner, which is basically corned beef, and cabbage, but it's way better than what we have here in the States. He made it for the guys before, but it's a shit ton of work.

"Dude, I'm going on very little sleep." He rubs his eyes. "I'm not even sure what I put in the sauce."

We all laugh at that, and Mel gives him another hug. I've never been envious of any of the guys, but I'm suddenly feeling a little strange, suddenly wanting a taste of what they have.

I push up to my full height and pull myself together. "If you needed help, you could have called me."

"Ah, three kids and your dad. Don't you think your hands were full?"

My shoulders sag and exhaustion overtakes me. "Okay, true."

"It's all good, Mountain." He puts his hand on my shoulder. "I'm glad you guys came over. We don't need to be in the Caribbean to have fun."

I'm having a lot more fun at home than I would have been having in the Caribbean but I'm not about to tell him that. It's a secret. Gina doesn't want anyone to know. Unlike my ex, who loved to put things all over social media, it's a little strange how her wanting to hide all of this is suddenly not sitting right with me. It should but it doesn't, and I can't quite figure out why. It's better for both of us that it's a secret. Jesus, Coach would kill me.

Melanie looks at me with warmth and gratitude. "Ash, it's so nice of you to help Gina out like this. I always knew you were a jack of all trades, a man of many talents, but I never knew you were so good with kids."

I try not to balk at the man of many talents comment as it takes me right back to the first time I put my cock in Gina. "I'm not good with kids."

"That's not what Gina says, and she wouldn't leave them with you if she didn't trust that you could properly care for them."

I school my features, not wanting to give the trained psychologist anything to work with—the last thing I want is her to see through me, and to be honest, I'm not quite sure what it is I'm trying to hide. "Yeah, well, she has Noah and Brighton's kids too, and she was in a bind, and helping her is what they would have wanted."

Gina steps up to the stove and something passes over her eyes before she looks away. "This really does smell amazing, Brady." She glances around, looking everywhere but in my direction. "Is there anything I can do to help?"

"Yes, you can refill our wine glasses," Mel says and slides the bottle her way as she starts slicing a baguette. As Gina fills the glasses, I nurse my beer. I'm driving tonight and don't plan to have another.

"Mommy, can we get a dog?" Zoe asks, coming into the kitchen with Jersey, a chocolate lab who is almost as tall as she is. She bends and hugs her. "I just love her, Mommy." When she lets her go, Jersey shakes her head, and drool lands on Zoe's clothes, but she doesn't seem to mind.

"Food," Brady explains.

Mel laughs. "You should see the drool when we cook a turkey."

Gina grabs a paper towel and starts to wipe the drool—Zoe refuses to take it off. "We'll have to wash this tonight."

"I don't want to. I want to sleep in it."

I don't miss the exchange between Mel and Brady. Do they think I'm getting too close to this family, that Zoe might be getting attached. Fuck, I really don't want to hurt anyone.

"Can we, Mom? Can we get a dog? Camryn and Tate have Mabel the big Bearnaise."

I chuckle at that. "Bernese," I correct.

Zoe looks at me like I'm deaf, or dense. I'm not the former but it's possible I could be the latter. I'm sure some would say I am, considering I'm messing around with a single mom.

"That's what I said." I don't bother correcting her as she turns to Gina. "Mom, can we?"

"We'll see."

Ah, her usual comeback.

She throws her arms out wide. "I want a big dog like Jersey."

"I don't know about that. Our place isn't that big."

"I don't like little dogs. Miss Tammy has that chewing dog, and it's always barking."

"Chihuahua," I correct, having no idea who Miss Tammy is.

"Did you know Dani used to have a Chihuahua?" Mel tells her. "Its name was Bear."

"That's a silly name for a little dog." Undeterred, she looks back at Gina. "Can we get a big brown dog like Jersey and name it Bear?"

"Honey—"

As if knowing the answer still isn't going to change, she switches tactics. "Ash has a big house. We could keep Bear at his house. Can we, Ash?"

I push off the counter. Wow, does this kid have my number or what, because yeah, I find it hard to say no to her? "Uh...we'll see."

She smiles at that, like she won the battle and now it's Gina and I who are exchanging worried looks.

Zoe inhales, her focus shifting once again. If she's redirected that easily, maybe she'll forget about the dog. "I'm hungry."

Brady drops the pasta into the boiling water. "Dinner will be in about eleven minutes."

"Here." Mel sneaks her a slice of bread, and Zoe giggles and runs out of the room with it. Mel slices the rest of the bread and sets it on the table, and I don't miss the way Gina is trying to busy herself.

Since I'm not needed, I gesture toward the living room. "I'll check on the kids." I walk into the living room and my heart squeezes tight when I see Dad laughing as he plays a board game with the three, Tate on his lap, snuggled up to him as they play snakes and ladders. Zoe's petting Jersey, who's after her bread. Am I a bastard for not giving the man grandkids, and even a dog? After all he's done for me, and he's not getting any younger...

Fuck, what am I saying?

"Who's winning?"

"Come sit with me," Zoe yells and holds her hand out to me. I drop down onto the floor, and she climbs onto my lap. Is this what it's like to be a girl dad? Maybe little girls aren't as scary as I thought they were. I don't miss the gleam in my father's eyes as he watches us.

Zoe reaches for the dice. "It's our turn, Ash." She puts the dice in my hand. "Here, you roll." I roll and she moves the pieces and groans as she hits a snake. "Oh no."

"I must be bad luck."

She turns to me, cups my face with her small palms and smiles. "It's okay, Ash. It's just a game."

My heart twists in my chest as she consoles me, and when I lift my head and catch the mixture of wonderment and worry in Gina's eyes as she leans against the doorframe and watches us, I get it. She's worried about Zoe getting too close to me, and I can totally understand that. From here on out, I need to make sure Zoe doesn't think of me as anything more than a friend. The last thing I want is for her to get attached. This hook up isn't going to last forever, and I don't want a little girl getting hurt when I distance myself.

Gina pushes off the doorframe. "Dinner time."

"Yay," Zoe shouts. "Don't worry, Ash, we can finish later."

"Okay." She jumps up and hurries to the kitchen with Camryn and Tate and I get up, turning to give my father a hand. He pushes my hand away.

"I can get up."

"I know you can, but you weren't feeling well last night and I was just offering a hand."

He looks like he's about to protest, then something in him softens, turns frail. "Fair enough." He holds his hand out to me, and I take it and tug him to his feet. Okay, that's a first. I eye him as he saunters off. What is he up to now?

Gina waits for me. I step up to her and dip my head. "You okay?"

"I am." She pauses. "I just worry about my daughter. She really likes you."

I actually like her too, but don't admit it. "What should we do about that?" I ask, not at all sure how to handle any of this. It's definitely not in my wheelhouse.

"Once she's back to school, and routine, I think it's all going to be okay and once Camryn and Tate are back home, she might forget about wanting a daddy." She sighs heavily. "At least, I hope so."

I look over her head. "Okay, let's go in there before we give Mel something to talk about."

She laughs at that. "It's hard to keep anything from her."

I touch her lightly to get her moving, but drop my hand as soon as we enter the kitchen. The three kids are seated around the table, as Mel pulls the bowls from the cupboard.

"How many meatballs do you want?" she asks each child. "Remember, they're really big."

"I want two," Zoe says. She looks at Brady, so damn serious, it's comical. "Do your meatballs have lumps?"

Oh, Jesus.

Brady frowns, and glances at his meatballs. "Uh, lumps?"

"Don't ask," I say quietly. "Just say no."

"No lumps," he tells her and puts two meatballs, along with some sauce on top of her noodles.

He sets it in front of her, and her eyes go big. "These meatballs are huge."

"I told you," Mel says with a laugh as she fills two more plates with noodles and hands them to Brady. She turns to Gina and quietly asks what the lumps are all about. Gina tells her as Brady finishes them off with meatballs and sauce, and as the volume in the kitchen rises, my chest swells. I kind of love all the rambunctiousness of this. It's clear Dad does too. He hasn't stopped smiling, and I'm so glad he's feeling better.

Once the kids have their meals, Brady serves the adults and we all sit around the table like a big family.

Found family.

I glance at Gina. It's just her and her daughter, like it is with Dad and me. This could be found family for her too. As if feeling me staring, her gaze lifts and she gives me a small smile.

"Mommy, Kayce has a daddy too." Zoe frowns, and puts her chin on the table. "My wish lumps aren't working."

Brady and Melanie glance at Gina, who looks a bit mortified. Gina opens her mouth, but no words come out.

Deciding I need to help her out here, I say, "I don't think it's that easy, Zoe."

"Oh, it is, Uncle Ash," Camryn supplies with an exuberant nod of her head, before she sucks back a long noodle, splashing sauce on her face.

"I think it's different for everyone," I weakly explain.

Zoe's gaze zeroes in on me. "Why can't you be my daddy, Ash? All you have to do is kiss my mommy. Right, Camryn?"

Camryn, with all her knowledge, adds, "He needs to give her a ring and they have to sleep in the same bed, remember?" After that helpful information, she jabs her fork into her meatball and starts nibbling on it.

Well, fuck me sideways.

Dad chuckles and my gaze flies to his, and I find him sitting there like Zoe's idea just solved world hunger. Christ.

"I heard you went skating today. Was that fun?" Melanie pipes in, redirecting the conversation, and when all the kids start talking, I exchange a look with Gina, who has paled quite a bit. Damn. I hope she's right about Zoe's life getting back to normal once she's back to her regular routine.

The kids talk nonstop as we finish our meal, and eat the pastries Gina brought. It's nearing the kids bedtime by the time we clear the table, and Gina needs to get them back to her place and into bed.

After we say goodbye, we head to the door to get into our coats, and Zoe complains, "I don't want to go home. I want to stay at Ash's again."

"Honey, no, you have school in the morning, and I have to drive Camryn and Tate home."

"I want to stay at Uncle Ash's too," Camryn pouts, with a big yawn.

"I think—" I begin when Dad puts his hand on my arm.

"I'm not feeling so good again, son."

Gina puts her hand to his forehead. "He actually does feel warm."

I'm about to point out that he likely put a hot cloth to his head when he disappeared into the bathroom, but I don't. Again, if something really was wrong, I'd hate myself for not taking it seriously, and let's be real here. I kind of want them all to stay overnight too.

Oh boy.

15

———

GINA

———

"**M**ommy, can we please stay at Ash's."

Grant coughs again, and it concerns me that it's only coming on at night. I glance at Ash. Perhaps he doesn't want his house full again.

"I...if..." I begin.

"You should probably stay the night again," Mel suggests and my gaze flies to hers. "Grant is looking a bit pale."

"Do you think we should take him to a clinic?" Ash asks, as he helps his dad into his coat.

"No, no clinic," Grant grumps. "I just need some more of Gina's medicine, and for her to tuck me in. That helped last night and of course, knowing she's close by if anything happens helps put me at ease." He turns from me. Wait, did he just exchange a look with Melanie? Do they know something I don't?

"It's your call, Gina." Ash touches my arm. "If you need to get the kids home, I understand."

I frown, and work out the logistics in my head. "I did bring clothes for them, so they do have something to sleep in."

"I want to sleep in Ash's jersey again," Zoe informs me with a pout.

I glance down as I consider it. "I am off work tomorrow. I suppose we could all get up a little earlier, and I could run Zoe into school, and then head—"

"How about I take Camryn and Tate back to Sparrow Springs? I'm sure Dad will be feeling better, and would like to get out for a drive."

"I'll probably feel better in the morning. Just need some meds," he tells me.

"If it gives you comfort for me to stay, then I'll stay."

"I think that's for the best," Melanie agrees quietly, and puts her hand on my shoulder. "We're right here if you need anything."

"Okay, thanks." I give Mel and Brady a hug and we all head outside. The kids are excited for another sleepover and honestly, I hate to admit it, but I am too. I should be putting a measure of separation between Ash and me even though we agreed to extend this friends with benefits relationship, but I just don't have the strength to do it. Come tomorrow, though, when I'm back at my own place, I'm sure things will be a little easier.

After we get the kids into one vehicle and Ash and Grant into the other, we drive the short distance to Ash's place. He left the outside lights on and there's such a warmth about his place. I can see why the kids like it here. I like it here too.

"Okay, little ones, we wash up and then it's straight off to bed. School in the morning."

"No school," Tate mutters, barely able to keep his eyes open.

"No, you don't go to school, but you must be happy to see your mom and dad and Mabel."

He hugs the stuffed toy in his hand. "I miss Mabel."

Mabel was kenneled this week while they were away. I couldn't take her. I have no space for a dog that big and Zoe is after me for a pet as it is. If she got used to having Mabel around, I'd never hear the end of it.

If she got used to having Ash around...

Grant gets out of the car ahead of us in the driveway and worry zings through me. Maybe tomorrow he should go to his doctor or a clinic for a checkup. I can be here tonight, but this is my last night. I'm back at my place tomorrow and Ash is back to hockey, and there won't be anyone around if anything happens. I make a note to talk to Ash about it.

As the kids excitedly head up to the house, a smile touches my lips. Everyone is so happy. Heck, I am happy too. It was so much fun getting out tonight and having dinner with friends. Having Ash and his dad there. There was a strange kind of fullness in my heart that I haven't felt since...ever.

I shake my head. I might hate what Lucian did to me, but what I got out of the deal in the end is priceless. I haven't checked his socials in years. A part of me suddenly wonders if his wife ever found out, and if she did, would she have stayed. They have two kids together, and I just couldn't be a home-wrecker.

As those dark thoughts invade, I push them down, and as Grant opens the door to the house and the kids pile in, Ash waits for me. With no one looking, he drags me to him in the dark, and lightly kisses me.

"You sure you don't mind staying?"

"No, not if Grant needs me."

"What if I said I needed you?"

My heart jumps into my throat. Do I want him to need me? I kind of think I do, but of course he only means sexually. His arms circle my body, and when I feel his swelling cock against my stomach, it confirms that theory. While I like that he needs me physically, I wasn't hoping that he needed me other ways too, was I?

God, this is so not going to be good for my mental health when it's over.

"Mommy, are you coming?"

I break away fast from Ash, and hurry up the walkway. Zoe has a grin on her face when I enter the house. "Mommy, were you kissing Ash?" she asks.

Oh, God.

"No, I had something in my eye, and he was helping me get it out." I blink to really pull it off, and then say, "I think we got it." She stares at me for a moment, like she's not sure she believes that or not, and I put my hands on her shoulder, and turn her around. "Bedtime, young lady."

She mumbles something about wishes, and hurries up the stairs. I follow them up and glance in to find Grant in his room.

"Are you going to come check on me?" he asks, his voice sounding weak. It's odd, he had so much fun tonight, and even ate seconds. He laughed with the kids, played games, and looked like he was having the time of his life.

"Let me get the kids settled then I'll be right in." I back out of the room and hit a wall of muscle. I turn to find Ash standing over me, and as I breathe in his arousing scent, my entire body craves his touch. "Didn't see you there." I laugh, and I hope it doesn't come out sounding as aroused as I feel. "Hard to miss a mountain."

He reaches around me and closes his dad's door and his closeness continues to mess with me. "I think Grant should see a doctor tomorrow."

"He won't go." I open my mouth about to protest and he exhales loudly. "Gina, I hate to say this. I hate to even think it, and would hate myself if anything happened to him...." A pause and then, "But I think he's faking."

"Why would he do that?"

"Did you see him tonight?" I nod. "The man couldn't have been happier. He's already in love with your daughter, Camryn and Tate, and I think..."

"Ohmigod, he's matchmaking. He's trying to get me to stay here, because he's trying to—"

"Marry us off and have the family he's always wanted."

"He's...he's...he's been playing with us." Even though that's wrong, it sort of breaks my heart a bit. I can see how much he adores the kids, and they adore him too.

"I think so. But what if I'm wrong?"

I consider all his ailments, and how they come and go. "I actually don't think you are."

He relaxes a bit, his shoulders drooping. "Good." Big fingers rake through his hair. "I always knew he was a stubborn bastard. I just never knew he was a sneaky one too."

"Well, I think we should play a game with him too."

He cocks his head. "What do you have in mind?"

"I'm going to think on it. First, I need to get the kids settled." I walk into the room and sort through the box of books as I wait for the kids to finish brushing their teeth. Ash hangs at the door, moving as each child comes barreling in.

"I want Ash to read to us again," Zoe insists.

I eye him and he just nods his head. Once again, we're all piled into the big bed, and it's crazy how much I like it. He reads to the kids and I find my eyes drifting shut. It's been such a long day, I could fall asleep right here. Once he finishes the story, I open my eyes and find him watching me, a new kind of concern about him.

I look at the three sleeping children beside me and force myself to get up. I have to check on Grant, and I'd love some quiet time with Ash, as well. I just wish I wasn't so darn tired. The early morning at the café wore me out. Thank goodness things are back to my normal routine tomorrow.

In the hall, Ash pulls the bedroom door almost shut. He puts his finger under my chin and lifts my eyes, his gaze carefully assessing me. "You're tired."

"I'm okay." I yawn, my actions defying my words.

"No, you're not fine. You need sleep."

"Actually, I need a bit of relaxation before sleep." A scraping sound reaches my ears, and I glance toward Grant's room. "Is he moving furniture in there?"

Ash rolls his eyes. "I have no idea. Let's go check on him."

Since I left my mom bag in his room last night, we head in and he hurries back to his bed. I glance around, note the lamp is turned on beside his bed, and a towel near it, but can't figure out what he was doing.

"How are you feeling?" I ask.

"Not so great. I think I have a fever." Wait, he wasn't using the lamp and towel to make his forehead hot, was he? I touch his head and it's scalding. My God, the man is going to great lengths to keep me here. It's kind of adorable, really, and I like him as much as he likes me.

"Is it okay if I take your temperature?"

"Okay." He seems to be proud of himself. "I'm pretty sure I have a fever."

I reach into my bag. "Oh no."

"What is it?" Ash asks, and looks into the bag with me. "My thermometer seems to be broken. I guess I'll have to use the rectal one." I pull out a thermometer, that is not for the rectum, but I assume Grant wouldn't know the difference. "If you want to just—"

"You're not using no damn rectal thermometer on me. Just give me some of those meds you gave me last night and I'm sure I'll be right as rain."

"Oh, no that wouldn't be responsible of me."

"I didn't have a fever last night and you gave me meds."

"I gave you something for your nausea."

"Oh, right, well I have that again."

I hold the thermometer up. "First, we check your temperature."

Grant's horrified gaze goes back and forth between the two of us, and when I can no longer hold in a chuckle as he tries to get out of this, his shoulders sag.

"You two..." He shakes his head. "I should have known."

"Yeah, well I was pretty sure I knew what you were up to all along."

He grins like a child who'd gotten their own way. "Well, it's too late for Gina to go home now. The kids are asleep."

I fold my arms and cock my head in challenge. "I can wake them."

He frowns. "The roads are bad."

I glance out the window. "It's clear out there. No snow, no ice."

Grumbles come from the depths of his throat, and then he puts his hand on his stomach. "I don't feel great."

I burst out laughing. "Really, Grant?"

"Okay fine. Is it so wrong that I think you two are perfect for each other?"

"Dad," Ash begins. "You can't fake being sick and you can't be interfering in my life like this. I'm a grown man. Who I see or don't see is up to me. We've had this discussion. You know where I stand on relationships."

Grant grumbles something under his breath. "Dad," Ash warns again and casts me a fast glance. From his deep frown, whatever it was his father said, Ash did not like.

"If you would have listened to me, things would have been different. You wouldn't be so...so...blind to what's right in front of you." Grant crosses his arms. "Get the light on the way out, will you." I don't miss the small smile he gives me, and I can't help but smile back.

I pat his arm. "Get some sleep and if you do feel ill and need me, just give a shout."

"You're one of the good ones, Gina," he tells me, and Ash just shakes his head.

"I like you too, Grant. Now get some rest. The kids will be up early and making noise."

I pull his blankets up as I fight a yawn. "Looks like you should be turning in too," Grant murmurs. "The room beside me is closer. You'll be able to hear me better from there."

"Are you still..." Ash shakes his head and putting an end to Grant's antics, he says, "Goodnight."

We leave his room, and out in the hall, I make my way toward the stairs. Perhaps a glass of wine will help me wind down, but Ash seems to have a different idea.

"Come with me."

He takes my hand, his fingers warm as they engulf mine, and guides me to his bedroom. I arch a brow when I take in his bed. "In there." He points to the ensuite.

"You want me to go to the bathroom?"

"Yes."

"I don't have—"

He picks me up and carries me in, setting me on his counter. I'm a little shocked at his caveman moves, not that I'm opposed to them. I kind of like not having to make all the decisions all the time. Two steps take him to his gigantic tub, and he bends to turn it on.

"This should make bubbles." He shows me a shower gel. "Eucalyptus. Do you like that?"

"I love it."

He nods and my heart wobbles a bit as he squirts it into the running water, and bubbles form. "You get in. I'll be back with a glass of wine for you. Then I'm putting you to bed."

He's not going to get a fight from me, and what he's suggesting sounds perfectly acceptable, and spectacularly delightful. He lifts me from the counter and I'm a rag doll in his arms.

I sigh, and start undressing as he disappears. I honestly can't believe this man ran a bath for me and is getting me wine. Not only that, but he's so good with the kids, taking them sledding, skating, playing board games, reading bedtime stories, and he treats his father so well.

Speaking of his father.

I slip into the bubbly water and breathe in the delicious scent as Grant's parting words rumble around in my brain. What did he mean when he said: *If you would have listened to me.*

What didn't Ash listen to? I stretch out and briefly close my eyes as I bask in the heat, and me-time, which I don't get very often, as I consider Grant's words.

"Hey," Ash murmurs quietly as he comes back with the glass of wine and the jersey I wore last night. I sit up and gratefully take the stemmed glass and as I sip it, and look into his blue eyes, he angles his head, his gaze moving over my face, reading me. He sighs. "You really want to get into it?"

16

ASH

I drop down, sit on the hard tiled floor, and dip my hand into the warm, soapy water. I study the gorgeous curves of Gina's face as her body relaxes. She takes a sip of wine, and puts it on the edge of the tub, to take my hand in hers. Our fingers automatically weave together, soft and rough joining as one. A new kind of tightness weaves its way around my chest, as I bring her hand to my lips for a soft kiss.

"You're wondering what my dad was talking about, right?" I finally ask, breaking the quiet surrounding us.

She nods, her eyes narrowing as she studies me. "Yes, but if you don't want to talk about it, you don't have to. I was just curious."

The fact is, Gina was forthright and honest with me when I asked about Zoe's father. I can't deny that her openness, the trust she put in me with that disclosure meant something, and while I don't talk about what happened with Liza, because it was nothing but bullshit. People judge anyway. Yet, something deep inside me lets me know, I won't get that reaction from Gina.

"Last year, I was dating a woman who wanted to be famous." Gina sits up a little straighter, her eyes meeting mine, fully interested and invested in what I have to say as I begin to open up. I snort out an uncomfortable laugh. "She was all over social media, posting numerous times a day, and I guess she thought that dating a hockey player was a great way to get attention. That's why she latched onto me."

"I'm sorry, Ash. It's not fun to be used like that."

"Oh, it gets better...or rather worse." I pause for a second. "I liked her in the beginning. She came off sweet and kind, and well...she wasn't at all who I thought she was."

A garbled sound crawls out of her throat. "I know all about that."

"Yeah, I know you do. Funny thing is, Dad could see right through her. I'm not sure how. Maybe that comes with age, or having experienced his own kind of betrayal."

She nods in understanding. "Look at us, more alike than we ever thought and yes, betrayal does make you leery, and not quite as trusting." I nod and groan as I shift on the floor. She crooks her finger. "Why don't you get in here with me. There's room."

"Are you sure?"

"Well, if you don't want—"

"I never said that," I blurt out quickly and it brings a smile to her face. "But this bath was about you relaxing. You've had a busy day."

"So did you and trust me, I'll be more relaxed if I'm snuggled against you." Since my body is tight, like it always is when I think about Liza, I decide it's a good idea. And of course, it's always a great idea to get naked with Gina. I stand, tug off my clothes and climb in behind her. She shifts forward to make room, and after I'm settled I pull her against me. As she nestles in, I run my hands through the water to create small waves. "Do you want to tell me more?" she asks.

I exhale and my body starts to relax. "I actually want to tell you everything."

She glances at me, a small smile curving her beautiful lips that I really want to kiss. "I'm listening."

"Like I said, at first, things with Liza were great. She was always taking pictures of us and I didn't mind. It was the new stages of a relationship and lots of endorphins and I wanted her to be successful at her job."

"Honeymoon stage. I get that. I also get that you wanted her to be successful. That makes you a good partner."

"But she wasn't getting the followers she wanted, and everyone seemed more interested in me, and what I was doing, than her." She goes quiet and puts her hands on my thighs and gives a little squeeze. "Wait, do you know about any of this?" The truth is, she might already know the horrid details. It's not talked about by the guys or the WAGs, they all know the truth, but the media frenzy around it was crazy at the time and it still comes up in interviews, which is why Coach told me to keep my head down and on the straight and narrow.

"No, not at all. I rarely go on social media. I only ever do pictures and updates on my café page."

She takes my hands. "I want to hear the truth from you." Her faith in me astounds me, especially after everything she's been through. I can't even begin to describe how that makes me feel.

I lay my head back and lightly run my fingers over her stomach. "When Liza wasn't getting the comments and attention she needed, and her fans made it more about me, she turned on me."

Her hands tighten around mine. "What did she do?"

"She used her audience to spread lies about me. She said I was abusive, a drunk driver, and that I was banging multiple 'young' girls at once." I hold her gaze, gauging her reaction. What I see is hurt and sorrow, not fear or belief. It prompts me to continue. "People love drama, Gina. God, they fucking love to get the dirt on people, especially people in the public eye, like hockey players. Those posts started getting her the attention she needed. At first, I didn't even know she was saying horrible things about me. It was done behind my back. We were still seeing each other. It was Brighton who told me."

"Brighton knew the truth."

It's a statement, not a question and it speaks volumes. Gina believes me, too. "Then the news channels started following me around, asking questions, and making me look pretty damn bad in the public's eyes."

"That must have been horrible, Ash. No one has said anything to me. I'm not sure I would have believed it anyway."

"We don't talk about it, and they all believe me, and take my side. If they didn't, if someone in the group thought I did those horrible things, I'm sure they would have whispered warning words or something to you."

"Maybe not." She widens her legs and as I glance at her beautiful body, my cock twitches against her back. "No one knows what's going on between us."

"Right." I resist the urge to ask exactly what is going on between us. Friends with benefits is one thing, but I've never spilled my guts to anyone outside my teammates before.

We remain quiet for a long time, just enjoying the quiet and each other's company. I run my fingers over her body and soft moans escape her lips. "Ash, is this why I've not seen you out with anyone?"

"Yeah." She turns sympathetic eyes on me, and falls silent, like she's waiting for me to say more. "I'm not good with relationships. My relationship with Liza really opened my eyes to how I was living my life and who I was dating. It turns out everyone wanted something from me."

"I was wondering what you meant when you told your dad he knew where you stood on relationships. I understand now, and I understand being scared to try again, because betrayal really hurts. But there could be a woman out there for you. I don't think all women go after hockey players because they want something. Look at Melanie, Brighton, Josie, and Maeve. All amazing, strong women."

I go quiet, and she leaves me with my thoughts for a moment. After a while, I explain, "I don't know what I did to make my mom leave. Do you have those thoughts too?"

She turns in the tub and faces me. "I do, but after having a child of my own, I learned it was her, not me. I love Zoe with all my heart and keeping her safe, protected and loved is the most important thing in my life. Nothing would ever make me leave her. Mom had problems. I guess yours did too." Her hands cup my face. "You can't blame yourself, Ash. Honestly, I can't understand how Lucian didn't want anything to do with Zoe. He had two kids, sure. But to simply discard the third one, it's cruel."

"It is cruel." Maybe she's right about all this. Maybe it had more to do about my mother than it had to do with me. "I had Dad," I murmur, and even to my own ears, I can hear the love and fondness in my voice.

"You're a great man, Ash."

My heart swells as a new kind of lightness comes over me. "He did good, huh?"

"He did good. You did good too."

I splash the water. "Jesus, now I'm going to have to give him the family he wants."

"No, you can't have a family to please your dad." She pokes my chest. "You have a family because it's what you want."

Is that what I want? Do I want a family of my own? Am I too much of a chicken shit to open myself up again?

She turns back around, picks up her wine and lays against me. A soft sigh escapes her lips. "Gina."

"Hmm."

"You're one to talk."

"Meaning?"

"You said you understand being scared because betrayal really hurts. What about you? You seem to be in the same position."

"It's different for me. I have a child. I have to be careful she doesn't get attached and then discarded." I digest her words, and for some reason they gut me a little. "Also, I'm a ready-made family, and finding a guy who wants that...won't be so easy." A small laugh that holds no humor escapes her throat. "I mean, who wants to hang out with someone who does old lady mother things," she adds, calling on Callie's cruel words.

"Jesus, you're not that much older than her, and if what we've been doing is old lady things..." I slide my hand over her stomach and reach up to cup one of her breasts. "Then bring it on."

She moans as I lightly brush my thumb over her nipple, but I don't want to start anything with her tonight. No wait, that's not true, I'm desperate to put my cock in her, but she's had a long day and needs a good night's sleep.

I kiss the top of her head, breathing in the sweet scent of her shampoo, and when the water begins to get cool, I shift, lifting her from my body. She sits up, and I push to my feet, pulling her up with me.

"Come on. It's getting chilly, and I don't want you getting sick. One sick person in the house is enough."

She laughs at my joke. "First, you can't get sick from cool water, and second, the sick person in the house is faking it." She smiles up at me. "It's nice how he cares so much about you, Ash, and really, he only wants what's best."

He thinks Gina is best for you, dude.

I grab a towel and wrap it around her. Dad was right about one thing, though. He did warn me about Liza. He saw things I didn't see. Maybe it's because of his experiences with Mom leaving. I don't know, but he saw the signs, and I didn't listen.

I'm certainly not going to listen to him this time either. Gina's not interested in more. She just told me that, when she said it was different for her because she had a child.

"Stay put," I order in a soft voice as she hugs the towel to herself. I grab another and quickly dry off and when I'm done, I pick her clear off her tired feet, and carry her to my bed. I set her down for a second, and pull the covers back. "Don't move."

"My, you're awfully bossy tonight."

I hurry back to the bathroom and grab my old jersey. Back in the bedroom, I step up to her and pull it over her head. She finds the arm holes and once it's on her, I step back and my heart beats a little faster.

"I like you in my clothes," I explain when her brows raise. "If you ever come to a game, you could wear it."

"Aren't there enough girls at the game wearing your number, Mountain?"

"None of them look as good in it as you do." She crawls into bed and I double check the lock on the door. I don't need any little ones catching us sleeping together, and I'll set my alarm early to take her back to her own bed.

I slip in beside her and pull her to me. She snuggles against me, her back to my chest and I drape one arm over her body. She laces her fingers with mine, and I really fucking hope she can't feel how hard my heart is pounding.

"Come to Thursday's game?"

"I don't have a sitter, remember. Margo is with her family."

"Bring Zoe. She'd love it. I'm sure Camryn and Tate will be there."

"But what if..." She nibbles her lip as she crinkles her nose. "We don't want to give anyone the wrong idea."

"No, we don't. I don't want that either," I agree, not bothering to explain that Coach would kill me.

"With Zoe...it's. just...I don't want her to think..."

"It doesn't have to be anything more than taking your daughter to a game to see her manny play hockey, Gina."

She chuckles at that, and my gut tightens, because yeah, maybe I want it to be more than that.

Fuck.

GINA

I can't believe I'm behind the glass, seated between Brighton and Melanie, watching the Bucks play Vegas on home ice. The action is fast, and while I can't really keep up to what's going on, not that I'm looking at anyone but Ash, the kids sure are having fun.

Zoe wasn't too happy when we went back home on Monday morning, and school started up again. If she could have it her way, she'd stay at Ash's forever. It's only her and me at home and I think she liked having both Ash and Grant around, as well as Camryn and Tate.

I glance at Camryn, Zoe and Grant standing just to the left of us, banging on the glass. I grin. Grant definitely needs grandkids of his own, and I don't want to think about how that might never happen for him. Tate is home with a sitter tonight as these games run too late for him, and while they run too late for the girls too, they really wanted to cheer on their favorite players. Naturally, Camryn's favorite is her father. It was all I could do to get Zoe out of her too big jersey, and get it washed. She tried to wear it to school Monday, but I put my foot down.

It's okay to wear it to a game. I just don't want anyone getting the wrong idea, even though it could be too late for that. With Mel on the other side of me, Kayce also with a sitter, I have no doubt she picked up on the tension between Ash and me when we all had dinner the other night—and the fact that Zoe adores him.

I am not in the jersey Ash likes me wearing. God, how could I put that on, knowing how he'd slipped it on me that night after the bath, after he'd shared a part of himself with me, and then snuggled me until I fell asleep. Dammit, I'm starting to feel emotional, so I shove my hand into my popcorn to swallow all the crazy things I'm feeling down deep.

"Go Ash, go!" Zoe and Grant scream and pound against the glass. He doesn't hear them, as his focus is on the game, but Zoe is jumping up and down right beside Camryn who's screaming for Noah.

Brighton nudges me. "Zoe looks cute in that jersey."

I nod. "When we stayed overnight, they didn't have clothes to wear. It's kind of huge on her, but she refused to take it off."

"Camryn told me all about it. Sounds like it was a fun night for them."

"They really enjoy his games room," I agree, and try to focus on the ice so my friend can't see how much fun the night was for me too. "They loved the pool table and pinball machine."

"I bet they did."

I can feel Mel's eyes drilling into the back of my head as I turn to face Brighton, working hard to school my features as I redirect the conversation. "I'm glad I could take them for you so you could enjoy the Caribbean."

"I'm always here to take Zoe if you need a break, or want to go on a trip. You and Ash both missed out. Maybe you two will want to make up for missing the Caribbean."

I snort at that, even though a trip to the Caribbean with Ash sounds like the most magical adventure ever. "I'm not going anywhere anytime soon." I hold out my fingers and start listing the reasons. "The café, staff sickness over the winter, Zoe's schedule."

A moment of silence and then Brighton says, "Okay, Gina, we've been dying to know what's going on between you two."

My heart leaps. Dammit, I was a fool to think I could hide anything from these two?

"Basically, what she's asking..." Mel begins, and wags her brows. "Did *you* play in any of *his* rooms and were there balls involved?"

I burst out laughing, half embarrassed and totally caught off guard by her blatant sexual words. But then I quickly sober and turn to see if Grant heard her. He's busy laughing with the girls and I'm pretty sure he's out of earshot. I relax a bit.

"You did not just ask me that?" Heat rushes into my cheeks, despite the coolness in the rink. Damn, I wish I was better at controlling my emotions—being nonchalant—but this is Melanie we're talking about. A trained psychologist who can see things for what they really are. Even though I have no idea what things really are between Ash and me. Not anymore, anyway. The line is so blurry, I'm going to need bifocals to see it. God, this is getting complicated and that's the last thing Ash and I ever wanted. Maybe I should just end this...now.

"Oh, I did ask," Mel says and glances around me to see Brighton, a smug knowing look on her face. She snorts out a laugh. "Forget it, Brighton. She doesn't need to answer, it's all over her face."

Brighton snickers. "I bet there was something all over her face."

"Ohmigod." My head rears back as the two women laugh. "Am I in a guys' locker room right now?" I shake my head. "What is happening?" I glance at the ice. "Marriage." I roll my eyes and groan. "Your men have corrupted you both." Honestly though, marriage looks good on them, and maybe I'm a little envious at what they have.

Brighton grins and nudges me. "Yeah and we love it. You should try it sometime."

Yeah, maybe you should, Gina.

"I'd have to be in a relationship, first."

"Still not admitting anything out loud, huh?" Mel teases and hits me with her shoulder. "For the record, sex is a form of a relationship. It's okay, you don't have to use words. We know what's going on, and don't worry, it can be your little secret."

Brighton leans in. "And ours."

"And also for the record," Mel continues. "You two are perfect for each other."

"Perfect," Brighton agrees.

"Guys—" I begin.

"You know, I don't remember the last time I saw Ash this happy. When he was with…" Brighton pauses and cringes. "Well, let's not say her name out loud. Actually, I haven't seen him with anyone in a long, long time."

"Whatever happened last summer in your kitchen," Mel says with a low whistle. "Must have rocked his world, because that man isn't looking at any woman but you."

Just then Noah gets a goal and we all jump to our feet and cheer. Zoe and Camryn are going crazy dancing around like fools, and it's completely adorable. From the corner of the ice, I spot movement coming our way, and I turn and catch Ash skating right at us, but it's the way he's looking at me, and the small, promising grin on his face that steals the air from my lungs, and teases the needy juncture between my legs. He skates up to the glass and bangs on it in front of the girls and they go crazy.

So does my heart.

I sigh, wishing my emotions weren't on a roller coaster today. Who am I kidding? They've been on a roller coaster since he fixed my air conditioner last summer. He's all I've been able to think about this last year, which is why I've kept my distance. But those walls shattered when he showed up and helped at the café. Ash Wheeler is anything but an Ash-hole and it's possible that I could be in a lot of trouble.

When he skates away, but not before casting one last glance my way, we all sit down, and a soft sigh escapes my lips.

"Girl, you got it bad," Melanie says, and I steal a glance at Grant again, to make sure he can't hear us.

Brighton nods in agreement. "Real bad."

I swallow down the lump punching into my throat and stick to my story. "We're friends."

"Friends with benefits," Brighton says, and my gaze flies to hers.

The fight drains out of me, and honestly, I find myself wanting to talk about Ash, wanting to tell these two what's going on even though we agreed to keep it a secret. "Friends with benefits." I set my popcorn down. "That's what we actually agreed on."

Melanie nods her approval. "About time."

I nibble my lips and focus back in on the ice, although I'm not seeing much as my mind races. "I have a daughter to consider. Ash and I are just having fun, and I don't want her to get attached."

Melanie glances at Zoe. "Looks like it might be too late for that."

I exhale as my shoulders sag. "Yeah."

"Too late for you too, huh?" she adds.

"Ash and I want different things," I tell her, reminding myself how last summer, he was quick to point out that we weren't a good idea, and again just last weekend when he asked me to come to a game. I said I didn't want to give anyone the wrong idea about us, he straight up said he didn't want that either. He'd been betrayed and is too afraid to put himself out there.

You've been betrayed too, Gina.

But Ash isn't like my ex. He's not hiding anything from me. Right?

"Oh God," Melanie shrieks and grabs my arm. I turn to her and her focus is on the ice. I gasp as two guys come flying down the ice, passing the puck back and forth. The next thing I know, Ash is moving, liquid lightning, his big body barreling toward the player with the puck and bam, they hit the boards so hard, the whole rink practically vibrates. They both go down, and without realizing it, I stand, my heart in my throat.

The refs skate over, and a second later, Ash is on his feet, his gaze seeking mine, and he gives me a devilish grin. I suck in a fast breath, refilling my collapsed lungs as I sink back into my seat.

"Is it always like this?" I ask, my insides still shaking.

"Always," Melanie tells me. "You'll get used to it."

"You think?"

"Mommy, did you see that?" I take in Zoe's excitement. "Ash stopped that guy from scoring."

"I saw it, honey."

Her eyes shine bright as she hugs her jersey. "Ash is my favorite, Mom."

Yeah, he's mine too, kiddo.

Little Miss Camryn—seven going on seventeen—whispers something into Zoe's ear and my stomach tightens. I'm sure whatever it is she's saying, it's not something I'm going to like. Zoe claps her hands, and they both turn back to the glass.

"The guys leave tomorrow morning for Tampa. We should plan a girls' night out. Go out to a nice quiet dinner, no kids. My treat, Gina. For watching Camryn and Tate."

"An adult dinner sounds perfect, but I don't have a sitter."

"I can watch Zoe."

My head swivels toward Grant and I find him staring at me with a big smile on his face. How long has he been listening? Or more importantly, what did he hear? Before I can tell him I don't think it's a great idea, he bends and takes Zoe's hands in his and starts swinging them. "Want to hang out with me this weekend? We can play that old board game Trouble that you love."

"Where I pop the six," she screams with joy.

"Yeah, we can make popcorn and watch movies. It will be fun."

"Can I, Mom, can I?"

Zoe looks over the moon excited, and while I think Grant is a great grandfatherly influence on her, I'm not sure spending so much time with him is wise. When it's over between Ash and me, it's going to kill her to have him torn from her life, but... dear God, how can I say no. They are both so excited and I'm not sure who needs this more, Zoe or Grant?

"Looks like that's all settled," Brighton says, a cheeky grin on her face. When I frown, she continues. "It's going to be okay, Gina. Even if it doesn't work out with you and Ash, there's no reason Grant can't be in her life. Look at what's happening with little Tyler. Conner's late brother had an affair, and the child was kept secret, now Conner's parents have taken Tyler under their wing and are giving him everything he needs."

"He's family, though. That's different."

"Okay, then look at me," Melanie says. "Brady and I don't have family to speak of, and Conner's parents are now Kayce's official grandparents. They took him and us in too. We are in no way related."

"Darci and Bill are really good people."

Mel smiles. "We can all be one big happy family, you know."

My stomach squeezes tight. The truth is, that's all I ever wanted. Zoe has two siblings out there somewhere that she'll never know. If she ever does find out when she's older, will she hate me for not telling her? God, I hope that never happens.

"I know, but I'm not a WAG. I'm just friends with you guys. I think that's different."

"You're sleeping with Ash, aren't you?"

"Shh," I whisper and my head swivels back to Grant to find him looking back at the ice with the girls.

"Yes, but it's only temporary."

"Doesn't matter." They both squish into me. "You're one of us. We're a big happy family, Gina."

My heart wobbles a little—okay, a lot. After I met Melanie on the beach that day, my life changed for the better. I don't want to do anything to screw it up, and not to be crude, but screwing Ash could be doing just that.

"But..."

"Stop overthinking," the psychologist beside me says.

"But that's my superpower," I tell her and we all laugh.

"Here's my unsolicited advice. Have some fun. Let your little girl find what she needs in Grant, and at the end of the day, there's no reason he can't be in her life, no matter how it ends with you and Ash."

Do you want it to end with you and Ash, Gina.

"She can even start calling him Uncle Ash, like all the other kids do." I blink as I let that sink in, and Brighton squeezes my hand. "You'll always be in this family, Gina. Ash will always be in yours and Zoe's life. Maybe just not in yours in the same capacity as he's been lately. Although I'm not sure anything has to change."

My stomach knots because I want it in the same capacity, and admitting that is huge for me. After Lucian's betrayal, I've been too scared to put myself out there, too scared to open up only to get hurt, for my daughter to get hurt.

"Okay," I say and smile at Melanie. "I am going to stop over-thinking and just have some fun."

"Now tell me, are the rumors true?" Melanie wags her eyebrows.

"What rumors?" I ask, my stomach squeezing. I know his ex wrote some nasty things about him, but he said it wasn't talked about amongst the group.

Melanie's eyes gleam with mischief. "When he fixed your refrigerator last year, Dani mentioned he brought a big tool. Just how big was it?"

Ohmigod!

Inside the locker room, Noah puts his hand on my shoulder. "Great save there, Mountain."

I snort. "You had some great plays too, Jonesburger."

"Seems nothing was getting by you tonight." He cocks his head and there's a gleam in his eyes and I'm not even sure I want to hear what he's thinking.

Theo walks over. "Who's the chick in the stands that he couldn't take his eyes off?"

My blood instantly boils as that asshole smirks at me. I get along with almost all the guys on the team and some of us are closer than others, but Theo Wagner is a fucking womanizing pig.

"None of your fucking business and have some respect."

He laughs and lets out a low, slow whisper. "Respect, that coming from you, Ash-hole?"

My fingers curl into fists. "What did you fucking say to me?"

"You think putting your dick in a single mom is going to help your image, Ash-hole? Wait until the media gets a hold of this. They'll spin that shit in a direction that will send your head spinning."

I turn to him, about to pound him against the lockers, but Elias steps in. So does Kalen Coolidge. Kalen has only been on the team a couple years, and he's mostly quiet, until someone he cares about might get hurt.

"Go fuck off, Theo," Elias barks out, and Kalen crosses his arms in a show of strength and support.

Theo holds his hands up. "Hey, just looking out for you, buddy. Hate to see you slammed on socials, again."

"None of this is your business," I toss back and his face hardens.

"It's my business when you get traded." He glances at the guys. "It's all our business when you get traded and we have to break in a new guy. You made one good play tonight, but mostly you've been playing like shit."

"I can't remember the last time you brought anything to the ice," Gunther points out, coming to my aid.

As they toss barbs back and forth I shake my head. Looks like Theo believed Liza's lies, and that's not a surprise. They were spotted out together a couple of times after she threw me under the bus. The relationship must have fizzled out—maybe being with him didn't get her enough Insta likes—because he's back on the bunny circuit again. Too bad really, they were made for each other.

"You good?" Noah asks, as Gunther shoves Theo away, before I get a chance to destroy him. I don't like him talking about Gina like that. Yeah, I'm overprotective of my friends, all my friends, even the one who is friends with benefits, and maybe more so. Jesus.

"I'm good." I tug off my clothes, grab a towel from my locker, and wrap it around my waist.

"We're heading to Kilting Around?" Noah asks. "Grab a beer before we head out this weekend?"

"Sounds like a good idea to me."

"Will Gina be joining us?" he asks in such a casual manner—so casual, it's clear he's trying to cover for something, so I turn back to him.

"No." I study his face as I harden mine. "She has Zoe. Tomorrow is a school day."

"Right, Zoe. I saw her in your jersey next to your dad and Camryn." A small smile touches my mouth and I quickly wipe it away. Noah grins again. "You've got something on your mind, Jonesburger?"

We start walking to the showers. "No, it's just that Camryn and Tate had a lot of fun with you guys when we were in the Caribbean. They told me all about the sledding, your broken nose..."

"It wasn't broken," I grumble.

"They loved the sleepovers and cutting up your clothes."

"Gina came to take care of Dad and they had nothing to sleep in. What was I going to do? We had no choice." Oh, so many excuses, that I'm not sure my buddy believes anything I'm saying.

He puts his hand on my shoulder. "Real good of you to step in and help like that."

I eye him and know he's got a lot more on his mind. Hell, Brady warned me about getting into trouble when I had dinner at his place, but then again, it wasn't a warning, was it? He said he thought it could help my image. I think Coach might see things differently.

I shrug. "Gina was in a bind. She had too many kids on her hands when her staff was off sick, during a snowstorm. Two of those kids were your kids. I did it for you, bud."

"Oh, you did it for me, did you?"

Tanner Bang, who knitted us all mitts for Christmas one year —he even knits on the buses and the planes when we head to away games—comes along. "Hey, heard you're Gina's manny."

"Jesus Christ." I snort out a sarcastic laugh. "Are you guys all in a knitting club or something? Sitting around gossiping about my love life?"

"Love life?" Noah arches a curious brow, as he quickly zeros in on that one word.

I step up to the shower, hang up my towel, and turn on the spray. "You didn't let me finish. I was going to say, or lack thereof."

"Ash," Noah begins, and I hold my hand up to cut him off.

"I don't need a lecture." Actually, I probably do, because I don't know what the fuck I'm doing anymore, other than falling in love with a single mom, and let's face it, her daughter too. I have never in my life felt like this before. It's messing with me in the worst way. But that single mom isn't interested in bringing anyone into her life. Relation-ships are nothing but complications to her—she has her and her daughter's heart to protect—which is why this is all a secret.

Maybe you should show her you're not a threat, Ash.

"Mountain," Noah continues, despite my protest as he turns on the spray and steps under it. "All I was going to say is, it looks good on you."

The fight drains out of me—they all know me too well—and my shoulders sag. "Yeah?"

"Yeah, buddy. She's a keeper." I glance at Tanner who's showering beside me and he's frowning.

"What?" I ask and brace myself. Is he the only smart one here who thinks messing with a single mom with trust issues is bad, and that coach and the media would have a field day with it?

"I was just thinking I needed to add an adult woman and youth mitts to my list this year."

I grab the soap and start washing. "Jesus, enough with the mitts."

"You don't like them?" He almost looks hurt.

"Yes, but I need a hat."

We all laugh and there's a new kind of lightness about me. The guys think this looks good on me. But it's Gina I'm worried about. She sees things differently. As more guys jump in the shower, I push those thoughts to the back of my mind and finish washing up. I don't expect Gina or Zoe to be outside waiting for me. I'm sure she took right off to put Zoe to bed. The thoughts of that sit heavy in my chest. Maybe I can call her later. Jesus, I got it bad.

I head outside and cameras flash in front of my face. I search for Gina, but my eyes are burning out of my head thanks to all the glaring lights. Digging into my back pocket, I pull out my cell phone and slide my finger across the screen, to see if Gina messaged. With my phone still in my hand, a girl comes running up to me, and the next thing I know she's wrapped around me, legs around my back, one hand behind my head as she snatches my phone from my fingers.

"Ash, you were amazing tonight."

I inch back and that's when I realize it's Callie, Margot's granddaughter, and she's in the jersey I signed for her. Fuck, she's young, and now everyone is probably going to think we're an item. This isn't a good look for me.

I try to set her down, but her legs are around me holding like a vice. Jesus. "Callie," I begin. "Let's get you on your feet."

She pouts and practically rubs her breasts in my face. I hear cheers from the crowd, and it's not like I can see anyone with the cameras still flashing. I finally manage to peel her off me, and she holds my camera out to take a selfie of us.

The camera flashes, and I'm sure I must look like a deer in the headlights. "Send me these," she says.

"I don't have your number."

She does something, then when her phone rings, she pulls it from her pocket and hands me mine back. "You do now."

She trots off, and blinking to get my sight back, I peer into the crowd, just in time to see Gina bend down to say something to her daughter. They start to walk away, and it looks as if Zoe is dragging her feet. She either doesn't want to go, or is dead tired. Probably both.

Shoving my phone back into my pocket, I push through the crowd, and touch Gina's shoulder to draw her attention. She has an uneasy look on her face when her eyes meet mine.

"Were you going to leave without saying goodbye?" I half joke. I want to lighten her mood, because in no way do I want her to think I liked Callie's little performance back there.

She glances around me, and winces as someone takes her picture. "You were busy. You have to go do your after-game thing."

"After-game thing?"

Zoe tugs at me. "You took that guy out hard, Ash." She rubs her tired eyes and I suddenly don't give a shit who's watching. Let Coach ream me out again. I bend and pick Zoe up, and she rests her tired head on my shoulder.

"Close your eyes, Zoe." I rub her back and glance at Gina. "Did you drive here?"

She nods and fights a yawn. "I'll walk you to your car." I note the dark smudges under her eyes. Maybe I shouldn't have asked her to come to this game. What a selfish prick I am. "Better yet, how about I drive you both home?"

"No, you need to go out with the guys and WAGs for drinks. The roads are good. I can get home by myself."

"Yeah, well, maybe I'm tired of you doing things yourself." Her eyes go wide. Shit, I didn't mean to sound so aggressive. "Gina." I soften my voice. "Where's your car, babe?"

Before she can answer, Dad steps up to us. "There you are." He looks so proud of himself when he shakes out the clothing in his hands. "Look what I got for you, Gina." He hands her a jersey that actually fits her. "I also got this for you, Zoe." Her head lifts as he holds out a children's jersey. "Now you can move around a little better when you cheer."

"I love it," she says and holds her arms out, and Dad leans in for a hug. "Can you be my grandfather?" she asks, and the noise of the crowd closes in on me. "Camryn and Tate have a grandfather. They call him grandpa. They have a grandma too. Wait, do you have a grandma?"

"No, Zoe. I don't," Dad responds, knowing she's really asking if he has a wife who could be her grandma.

"If you put a ring on a girl's finger, and sleep in the same bed, you could have a grandma." She yawns. "Oh, you have to kiss her too. Tate said he doesn't want to kiss a girl."

Even though Dad is cocking his head in confusion, he grins. "Is that all I have to do?"

"If you want a grandma. I could give you one of my lump wishes."

On that note—and while I think that's the sweetest fucking gesture ever for a little girl who is saving her wishes for a daddy—I say, "Let's get out of here." We head toward the parking lot, where Gina parked, and I get Zoe buckled into her booster seat. I fish my keys from my pocket and hand them to Dad. "Can you follow us to Gina's?"

"Sure thing. You go ahead. I'll catch up." He winks at me. "I know the way."

He begins to whistle as he walks away. "You can find my car okay?" I ask. He turns back and glares at me. I hold my hands up, palms out, and bite back a grin. "Right, I get it. Sorry."

I catch Gina's smirk. "He loves to prove his independence, doesn't he?"

"Until he's sick." I pause to do air quotes around that one word. "And then needs my girlfriend to take care of him."

As soon as the word girlfriend slips from my mouth, I realize what I'd said. Gina's wide eyed gaze locks on mine, and I quickly backtrack. "You know what I mean." She might, but that doesn't mean little miss Zoe does. I quickly glance into the car and exhale a relieved breath when I find her head tilted, her eyes close.

I note the jersey in Gina's hand. "You don't have to wear that or anything." I laugh. "I don't think Dad has given up."

She slides into the passenger seat and I drop into the driver's seat, adjusting the seat back, because I'm practically sitting on the steering wheel. She laughs.

"My mountain man. Too big for my car."

"When the seat is this close, I am." Her grin fades, and I'm not sure what's going through her mind. I adjust the seat, and try for casual. "You know I didn't mean that about girlfriend." My eyes are on her as I adjust the rearview mirror.

"Of course." A soft groan rumbles in her throat. "I just hope no one heard it." She glances out the window and bites her lip, and I note the tightness in her shoulders.

I reach across the seat and take her hand in mind, giving it a little squeeze. "Are you okay?"

"I'm not used to being in the spotlight like that."

"I love my fans, I really do, but it can be overwhelming, for sure."

"Callie sure was all over you."

"I pray to fucking God that's not splashed all over the news tomorrow. I can see the headlines now."

"Better her than us," she murmurs quietly.

My heart drops into my stomach, and churns. "I'm really sorry, Gina." Fuck, I had no idea that being seen with me like that would upset her so much. I guess she really is serious about keeping this a secret and I'm obviously finding it harder and harder to keep things under wraps. A few of the guys already know and I wasn't able to throw them off or convince them otherwise.

Why is that?

Oh, because I didn't fucking want to.

I want to talk about Gina. I like talking about Gina.

I ease her car out of the busy parking lot and she falls quiet as I take her home. I glance in my rearview mirror, looking for signs of Dad, but he must be stuck back in traffic. We finally reach her place, and I park.

"I'll carry her in, okay?"

"Thank you."

I unbuckle Zoe, tug her into my arms and carefully make my way up the slick driveway. It had rained earlier and the temperature is dropping. I need to get home fast before things ice up. I just hope Dad is okay driving here.

We head up the stairs and I take Zoe straight to her room and set her on her bed. Gina closes the door quietly, and looks at me. "I don't let her go to sleep without brushing her teeth or washing up, but I think I'm going to have to make an exception for tonight."

I cup the back of her neck and bring her lips to mine. "I loved seeing you guys tonight," I whisper into her mouth.

She pokes me. "You scared me when you hit that guy. I thought you were hurt."

I lightly rub her cheek with my thumb. "Worried about me, babe?"

"Yes, I was."

I kiss her deeply, and my cock aches for her. Voices from outside reach my ears and I inch back. "That must be Dad." My gaze rakes over her flushed face. It kills me to move away, but I need to get Dad off the roads. "I'll see you later." She nods and I head outside. I hurry down the stairs, only to reach the sidewalk and see that it's Callie and some girls chatting away.

I stay in the shadows and wait for Dad. Minutes tick by and worry invades my gut. Digging my phone from my pocket, I call him. He picks up on the second ring.

"Everything okay?" I ask quickly.

He grumbles something under his breath. Probably cursing me for checking up with him. "Everything is fine," he blurts out, like I offended him.

"Where are you?"

"I'm at your place. Where do you think I am?"

I shake my head. "Dad, you were supposed to follow me to Gina's."

"Oh jeez." I hear a slapping sound and envision him whacking his forehead with his palm. "I completely forgot. Must have been going on autopilot, straight to your place." I hear rustling sounds in the background, and he grunts, like he always does when getting out of the recliner I bought specifically for him. "I can come now, son. Oh wait, it looks like the roads are getting slick. Can't you just stay over, and I'll come by in the morning?"

"I have to be up early. We're headed to Tampa, remember?"

"Of course, I remember. I can come early."

"I can just take a cab home. No sense in you getting up early." I pause and sink deeper into the shadows when the light next door flicks on and falls over Callie and the girls. I thought she didn't know anyone in town. Wasn't that why her grandmother suggested I take her out?

"No, no. I'll come early."

"Are you meddling again?"

"What? No. Why would you accuse me of that? I made an honest mistake, son." Another grunting sound as he drops back down into his chair. "Maybe I'm not as sharp as I once was."

Okay, that's bullshit and the fact that he's using that as an excuse is exactly what he'd do if he was meddling. Fuck. Maybe I should just call a cab right now. I do have an early morning.

"Goodnight, Ash."

With that the call ends, I open my app to get a car. As the light shines on me, a recognizable voice calls out from the sidewalk next door.

"Ash, is that you?"

"Fuck." I step from the shadows and the streetlight falls over me. "Yeah, just calling a ride. Dad was supposed to follow me here."

"What are you even doing here?" She glances up at Gina's place. "Are you—"

"Zoe and Gina were exhausted. I gave them a ride home."

She comes a bit closer, her hand on my chest. "And now you're looking for a ride."

"Uh…"

"Emma, Charlotte, come here."

They hurry over and both gasp when they see me. "Told you I knew him. Come here."

Before I realize what's happening, they surround me, and Callie starts taking a bunch of selfies.

"Uh, okay. I better get going."

"You're not staying for a ride," she murmurs, rubbing up against me.

"I have an early morning. Travel day tomorrow."

She pouts. "Call me when you get back? Maybe we can hit up a pub before I go home."

"Uh…"

"Yeah, I don't know. I'm pretty busy."

"Ash," she cries out and tangles herself around me. "Please."

Taking a play from Gina's book, I say, "We'll see." Honestly, I have no intentions of calling her. I just said it so I could untangle myself from this situation.

"I look forward to it."

"See you, Ash." The girls trot off, and as Callie opens the side door to her grandmother's house, I glance up and see Gina move past her window. I need to get the fuck out of here. But then, as though moving of their own accord, my feet move, and I find myself headed back up the steps, two at a time. Even though I have a key, I knock on Gina's door, and when she doesn't answer, I call out. "Gina, it's me. Dad went to my place by mistake."

The door swings open and the second I see her, standing there in the jersey Dad gave her, her hair flared around her shoulders, her cheeks a pretty shade of pink, my heart starts pounding hard.

"Gina," is all I manage to say as I step inside and lock the door behind me. "You..." My gaze moves over her again, admiring her bare legs, and the way her hard nipples are poking against the jersey. "Do you have any idea what seeing you in this does to me?" I lightly rub the sleeve between my thumb and index finger.

She grins, because yeah, she does know. "You were really good tonight, Ash," she tells me, her voice low and breathless.

My heart thumps and I too am a bit breathless when I murmur, "Yeah."

She quivers when I exhale that one word and I can't stop looking at her in my jersey wondering if she's wearing panties, or is completely naked beneath the shirt. My fingers itch to touch her, to explore all that's hidden from my hungry gaze.

"But now..."

"Now what?" I ask.

"Now I want you to be bad."

19

GINA

He called me his girlfriend.

Sure, it was a slip, a mistake—Freudian perhaps— and then he tried to walk it back. Yet, despite all that, I liked it. A lot. It was a healing salve to my damaged soul. I can't explain why or how, but suddenly, I'm tired of being afraid, of worrying that every man is going to hurt me or my daughter because they're not who they say they are.

Ash Wheeler is a good guy. He's proven that over and over again, and while I no longer have any idea what's happening between us, I do know that I'm finding it harder and harder to fight what I'm really feeling for this man. Is it love? I can't say for sure, because I'm not sure I ever knew what love was. What I felt for Lucian, well...I thought that was love. Now, I know it wasn't.

But I am sure that Ash cares about me, my daughter, his father, and his teammates. He'd do anything for any one of us, and I used to think he took care of me because I was friends with the WAGs. I'm not so sure about that anymore, either. Seems like I'm not too sure about a lot of things.

Maybe the WAGs—my good friends—are right. Maybe Ash and I are perfect together—a word he's used a time or two where I'm concerned—and while I worry about Zoe getting too close, maybe she could still have Grant in her life if Ash and I go our different ways. Wow, I just used the word *if*, not *when*.

Does that mean I want something more? I think it does. Does it mean even if Ash doesn't, Zoe could still have a faux grandfather? I think it does. Zoe and Grant seem to love hanging out, both seem to need each other in their lives. Right now, however, what I need is the man standing before me—in my life and my bed. He swallows as he gazes at me like he's dying to see what's underneath the jersey. Perhaps I shouldn't keep him guessing.

I take his hand and lead him to my bedroom. Inside, I shut the door tightly, and give him a little shove. He arches a brow as he backs up toward my bed and drops down. I'm the one who said I wanted him to be bad, but I might want to drive him a little mad first.

Sliding my finger across my phone, I put on some music and Ash's big fingers dig into my bedding as I slowly start moving my hips. His blue eyes darken with heat and lust, and I grip the hem of the jersey and lift it slightly, just enough to expose my upper thighs, but not enough for him to see if I'm wearing anything underneath. His deep, animalistic growl warms the needy spot between my legs, and I slowly turn, presenting him with my backside.

I lift the jersey again, exposing the bottom of my cheeks, and when I glance at him over my shoulder and watch his chest rise and fall rapidly, a thrill goes through me. Wiggling, I hike my jersey up a bit higher and his tongue practically rolls across the floor. I guess this old lady mother has still got it. Take that, Callie.

Seconds from turning around, a grin on my face, his body presses against mine. "Oh," I murmur, as he puts his hands on my hips and pulls my ass against a very hard erection straining, no doubt painfully, against his pants.

"You keep teasing me like this, and I'll toss you on the bed, hold you down, and fuck you so hard you'll forget your own name by the time I'm done with you."

I gulp, loving the idea of him taking charge like that. It's been so long since I've put myself in anyone's hands, so long since I've trusted a man's hands, and I do trust Ash. I push away from him and turn to face him, offering him a mischievous grin.

"Me, teasing?" I nibble my bottom lip, and his growl provokes me even more. Gripping the hem of my jersey, I lift it. His gaze drops to take in my pussy, which is so wet for him. I wiggle a bit as I peel the jersey off and stand before him, open, vulnerable...and completely naked.

"Okay, that's it." With one big step, he's hovering over me, and he picks me up like I'm lighter than his hockey stick as he carries me to the bed, lays me out and falls over me. Pinned between his hard body and my soft mattress, I writhe as he takes my hands in his and pulls them over my head.

Oh my.

His mouth finds mine for a hard kiss, one born of passion and need and maybe...just maybe...something else. I kiss him back, taste the depths of him as I spread my legs to offer him my body. One hand slides between my legs and the groan that crawls out of his throat when he inserts a finger and finds me soaking wet, nearly makes me climax. When was the last time I ever had so much fun?

Once my lips are thoroughly and beautifully bruised, he inches back. The intensity about him fills the room with heated energy. He presses my hands into the mattress. "Don't fucking move," he commands in a low tone. A hard quiver goes through me.

"Wouldn't dream of it."

Growling, he inches back, running his fingers down my neck and between my breasts. "You are so beautiful, Gina." This time there's a softness in his voice, a tenderness that I've only ever heard in the bedroom. Is it reserved for just me? It's insane how much I want that to be true.

He stands beside the bed and takes off his clothes, and I let my gaze rake over him, feeling zero shame in the way I'm admiring his rock-hard body. There's a small grin on his face when my eyes finally make their way up, back to his. He likes the way I look at him. I crook my finger, everything inside me craving him. I swear if he doesn't put his cock in me in the next second, I'm going to explode.

"Get over here. There's a mountain I need to climb."

He falls over me, his cock centered between my legs, and in one fast thrust, he's inside me, like he too is desperate for this connection. He fucks me long and deep, his grunts and growls turning me inside out. My palms explore his shoulders and back, and the way he quakes under my touch wraps around my heart and squeezes.

"Ash, that is so good." He nuzzles my neck and slips a hand between our bodies to rub my clit, and I go off like a firecracker.

"Fuck, I feel you, babe."

He continues to drive in and out of me, my muscles clenching hard around his pistoning cock. I soak him, and glance down to see my slick juices all over his body. I love everything about that, but I want more. I'm about to push him off me, not entirely sure I can, and as if reading my mind, he grips my hips.

"What was that you said about climbing a mountain?" In one easy move, he rolls. A moan laced in pleasure rumbles in my throat as he positions me on top of him and takes my breasts into his big hands. "Do you have any idea how much I like making you come?"

"Do you have any idea how much I like it when you make me come?" I return, and it brings a laugh to his throat.

God, I love this man.

My heart stalls.

I love this man.

As that realization hits me, I stop moving, stop thinking... stop breathing.

Concern jumps into his eyes. "Babe, are you okay?" He sits up a bit, and puts his hands on my cheeks. "You disappeared for a second there. Did I hurt you? Jesus, if I hurt you..." His voice falls silent as the fear in his eyes says it all.

I struggle for words, to form a coherent sentence as his gaze races over my face. "No, you didn't hurt me. It's just the opposite, Ash. You make me feel better than I've ever felt before." My heart races as a bevy of emotions fill my soul. "I love...I love..." I catch myself at the last second, reining in the things I'm feeling. If I tell him I love him, will that scare him away? "I love having sex with you."

He relaxes and exhales his words. "Okay, good." He brushes my hair back. "I love having sex with you too, babe."

I slowly move my hips in a circle and his mouth falls open. Damn, I love how much I affect him. "Then maybe you should get back to it."

He growls, grips my hips and starts moving me over his cock, up and down, grinding deep and hard, and with each thrust, he stimulates my clit. This...right here...it is so good. I close my eyes as pleasure takes hold, and as the world closes in on me again, I tumble into another orgasm. My muscles tighten around his thick cock, and he pulls me down and holds me still as he pumps into me.

What would it be like to make a baby with this man?

My eyes fly open. Why are all these thoughts jumping into my brain tonight? His eyes meet mine, and they're so full of pleasure as he fills my body with his seed. I fall over him, place my cheek against his chest, our bodies fusing as one. I close my eyes, a new kind of peace swirling around me as his fingers lightly roam my back.

"You're incredible, babe."

I lift my head, and he pushes my hair from my face and brings my mouth to his for a kiss. It's then that I realize just how tired he is too. He had a big game tonight, and tomorrow he's headed to Tampa.

I slide off him, and a quiver goes through me as he leaves my body. "Let's get you to bed."

He laughs and glances around. "Haven't we already done that?"

"Yes, but I mean, you need sleep. You take my bed, and I'll go to the spare room."

I try to leave, but he pulls me down. "Maybe I want to sleep in this bed with you tonight."

"As much as I like that too, I have a little one to worry about."

"Yeah, we do, don't we?"

Everything in the way he says 'we' once again makes me feel like we're a team in this thing called living.

"If she catches us, she's going to think you're going to be her daddy."

He glances down, and he's not frowning or smiling. No, he seems like he's deep in thought and I'm not sure if he likes the idea of Zoe thinking that or not.

After a moment, he gives a curt nod. "You take this bed. Zoe expects to find you in here tomorrow, not me." He leans in and gives me a soft kiss. Standing, he tugs on his clothes, and before he leaves the room, he adjusts the blankets around me. "Don't move."

I laugh. "When did you become so bossy?"

He disappears down the hall, and comes back with a bottle of water for me, and my heart wobbles. I stare at his big hands and he uncaps it. "I'll be gone before you guys are up in the morning." I nod. "Can I call tomorrow night?"

"I'd like that."

"Good." Another kiss where our lips linger a little longer, and then, "Okay, babe, you get some sleep."

Body tired, I collapse on my pillow, and the next thing I know, my early morning alarm is going off. I stretch out, and my sore body reminds me of last night's glorious lovemaking. Lovemaking? Maybe, or maybe it was just sex.

Little feet pounding on the floor give me little time to think about it. I jump up and grab my robe. "Morning, Zoe. You seem pretty happy and energetic this morning after being up so late last night."

"I found this on my pillow." She hands me a note, and I frown as I take it. That frown turns into a small grin as I read it to her: *I'll be back Saturday, and I'm going to have a present for you. Have a good day at school.*

"Look, Mommy, look. You have a note too." An apple-sized lump pushes into my throat. I work to force air into my lungs as my heart pounds against my ribs. My God, Ash left us both a note. Could the man be any sweeter?

Zoe begins to hop around as I pick up the note and read it. "What does it say?" she asks.

I read his scribbled words: *Hey babe. Hope I didn't keep you up too late last night. I'm on the road, and will call you tonight. Have a great day, and I'll be bringing a present back for you too.*

I can barely talk when I say, "Just that he'll have a present for me too." I sit on the edge of the bed, thinking about what that big present might be. I pull my daughter toward me and hold her hands. "Zoe, you like Ash, right?"

"I do." She tugs one hand free and points to the jersey she insisted on sleeping in, again. "He's my favorite player."

I am not entirely certain what my future holds with Ash and me. Brighton and Melanie made it perfectly clear that I'm part of this hockey family and always will be. Since being a part of a big family is something I've always wanted, I intended to keep this whole relationship a secret for fear of friendship complications and I didn't want my daughter to get hurt. I do know that Ash and I agreed to end this thing at the end of the month—and I need to be prepared for that—but it doesn't mean my daughter has to end things too. Ash can and will always be a part of her life.

As she stares at me with big curious eyes, I begin, "Do you know how Camryn and Tate call him Uncle Ash?"

"Yeah."

"He could be your uncle like that too."

"No," she says, and shakes her head so hard, she's giving me a headache. "I'm never calling him that, Mommy." She pulls away from me and runs from the room and that's when I get it.

She doesn't want to call him Uncle Ash, she wants to call him daddy.

Oh boy.

ASH

It's been a long fucking day traveling to Tampa, and I hate flying on the best of days. Add in bad weather and turbulence, I'm ready to call it a night. I make my way toward the elevator, anxious to get to my room to call Gina, when Coach steps up to me.

"Can I speak to you for a moment?"

Fuck.

His brow is furrowed, and I'm guessing he has something very important on his mind, something that probably has to do with me hanging out with a single mom. I really fucking tried to keep my head down, but this is sweet Gina we're talking about. I didn't have the strength to resist her. Which is why after fucking her in her café kitchen last year, I've been sniffing around like a goddamn stray cat, hoping for scraps. But dammit, she gave me so much more than scraps and I'm fucking addicted.

If the coach tells me to back the fuck off, what the hell am I going to do? Hockey is my life. I worked hard to make a name for myself. Not only for me, but for my dad. Not only so I could provide for him but to show him how good of a job he did, single-handedly raising me.

I exchange a look with Brady as he and a couple of the guys step into the elevator, and the strangest sense of doom washes over me as the door closes. Coach puts his hand on my shoulder, and I follow him across the lobby to a set of chairs in the corner.

How decent of him to tear me a new one in private. "What's up, Coach?"

"You don't know?"

I sink back into the cushioned chair. How do I play this? "Listen, if you're talking about Gina—"

"I am talking about Gina. Gina Martin."

How the fuck does he know her last name? Then again, he does seem to know everything about all of us and I guess that's part of his job. If one of us is in a slump because of personal issues, he needs to know these things.

"And her daughter, Zoe."

Well, fuck me sideways.

"I know," is all I can get out as my chest squeezes tight.

"I realize you aren't on social media, since well...and you guys have been traveling today, so I'm going under the assumption that you haven't seen any of the headlines."

Headlines?

I sit up a bit straighter. Jesus Christ, did those pictures really make the news. I snort out a humorless laugh. Of course, they did. Social media posts get way more hits when they're sharing juicy gossip.

"I'm not sure who the younger woman was who latched onto you—"

"She's nobody you need to worry about." I glance at the phone in his hand. "What are they saying?"

"Basically, who wore it better?"

"What the fuck." I nearly fall off my damn chair as I lean forward to see what the fuck he's talking about. "Who wore what better?"

"They show you with that young woman wrapped around you, and you with the little girl in your arms, and her mom Gina by your side." He holds his phone out to me, and my blood drains. Gina didn't want this. She didn't want any of this attention.

Why?

Oh, because we're just having sex...with a fucking deadline.

Maybe I should just end this before she walks out of my life. My father's life. We both know what that's like. Why the hell did I set us up for that again? But more importantly, I wasn't able to protect Gina from the spotlight, from the possibility of our secret getting out.

I glance up and catch Theo walking by, his ears perked, far too interested in our private conversation. I shift a bit so he can't see the phone. Something tells me the douche bag already knows anyway, and from his grin, he looks like he's happy to see me getting reamed out. But I'm not getting reamed out. Coach has a pensive look on his face, not an angry one. What is actually happening here?

"You like her."

It's a statement, and it's a true one. "Yes," I blurt out before I can stop myself.

He nods, and goes quiet again. I prepare myself for him to tell me to break it off, and I can't help but think it might be best for Gina and Zoe. "This is good for you, Ash."

"Yeah, okay I'll end...wait, what did you just say?" Holy Christ, Brady was right. He said Coach might see things this way. I glance up and meet his gaze. When I do, his dark eyes hold nothing but delight and satisfaction.

"You like the idea of me being with a single mom?" My brain is racing, so I'm not entirely sure I heard him correctly.

"It's stability, Ash. She seems like a nice woman and obviously you adore her daughter as much as she adores you." He snickers. "There's a lot being said about her wearing your jersey. Fans are going crazy about that."

"Really?"

I try to see his phone again, but he tucks it away and sits back. "There's not going to be any drama with Zoe's father, is there?"

"No. He's not in the picture."

He nods again. "I like this for you. It's not conventional." As he falls silent, I realize he's right. Nothing about Gina or her life is conventional. Her mom leaving her, being raised by her grandparents, a married man who tossed her away when she was pregnant, a nurse running her own café. A sweet, loving woman who's been doing it all on her own for years now.

"Still," Coach begins again, pulling my thoughts back. "It's a good look for you. Good for the team's image. Besides that, you were on fire last night, and I couldn't help but think it was to impress your girls."

My girls...

Fuck me sideways. I love the sound of that.

"Keep up the good work, Ash."

"Just to be clear, you want me to be seen with Gina and Zoe," I ask, because I'm dense like that. Truthfully, I need to hear it again, because there's a part of me that thinks my brain might just be making this shit up.

"Yes. Now go, call your girl. That's obviously why you were racing to the elevators."

I stand and none of this sits right with me. While I'm glad Coach isn't ripping me a new arsehole, being with Gina, and stepping out to get our pictures taken for all to see, seems a little...manipulative. I want to be with her because I'm damn crazy about her. The last thing I want is to exploit what's going on between us because it's good for the team's image.

Shit, this might have gone down worse than I thought.

I walk to the elevator, head down when I hear hushed voices, people recognizing me. Normally I'd stop and sign autographs. Tonight, I'm not in the mood to be around anyone but Gina. Too bad she's in Boston and I'm in Tampa. I steal a glance at my phone to check the time before I stab the button for the elevator. She had dinner with the girls tonight, and while it's late, I told her I'd call and I want to keep my word. I don't, however, want to wake her.

I hurry to my room, happy the guys have all gone to bed, and happy that I have my own room. After I let myself inside, I flop down onto my bed and pull out my phone. I see a text from an unknown number and ignore it.

Relaxing on my pillow as best I can after that weird conversation with Coach, I call Gina and she answers on the second ring. It's insane what the sound of her voice does to my insides, but as soon as I hear it, and the unease beneath her one word greeting, my stomach tightens. Has she seen all the media hype about Callie, her and Zoe?

"Hey," I murmur softly. "Not catching you at a bad time, am I?"

"No, not at all." I hear rustling noises in the background. Is she too in bed? "How was your flight?"

"Delayed, delayed, delayed."

She chuckles softly. "Yeah, I knew that. Brighton was getting updates from Noah at dinner. Sorry to hear about that. You must be exhausted."

"I'm okay. How are you?"

"I'm a bit tired."

"I kept you up too late." I kick off my shoes and push my blankets down.

"I don't mind late nights."

The softness in her voice, the warmth tone curls around me, and I close my eyes as I envision myself next to her. "I love the late nights." A beat and then, "Did you girls get my notes?"

My girls.

"Zoe loved it. She can't wait for you to get home."

"What about you?"

"I liked the note too."

I chuckle, because she knows what I was really asking. "Can you wait for me to get home?"

"No, I can't," she admits honestly, and it fucks with my heart in a million ways. "Also, you should know, your dad is asleep in the guest room."

"Really?"

"It was late when I got home, and I figured he might as well stay over. I wouldn't want him on the roads in the cold and getting *sick*." She draws out the word sick.

"We wouldn't want that. That would mean you and Zoe would have to spend more time at my place."

A soft sigh escapes her lips, and my heart jumps. Does she like the idea of that?

"We never did play pinball," she reminds me.

Fuck, I love talking to her like this, my eyes heavy, drifting shut as I lose myself in her soft voice. "You mean I never did beat you at pinball," I tease. My phone pings and I briefly pull it away from my ear to check to see who's messaging. Does Coach have more to say to me? I don't recognize the number. Well, actually I do. Whoever it is calling, has been at it all day and it's starting to piss me off.

"Everything okay?" she asks.

"Yeah, someone's calling. I don't recognize the number."

"Maybe you should answer."

"The only one I want to talk to is you. Besides, if I answer now, I'll probably tell the person off."

"Maybe it's a debt collector. They can be relentless."

I chuckle softly. "It's not."

"Does that happen often? Calls you don't recognize?"

I note the way her voice has changed, maybe a hint of worry, or even jealousy in it. "Random calls? No. I don't give my number out to just anyone." She's quiet again, for so long I'm about to ask if she doesn't believe me, only to shut my mouth when she speaks.

"Ash."

"Yeah." I wake up a little more at the seriousness seeping into her tone.

"You need to know something else."

I gulp. She saw the social media posts. Before I can apologize, she says, "Zoe has taken to calling Grant grandpa, and over pancakes this morning, she sent out a wish for him."

I'm not sure how I feel about that. "I guess I'm okay with her calling him that if you are. I'm sure he's in his glory." She remains quiet and I continue. "The kids all call me Uncle Ash. We do consider ourselves a big family."

"I just…you and me. I guess what I'm trying to say is Brighton and Melanie assured me that no matter what happens between us, we'll all still be a family and Grant can be a faux grandpa."

"You told Brighton and Melanie."

A little sound escapes her lips and my heart jumps with a

strange kind of joy. She was talking about me. "I'm sorry. It just came out."

"If we're being completely honest, Gina. I told Brady, and Noah and Tanner know, too."

She laughs quietly and it wraps around my body. "So much for us being able to keep a secret from our friends."

"Yeah, so much for that, but you can be assured Dad will always be in her life." A beat and then, "Gina, I'll always be in yours and Zoe's life too."

"The girls said that." I hear a little sniff. "You know I've always wanted to be a part of a big family."

"It's always just been Dad and me against the world, and while I never really thought about that growing up, I wouldn't trade it for the world."

"Ash?"

"Yeah."

She pauses for so long, I inch up and my stomach tightens. "I saw some social media posts from last night. Brighton showed me at dinner. She wasn't sure whether to or not, and in the end decided I should be aware."

"Jesus, I hate social media. Are you okay? I know you didn't want the world knowing anything about us." Telling our closest friends is one thing, but this is something entirely different. "Who wore it better. Christ, what the fuck is that?"

"You saw them?" There's genuine surprise in her voice.

I clear my throat as my conversation with Coach races through my mind. Should I tell her he wants me to be seen with her. Fuck, I don't want her to think I'm with her just for the image.

"Coach showed me."

She sucks in a breath. "Is he upset?"

"No, it's all good."

"Thank goodness. I mean, after what your ex did to you. I don't want to cause you any trouble."

"You're not trouble, babe."

"Well, I could be." Her voice turns seductive, sexy.

"Oh yeah."

"Sure." More rustling sounds and then, "Want me to tell you what I'm wearing?"

21

GINA

It's Saturday morning, Ash has a game tonight that I can't wait to watch, and with a full staff, I don't have to go downstairs to work. Voices from the kitchen pull me awake and I stretch to see that it's still early.

Pulling on yoga pants and a big, oversized sweater, I make a quick trip to the bathroom and then make my way down the hall. It's crazy. On school days, Zoe complains about getting out of bed early, on weekends she can't get up early enough.

I stop and stand just outside the kitchen archway to listen to the exchange between Zoe and Grant. Wrapping my arms around myself, I hug tight as my heart nearly explodes in my chest. My God, Zoe is absolutely crazy about Grant, and vice versa. It does give me a measure of comfort to know he'll always be in her life. I'm glad Ash assured me of that.

Honestly, nothing about my daughter calling my secret boyfriend's father grandpa is conventional, and some might think it's strange, but it's growing on me fast. Crazy, considering how worried I was about protecting Zoe from any kind of relationship with someone who wasn't family. I've come to realize that we are a part of the hockey family and I need this in my life as much as my daughter does.

Boyfriend.

Wait, did you just call Ash your boyfriend, girl?

My God, I did. I truly did, and I'm not mad at myself about that.

"Grandpa, not like that. You're stirring too much. I won't get lumps that way."

Her words prompt me into action. "What's happening in here?"

"Mommy, Mommy," Zoe screeches, and I press my finger to my lips.

"Inside voice, honey."

"We're making pancakes and then me and Grandpa are going to watch all the cartoons." She offers me a bright-eyed look. "You can watch with us."

I like to limit her TV time, but shut my mouth when I see the big grin spreading across 'Grandpa's' face.

"That is going to be a great morning."

"If you have any errands to run, or anything you need to do, I can watch Zoe." Grant stops stirring the batter, and pulls a spatula from the container on the counter. "We had fun last night, didn't we, Zoe?"

"We did. Mommy, we played board games and had popcorn." She laughs hysterically. "Grandpa couldn't pop a six at all, and I won the game."

"What can I say?" He throws his hands up in defeat. "The dice doesn't like me."

"Oh, Grandpa, you're silly."

I breathe deeply and work really freaking hard to swallow down the lump punching into my throat, and when tears begin to press against the backs of my eyes, I go in search of coffee.

"I really appreciate you watching her, Grant."

"No problem at all."

"Coffee?"

He checks his cup. "I'm good for now." Switching gears, he asks, "Are you going to watch the game tonight?"

"I want to watch Ash play tonight," Zoe pipes in. As Grant takes a drink of his coffee, she mimics him and reaches for her juice to take a big gulp.

"I'll record it for you." I tap her nose. Pouting, like she's about to protest, I add, "You've had enough late nights lately."

I toss a pod into the coffee machine and get it brewing. "Yes, I'm going to watch the game tonight." Until I moved here, I never watched hockey.

Oh, and why are you watching it now?

Because I'm friends with numerous WAGs.

Oh, puleeze.

Okay, fine. It's because I'm in love the with the star defenseman.

"You getting together with the girls to watch?" Before I can answer, he gives an easy shrug and continues. "You can if you want. I can stay with Zoe again."

"They did mention all getting together at Brighton's for game night. While that sounds nice, I'm up for a night in." I glance out the kitchen window. "I don't love being on the roads late at night."

He frowns and looks down. "How is this, Zoe?" he holds the batter out. "Enough lumps for you?"

She peers into the bowl and holds her hand up for a high five. As they slap hands, thick as thieves, I can't help but laugh at their antics.

I grab the milk from the fridge and set a frying pan on the stove. "Are you watching the game?" I ask.

"I wouldn't miss it."

I glance out the window again, and for the briefest of seconds, I'm sure someone is in my yard. I lean forward and peer outside, but don't see anything. Maybe it was an animal. Last week the garbage cans were knocked over, and I'm betting on hungry racoons.

"If you were serious about watching Zoe for a bit, I wouldn't mind running some errands." Normally I'd take her. Today it's clear she'd rather hang out with Grant.

He gives me a big smile. "Not a problem at all. We have a morning of cartoons to watch. It looks like it might be a nice day, so maybe we can get out for a walk too. Do you want to go for a walk, Zoe?"

"Can we go to the playground?"

"Sure."

These two are killing me. "If we're going to watch the game, I need to go to the grocery store to get all the best snacks for us."

He stares at me for a second, and his smile widens when understanding hits. "I make a mean pizza."

Zoe throws her hands out. "I love pizza."

I grab a notepad and pen. "I'll make a list."

"I usually buy the dough from Bucky's down on Tremont."

"I actually make a mean crust," I tell him.

He nods his approval. "Then all we need is sauce, and lots of pepperoni, and cheese."

I eye him, and the big grin he's giving me. "Wait, is pizza on your diet?" The man does have heart disease, and I'm not about to do anything to put him in harm's way.

"Of course."

I grab my coffee when it beeps and take a much-needed drink. "Do I have to ask Ash about that?" Why is it that I like saying his name.

Grant gives me a dismissive wave. "We don't want to bother him on game day, now do we, love?"

Love? Okay, the man is buttering me up and that tells me all I need to know. But hey, if he's good enough to watch Zoe, he deserves pizza. I just plan to buy some plant-based deli meats instead of the ones that are basically nitrates holding hands.

"Okay, are you ready to cook this?" he asks Zoe, and it amazes me how he pulls her chair over next to the counter. Ash did the exact same thing with her and I take that moment to envision a young Ash and his dad cooking together.

"What was Ash like as a kid?" I ask. Funny, I never thought I'd be talking to Ash's father about Ash's childhood.

"He was a good boy, Gina." He beams at me with pride. "Had to take on too much responsibility, I will say that."

"I don't think it hurt him at all."

"No, but we only want what's best for our kids, and I didn't love that he had to be so responsible at such a young age."

"I understand that."

He sprays oil into the pan, and tosses me a look of understanding. "I know you do. You and me. We're not so different, are we?"

"No, not so different at all." A week ago, I never thought I'd be saying this, but I'm really glad he stopped at the café that day.

I lean against the counter as Zoe climbs off her chair and runs to the fridge to get the syrup and fresh fruit. Yes, she's been eating too many pancakes, but at least she's getting fruit into her.

"Tell me more about Ash when he was a kid."

"Well, there was that one time that he nearly burnt down his school."

My mouth falls open. "No way."

Grant laughs, and nods. "Unfortunately, yes." He lifts his pancake slightly and checks the bottom. "Do you want one?"

I wave my hand. "No, coffee is good for me. I'll grab something later." I fall quiet and he continues to tell me stories about Ash, as he finishes up the pancake and pulls Zoe's chair back to the table. Grant and I laugh over stories, which I love hearing, until he gets his own pancake made, and joins Zoe at the table.

Zoe holds a piece of her pancake out. "This lump is for you, Grandpa."

"Kiddo," he begins. "This last week, I've gotten more than I ever could have wished for."

Zoe beams up at him. "Did I tell you Ash is bringing me back a present?"

He laughs and takes a sip of his coffee. "Oh, only about two hundred times."

As they eat, and knowing I'm not really needed here, I finish jotting down the groceries I need, take the last sip of my coffee and check the time. "Okay, I should shower and get going." I kiss Zoe on the head. "You have fun and be good. Call me if you need anything, okay?"

He holds up his phone. "I got your number."

As I head back to my room, my mind goes back to last night's conversation with Ash. I don't really think he had a bunny calling him, even though I do know the rumors about girls flocking to the hotels of the visiting team when they're in town for a game. I'm not sure why I even thought that about Ash. He's been with me every moment when he's here.

Ah, but he's not here now, is he?

I shut down that inner voice that likes to challenge me and remind me of my past mistakes.

In my bedroom, I grab some clean clothes and I'm about to head to the shower when I catch sight of my laptop. My heart beats a bit faster as I look at it. Should I? Ugh. I don't normally go on social media. Today however, with curiosity getting the better of me, I pick it up, and carry it to my bed.

The sound of cartoons in the other room blasts through the house. With no one paying any attention to what I'm doing, I peel my laptop open, and tap on a couple of social media apps. I do a search of Ash's name and the second I see pictures of Zoe in his arms, ones I didn't see last night on Brighton's phone, an uneasy knot tightens in my stomach.

I scroll, going down a rabbit hole that can only fill with dirt and suffocate me, yet here I am doing it anyway. My heart beats faster at the clear images of my face, and I don't know what to think at the captions calling me Ash Wheeler's new mystery woman. In other posts, my name is right there, for all to see. Someone did their homework, and fast.

I swallow, unable to help it but I feel like my privacy has been violated. God. It was just last year when Maeve had a stalker. It was horrifying for her. Not that I think I'm going to have a stalker from all this. But still...

I come across old posts from a woman named Liza, and instantly know it's Ash's old girlfriend. My God, she's gorgeous and younger than me. *Old lady mother things.* What the hell is Ash doing, tied down single mom, when he can be with a woman like her? Although she was horrible to him, I have no doubt there are many more gorgeous young things who'd give a kidney to be with Boston Bucks star defenseman. My stomach churns as I read the vile things she's said about Ash. My feed refreshes and a new post from Liza pops up. Wow, she's all over this. I guess she must think it's going to bring more attention to her. Playing the victim is one surefire way to get people on your side.

I lean in and when I see that she's sending a warning out to the mystery lady—me—anger floods my veins. Hating all the negativity, I slam my laptop shut, and work to erase all I've read from my brain. Not that I think that's possible.

Darting to the bathroom, I quickly shower and dress, needing to get outside. Maybe the fresh air will help clear the rest of the vileness from my thoughts. Once I'm ready, I head to the living room, and check in with Zoe and Grant again before leaving.

As they laugh their butts off at the silly cartoon, I make my way downstairs to the café to make sure I'm not needed. After chatting with the staff and seeing that everything is under control, I leave the kitchen. The bell over the door jingles and I glance out to see a man hurry out, and the strangest feeling grips my stomach.

I make my way to the front door, step outside and look up and down the street, but he's nowhere to be found. How could he have disappeared so fast?

As I stand on the cold sidewalk, noticing all the cars going by, I suddenly have the feeling that I'm being watched. Sure, my name was just posted all over social media and maybe the news outlets are looking to get dirt on Ash Wheeler's mystery woman.

Why then do I get the feeling that this has nothing to do with any of that?

22

ASH

It's game day, and after our morning skate, most of us are hanging out and relaxing. We all have our own routines and superstitions. I always eat the same food, and either read or play games with the guys and I always give Dad a call before we play. Right now, it's nearing noon, and I'm in Roman's room playing video games. Roman and I don't hang out much outside of hockey, although I like him, but when we're on the road, gaming is a good distraction and keeps my mind sharp and ready for game time.

"Dude, where's your mind? I just slayed the fuck out of you."

"Yeah." I toss the controller onto the coffee table. So much for a distraction. I've been uneasy since those pictures came out and Coach said he liked the idea of Gina and me. I mean, I'm happy about that, but I don't want to be parading her all around town because it helps the team's image.

He leans forward on the sofa, his gaze latched on me. "Is this about that chick you were photographed with?"

"Don't call her that."

He laughs. "I should say, that *mom* you were photographed with."

I jump up, and rake my hands through my hair. "You've got something against moms?"

"No man. I have one. I'm just not about to date one." He eyes me. "Dude, you got it bad."

I shrug, not about to deny it. "Someday it will happen to you."

"Nah, I'm not about to settle down anytime soon. I've got lots of living to do."

"Just be careful not to get in shit with Coach, while you're doing all your *living*." I do air quotes around that last word.

"I'm careful. No way do I want Coach warning me to walk the straight and narrow, like you."

I snort. Walking the straight and narrow with an amazing woman like Gina...well, that's not so bad. My phone rings and I snatch it from my pocket. Disappointment must move over my face, and Roman laughs.

"Dude, go call her."

I stare at the random number that's been calling for days, and hit decline. The only one I want to talk to is Gina, and dammit, I'm going to call her. "Yeah." That's all I say as I walk to the door and let myself out.

I hurry back to my room, throw myself on my bed and call Gina. She sounds breathless when she answers on the third ring.

"Ash, I didn't expect to hear from you today."

"I have a bit of downtime before the game. Just wanted to check in to see if Dad's been behaving."

She chuckles. "He's actually watching Zoe at my place right now. I'm out running errands and getting snacks for tonight. Your dad and I are going to watch the game together and apparently your father makes a mean pizza."

Shit, he knows better than to be eating pizza.

"Don't worry," she adds, clearly reading my mind. "I'm getting plant-based everything and the cheese is low fat."

This time I laugh. "He's going to kill you."

"Don't worry. This stuff tastes great." I hear a squeaky wheel and voices in the background. Somewhere in the distance, a child screams. "He won't even know." She goes quiet, her breath a bit heavier.

"Is everything okay?"

"Yeah..." she sounds distracted. "I don't know. It's probably my imagination."

I sit up straighter. "What's going on?"

"I...I'm sure it's nothing."

Clearly, it's not nothing, judging by the fact that she brought it up and seems out of sorts. "Gina."

"It's just, after the pictures came out, I feel like I'm being watched." Something dings on the other end of the phone. "It's weird, I know."

"No, it's not weird." My heart jumps into my throat. "You remember what happened to Maeve last year."

"Yeah, but that turned out to be her jealous friend. I guess I really shouldn't be calling her a friend, after what she did to Maeve. Maybe I'm just being paranoid because of that situation. I'm sure no one is stalking me, and I'm sure all the frenzy about your new mystery woman, *mom*, will die down soon. I'm not that newsworthy."

"Where are you?"

"I'm at the grocery store. I'm headed home in a minute. I'm sure it's nothing, Ash. I shouldn't have said anything. You have a game to focus on."

"I care about more than just hockey, Gina."

A beat and then, "I'm okay, Ash. I'm sure it's just someone trying to get dirt on Ash's mystery woman."

"What kind of dirt can they get on you?" I ask. She's the sweetest, kindest person I know and if they dig, they'll see that too.

She doesn't answer that question, and instead says, "Some places actually put my name right out there, and my café." She snorts out a humorless laugh. "Maybe it will bring new business to the café."

"Fuckers." Okay, that came out loud and harsh and from Gina's slight gasp, I'm pretty sure she's sorry she said anything. "I'll fix this when I get home, okay." I honestly have no idea how to fix it. People post what they want to post, and people believe what they want to believe. "I won't let anyone get close, Gina. I won't let anyone hurt you or Zoe."

"I know, Ash." I walk to my window and look out, wanting nothing more than to be home. "I'm looking forward to your game tonight. Promise me you won't get hurt."

"I can't promise that, babe." My heart misses a beat at the genuine concern in her voice. "But I'll do my best to get home to you in one piece."

"You'd better. Zoe would be very upset to see her manny hurt."

I laugh at that. "I'll do my best."

"She's also very much looking forward to her present. It's all she's been talking about."

On that note, I remind myself to hit the hotel gift shop. Knuckles rap on my door.

"Let's go, Ash. I'm starving."

"That's Brady. It's feeding time and Lord knows that man doesn't like to miss a meal."

"He's the goalie, he needs his fuel."

"Okay, babe. I should go…" I run my hands through my hair. "Ah, we're headed home after the game. It will be late…"

"You have a key."

My heart soars. "Yeah, but Dad is there. You don't have any spare rooms."

"You can crawl in with him. It's a big bed."

"I'd rather crawl in with you."

"I'd rather that too, but—"

"Zoe, I know." Goddammit, I'm tired of hiding what we're doing. In fact, I'm just about ready to scream it from the rooftop.

"But if you sneak out before she—"

"I can do that." As she laughs, I grin at the excitement I hear in my voice.

"Kick butt for us all tonight."

"There's only one butt I'm interested in. Later, babe."

"Later, Ash." With that, I end the call and my heart pounds a little too hard as she says my name and the next time I hear it on her tongue, I want my cock inside her.

As the pounding on my door continues, I walk toward it. "I'm coming. Jesus, where's the fire." I pull it open to find Brady standing there. Theo walks by and smirks at me, but nothing can bring my mood down now.

Brady cocks his head and smiles. "What?" I ask.

"Why are you smiling like the village idiot?" His gaze drops to the phone in my hand before I can hide it. "Oh, talking to Gina, I guess."

"Fuck off."

He throws his arm around me, and I pull my door shut. "Come on, let's go carb up." We take the elevator down to the main level, and I glance at Brady. "You were right about Coach. He likes the idea of Gina and me."

"Told you."

"It just pisses me off that her face and Zoe's was splashed all over the news, though."

"I know, bud, but it will die down. They're just looking for dirt. You know how the game is played."

Unfortunately, I do. "They won't find any." My heart lurches, because maybe I'm wrong about that. Are they going to dig into Gina's past? If they do, are they going to find Zoe's father? Blood drains to my feet, as the doors ping open. Jesus Christ, if anything happens to Gina, because of me, I'd never forgive myself.

"Are you okay?"

I take in the worried way Brady is looking at me. "Yeah, just hungry."

He looks like he's about to press, but stops when we step off the elevator to a group of girls standing in the lobby. The second they see us, they come running and the next fifteen minutes are spent taking pictures. A necessary evil of being a professional hockey player. At least Brighton and the other wives know it's part of the game we play, and trust us whole-heartedly. Will Gina extend me that trust? Believe that I'm not jumping from bed to bed when I'm not with her? If she does a search of me, and sees any of these pictures, it could skew her view.

From my peripheral, I spot the gift shop. "I'll meet you in there. Save me a seat."

Brady nods and makes his way into the restaurant where the guys are all gathering. I hurry to the gift shop and take a fast look around. What the fuck does one buy a little girl? Shit, I'm really out of my element here. Although I do know she loves books and games. I also know she's not as scary as I once thought she was.

My gaze falls upon the jewelry section and I see a beautiful dolphin gemstone pendant necklace.

"Can I help you?" I glance up to see the clerk behind the counter smiling at me. "That's a beautiful piece." I nod in agreement. "For someone special."

"Yes."

As I answer quickly, she picks it up and holds it out for me to see. "Do you know the dolphin represents protection and guidance?"

"No, I didn't." Could that be Gina's draw to dolphins? I'm not sure but what I do know is now that I'm in her life, she can always count on me to protect her.

"It's exquisite. I'm sure the special person in your life will cherish it."

"I'll take it." She nods. "I also need a special gift for her little girl. I don't think she'll appreciate jewelry."

"No, probably not. What's on her wish list?" the clerk asks and I laugh.

"If I could give her what she really wants, it'd be a daddy and a baby brother."

She grins at me. "Oh well, we don't sell those here." A wink and then, "But something tells me she might get those wishes in the future."

"Do you think?" I ask, like a goddamn idiot. But honestly just hearing a stranger say that to me, has my heart racing a million miles a minute because the truth is, Gina and Zoe are everything I never knew I always needed.

"Yeah, I think so. For now, how about a plush toy or a puzzle?" She waves her hand toward the kid section, and I walk over and spend far too much time looking at all the toys. It just doesn't feel right, though. Nothing about these things are special enough. I can't go home empty-handed though, so I reach for a plush toy, but when I do, something on the counter catches my eye. I switch focus and pick up the oval box, opening it to inspect the contents.

"I don't think a little girl would want that," the clerk kindly points out. "Here." She picks up a stuffed unicorn. "I don't know a girl who wouldn't love this."

I'm sure she would love that, but this...I examine the contents again, and grin. This is the absolute perfect gift for Zoe. I'm not one hundred percent sure Gina will agree with me, and I probably should run it by her first. Either way, I put it on the counter.

"I'll take this."

The clerk eyes me like I might have taken one too many hits to the head, and while that is true, I have full clarity and know exactly what I'm doing. She finally shrugs, and picks up the gift, taking it to the cash register.

"I guess you know her better than I do."

"I do." Squeals sound in the hall and I guess a few of the players have been spotted by their fans. Will I be able to make it to the restaurant unscathed?

"Well then, that's one lucky little girl and a very lucky mom," the clerk tells me as she rings up my purchases. I smile, all the while knowing that I'm the lucky one. A few minutes later, gift bag in hand, I head into the lobby. My phone rings again, and I snatch it from my pocket, hoping it's Gina. Once again that unknown, but now familiar number shows up and I shake my head.

Who the fuck keeps calling me?

That's when I realize I should probably answer it. What if this has something to do with Gina, and who might be following her. I'm about to slide my finger across the screen when a bunch of women rush me, and my phone is knocked out of my hand. It takes a hard hit to the floor, and while I want to get behind who's calling, after selfies with fans, the rest of the day is spent in a whirlwind of events before the game, leaving me with no time to myself.

And that's not fucking good...

23

GINA

I'm in a very good mood by the time I make it home with the groceries. Talking to Ash this afternoon made me feel so much more secure about this whole stalker situation, and he said he'd take care of it, even though I'm not sure there's anything he can do. Still, his protective nature over me, my daughter, his father and friends, gives me such a sense of comfort, I can't help but feel warm inside on this cold February day.

I ease into my spot outside my place. Hugging myself to ward off a chill, I step from the car and once again a strange, eerie feeling wraps around me. I search the sidewalks and find people bustling about, going about their Saturday afternoon shopping. No one particularly stands out, so I head inside the café and breathe in the delicious scent of cinnamon.

I chat briefly with the servers and when I notice the place is almost empty, I turn the sign from open to closed and let Carla know they can all head out early. Yes, I'm in a generous mood today and my staff work hard for me on my days off.

Hopefully come Monday, Margot will be available to watch Zoe after school, and I'm thinking about hiring new staff so I don't get bogged down on weekends with the flu season upon us. I make my way back outside to grab the bags of groceries for tonight, and for Zoe's lunches this week.

By the time I make it upstairs to my place, I'm ready for a hot cup of something and to spend the day relaxing with Zoe and Grant. Problem is, they have other plans, and they don't really involve me.

"Where do you think you're going?" I ask, as they both slip into their coats.

"Got a call. Need to help my buddy with a car repair over at his shop."

"Oh, well. Zoe, you don't have to go. I'm home now. Sorry, Grant. I wouldn't have taken so long had I known you we're needed elsewhere."

"No worries at all. I just got the call, and Zoe wants to go, don't you, Zoe?"

"Mom, I want to learn how to fix a Cadillac converter. Grandpa is going to teach me. He says mechanics is a good skill to know for when I'm older."

I do everything in my power not to laugh, because it's actually a catalytic converter, or cry, because this is the sweetest thing I've ever heard.

"You really want to learn to work on cars?"

She nods quickly. "Grandpa said he could teach me all the things he taught Ash, and that made him a jack in the box."

Ohmigod.

"Jack of all trades," I correct gently.

"He said Ash is a man of many talents."

"Yes, he sure is." As I think about how he's going to put those talents to use tonight, when he comes home from travelling, I swallow, begging my body not to react.

"Don't mind if I put this on, do you?" Grant asks, holding up the hat I'd given Callie to wear that day she showed up here to get her jersey signed.

"Where did that come from?"

"Callie came by to return it. She seemed a bit bored. Said her mom and grandmother were going out to play bingo tonight." He tugs the hat on and adjusts it in the hall mirror. "She said you might want to join them at the bingo hall."

Good lord.

"No, I'm not interested in playing bingo tonight, not when we have plans for the game." I walk past them and set the groceries on the side table. "We're still on for that, aren't we?"

"We sure are, love," Grants says. "I told Callie that and well..." He pauses and I suck in a breath as I eye him. "I asked her to join us. I hope that's okay with you." He hangs his head. "I'm sorry. I know I should have asked first. She just seemed so lonely. If I overstepped—"

"It's okay, Grant. The more the merrier." Honestly, I love how he cares about others and how inclusive he is. His son is the same way, although I'm not sure he would want to be hanging out with Callie, not with the way she puts her hands all over him.

He smiles, and looks somewhat relieved that he hadn't overstepped. "You're good with us going to the shop?"

"It's safe?"

"I wouldn't let anything happened to this little chicken nugget." He puts her hat on her head, and pulls her zipper to her neck.

Zoe laughs. "Mommy, Grandpa calls me chicken nuggets. That's so silly."

"It is silly," I agree as Grant beams at me. "You be good, okay?" I tap my daughter's nose. "You listen very carefully and don't touch anything you're not supposed to touch."

"I won't."

I pause for a second to think about what I'm doing. While I'd like to keep my child in bubble wrap, learning new things is good for her. So is spending time with her new best friend. I hand my keys over. "Why don't you take my car? The booster seat is in the back."

"Sounds good. Need anything while we're out?"

Those words give me pause, and my heart squeezes tight as my brain takes a quick trip down memory lane. How many times did my grandfather run errands and ask my grandmother if she needed anything? This, right here, is what home and family is all about and I want it more than I ever wanted it before.

"I think I got everything for tonight."

He steps up to the grocery bags and peeks in. "What the... you got fake meat."

"It's plant-based, not fake."

"You been talking to my son or something."

"He called when I was at the grocery store, but this was my idea." He looks like he's about to protest. "Trust me, Grant. You're going to like it."

He takes Zoe's hand, grumbling about everyone trying to ruin his life, as they head down the stairs, and I grin. As much as he grouches, he likes that we all care about his health.

I move to the window and watch Grant get her into the back seat and buckle her in. Wow, she lets him buckle her in and if I dared to try, she'd throw a fit. Snatching up my bags of groceries, I take them to the kitchen, and begin unpacking. For the next little bit, I work on making a dough, and getting it chilled before dinner, then I make up dips for snacks tonight, and do a bit of tidying around the place.

By the time I finish, Grant and Zoe come barreling back into the house, bringing the chill of the outdoors with them.

"Mommy, that was so much fun. I got to use tools and turn screws, and everything." When I reach them at the door, I laugh at the grease stains on her face, and I grab my phone to take a picture of her and Grant. I send it off to Ash. Not that I expect to hear from him. I'm sure they're all getting into game mode, but it will give him something to laugh about after the game.

"You're not putting that up on social media, are you?"

"No, I don't really use social media."

"It's garbage. Nothing good about it."

"I totally agree." A hard quiver goes through me as I remember the things Liza falsely said about Ash. Who does something like that to get ahead in life? "The pizza dough is chilling. Why don't you go ahead and get started on making dinner, and I'm going to take this chicken nugget to the bath."

"I'm on it."

Grant gets out of his winter clothes, and hangs them in the closet like he now lives here and it makes me chuckle. Honestly, I like having him around.

"Mommy," Zoe begins, and as I take her to the bath and get it going with warm water and bubbles, as she strips down, I listen to her talk nonstop about her time at the shop and some guy named Dodge that she met. I'm not sure if she's actually talking about a car or one of the mechanics, but she's pretty intrigued by it all and I can't help but think opening her up to seeing new things is a good idea. I know I certainly can't teach her anything about cars, and her own father isn't about to bring her into his world and teach her anything about medicine or psychiatry. "I've never been to a garage, you know."

"Oh, I know." I try not to laugh as she blinks up at me. She takes the washcloth from me as I try to wash her face.

"I can do it." As I watch her, my throat squeezes tight. She's growing up so darn fast. What is this place going to be like when she goes off to college? I can't even imagine the quietness or the loneliness. Maybe I should have another baby, or two.

Whoa, where did that thought come from?

I finish getting Zoe washed up and into her pajamas. By the time I'm done combing out her wet hair, there's a knock on the door, and Zoe darts down the hall and pulls it open.

"Hey, Zoe." Callie glances up at me when she sees me coming. "Gina." I smile at her, and she continues, "You don't mind me joining you guys for pizza and the game, do you?" I note she's in Ash's jersey.

"No, of course not. Come on in."

She steps in and I shut out the coldness behind her. She breathes in deeply. "Something smells good."

"Grandpa is making pizza," Zoe blurts out and darts to the kitchen.

Callie arches a brow. "Grandpa. Is there something I should know? I mean, last time we talked—"

"No. No." I am not about to tell Callie anything about my sex life or relationship with Ash. "It's just something she calls him. No relationship."

She lets loose a relieved breath. "Thank God." I really don't know why she's thanking God. From what I can see she doesn't have a relationship with Ash. "Did you see the pictures of us on social media." A light laugh rumbles in her throat. "Who wore it best? Hilarious."

"Yeah, hilarious."

"It's not even like you 'wore' him." She does air quotes around that word and I guess she considers the fact that she jumped on him and wrapped her legs around his back, meant she 'wore' him. "Oh, I mentioned it to Grant earlier. Mom and Grandma are going to play bingo if you're interested."

Good, God. I'm not that much older than her.

"No, I want to watch the game." Why do I suddenly feel like putting on my jersey, like I'm in competition with Callie? I really am far too mature for that. Maybe I should go play bingo. "Come on in. Can I get you anything to drink? Wine? Beer? Soda?"

"I'm not driving, so I'll have wine."

"Great." We walk into the kitchen, and she pulls her phone out and shoots off a text. She waits for a second, before shoving her phone back into her pocket. I pour us each a glass of wine and I might need more than one to make it through the night.

Grant puts the 'fake meat' as he calls it on the pizza, slides it into the hot oven and sets a timer. "That does look amazing," I tell him. "Crust was okay?"

"Crust was good," he huffs out. "But I can't guarantee the taste. Not with that low fat cheese and cardboard that's trying to pass itself off as meat."

I laugh at his antics. "I bet you'll love it."

"What do you want to bet?" he asks, mischief all over his face.

I fold my arms and eye the man who likes to matchmake. "What are you up to now, Grant?"

He whistles innocently, and I catch the curious way Callie is watching the both of us.

"Nothing," he grouches.

"Forget it. I'm not betting." I pull four plates from the cupboard and set the table. Callie sits, making herself comfortable as she once again does something on her phone.

"Callie, do you want to play a game with me?" Zoe asks.

"I'm not much into games."

Zoe looks a bit sad. "I wish Ash was here. He always plays games with me."

Callie perks up. "Oh, what games does he like?"

"He likes the pop one."

"Why don't you show me?"

I eye Grant as he watches her leave the room with Zoe. He leans in and whispers. "Looks like she's got the hots for my son." I can't help but laugh at that. "Poor girl doesn't know he's totally into you, though."

"Grant," I warn and he holds his hands up.

"Just making an observation."

I shake my head and set out napkins and pour a glass of milk for Zoe. "Beer?" He nods and I grab him one from the fridge.

Soon enough, the timer goes off and Grant pulls a delicious pizza from the oven. I call everyone to the table, and conversation is light and easy as we all eat. I ask Callie about her courses and career plans after graduation, only to learn, it's her goal to marry an NHL player. Alrighty then.

Once dinner is done—Grant grumbled about the fake meat but he gobbed it up—we clean up and head to the living room. After a few more games with Zoe, I get her cleaned up and tucked into bed, and we all settle in to watch the Bucks play Florida.

Grant's phone rings and he smiles from ear to ear as he talks to Ash before the game, something they always do. Callie watches on almost angrily and I tell her about their traditions, or maybe they're superstitions. Many of the guys have superstitions.

Eventually the teams make their way on the ice, and we all lean in to watch the game. Whenever the camera zooms to Ash, Callie squeals a bit, and I work really hard not to. Noah gets our first goal just before the first period is over. Florida comes back to match it in the second, and I wince every time Ash takes or gives a hit.

During intermission, I lay out all our snacks and we dig in. While I'm not hungry, I continue to stress eat. Hockey is nerve wracking, especially when you know the players, and you're sleeping with the defenseman.

As the third period nears the end, the teams tied, Jesse Campbell and Elias head down the ice together, working like a dream team as they pass the puck back and forth. Kalen is right there behind them. I'm on my feet when Florida's defense come after them, but Jesse and Elias's slick practiced moves prove too much. Jesse passes to Kalen, and he shoots, and scores. The light goes off and the guys all cheer, so do the three of us.

"I don't know how much more I can take of this," I blurt out, and wipe my brow with the back of my hand. With three minutes left on the clock, Florida pulls their goalie, and I hold my breath. Ash is killing it on defense, and as much as I want to look away, I keep my eyes glued to the countdown clock. It finally goes off. We all start cheering and jumping up and down and when the camera pans in on Ash and he grins, my heart races, because I think that secret smile is just for me.

"What a game," Grant says, pride all over his face.

Callie hugs herself, or rather her jersey. "That was intense." We all sit back down and stay put until the guys leave the ice, and once it's over, we all clean up the dishes and put things away—this time, Callie helps.

"Thanks so much for letting me watch the game with you guys. It would have been boring being at Grandma's alone."

"I'm glad you could join us." I walk her to the door and a cold breeze blows in as I open it. "Sleep well," I tell her as I think about how little sleep I'll get when Ash joins me in the middle of the night.

"You too." Her phone rings and she pulls it from her pocket. Her eyes go wide as she glances at the number. A second later, she slides her finger across her screen, steps outside and answers, "Ash, hi. Ohmigod, you played amazing tonight."

24

ASH

"How did you get this number?" I ask the second I hear Callie's voice.

"Aww, you're not mad, are you?"

Of course, I'm mad. She's been texting and calling me nonstop, and I don't answer unknown numbers. The only fucking reason I called back after the game was because I was worried it had something to do with the social media posts and Gina feeling like someone's been watching her.

"Callie," I warn in a tired voice.

"The other day when I took a selfie, I grabbed your number. Remember I asked you to send me the selfie and you said you didn't have my number? I put it in your phone and called myself."

Jesus, I forgot all about that. "Are you with Gina and my dad?"

"No I just left." Her voice is muffled by the wind. "I'm just headed home. I'll run up to my room and we can talk in private."

Fuck, did Gina hear her answer? Does she think I've been calling Callie. For Christ's sake. "I have to go. We're boarding the bus to head to the airport."

"Can you call me when you're free."

"I'm not free, Callie." I don't want to sound cruel or mean, but what she did was wrong and I don't want her to think I'll be calling her, any time soon, or ever. "Safe travels back to California," is all I tell her before ending the call. I'm ushered onto the bus before I can call Gina, and my gut is in a knot as I find my seat. Once everyone is boarded and we're in motion, I shoot off a text to Gina.

Me: Hey, did you enjoy the game?

Gina: It was stressful.

Me: Listen, I called Callie. I didn't know who I was calling. She put her number in my phone when she took a picture of us, and sent herself a text. She's been calling non-stop. I only called the number back because I thought it might have something to do with you. I hope you don't think I've been talking to Callie.

Gina: I never thought that. I had a feeling something was off. Just so you know, I think she wants to marry you.

I laugh at that, as my shoulders relax and I sink into my seat, wanting to text with Gina all night as I think about crawling in with her later. We send texts back and forth until we reach the airport, and I know it's late and she needs her rest.

Me: I'll see you soon.

Gina: Can't wait.

I board the plane and close my eyes as we take off and head back to Boston. It's the middle of the night by the time we land, and I head straight to my car and make my way to Gina's. I find parking near her place, grab my bag and step out onto the slick street. Oddly enough, when I see a car across the street, a strange, uneasy feeling comes over me. Numerous cars park on this downtown street, so why this one is drawing my attention is a mystery. Maybe I'm just paranoid because I'm worried about my girls safety and privacy.

Deciding to check it out, I cross over to it, and glance inside. I find it empty and look up and down the street as the hairs on the back of my neck tingle. I don't like this. Not one fucking bit. I hurry to Gina's and climb the stairs, using my key to let myself into her place.

On tip toes, I make my way to her room and cringe when the door squeaks open. I tug off my clothes, climb into bed, and pull a sleeping Gina close. I lightly kiss her shoulder and while I don't want to wake her—okay, I kind of do—she stirs.

"Hey," she whispers and rolls to face me. It's dark in her room, prohibiting me from seeing her features, but the sound of her voice washes over me and brings a new kind of warmth to my blood.

"I didn't mean to wake you."

"It's okay. I'm glad I'm awake." She puts her hand around my head and pulls my mouth to hers. I sink into her kisses, and moan with longing as I drag her closer. "I couldn't wait for you to get home," she admits honestly, her voice low, sleepy...seductive.

I brush a strand of hair from her face. "Why is that?"

"Oh, just that I wanted this." She reaches down, takes my swelling cock into her hand and lightly strokes it.

"Babe..."

I slide my hand down and find her wet, and warm and oh so ready for me. Inching one finger inside her, I move it in and out, just to make sure she's totally ready, and when she moans for more, I roll over her, spread her legs with my body and we both groan as I slide into her.

Her fingers snake around my body and she palms my back, holding me tighter to her, and as I push in and out of her, I know I want so much more.

"I missed you," I say.

"Same."

I snort out a laugh. "You just missed this?" I push deeply, hitting parts that pull a deep moan from her.

When her moan falls off, she counters with, "Didn't you?"

"Yeah, I did, babe." I go up on one elbow and cup her cheek, my gaze moving over the curves of her face. "But there's so much more I missed, too."

She goes quiet for a moment, and panic grips my chest. Have I said too much, am I pushing this too far?

"Same, Ash," she whispers quietly and brings my mouth to hers for a searing kiss that burns through my body and wraps around my heart. Our bodies, so accustomed to one another, move in sync, meeting and welcoming each thrust in that easy way of long-time lovers. Nothing about this is fast and frenzied, despite our desperate need for one another, but there's something so moving, so profound in the way we're making love. Dammit, I should go away more often, although I don't want to be away from this woman—this small family.

Her muscles clench around me and I too let go, pleasure washing over us both as my eyes drift shut. I stay inside her for a long time, and her hand trails down my back. As soon as they stop moving and her breathing slows, I pull out, turn her back to me and pull her tight against me as sleep nearly overcomes her.

Feeling very much in love and very overprotective, I say, "We should stay at my place."

"Why?" she asks quietly.

"I don't like the idea of someone watching you."

"I can take care of myself."

"Is it so bad that I want to take care of you?"

"I'm just used—"

"I know what you're used to and I want to change that for you, Gina."

A beat of silence and then, "I'd like that, Ash."

The next thing I know, voices from the kitchen reach my ears and I turn to see Gina still asleep beside me. Shit. I meant to get up in the middle of the night and go to the sofa. I grab my bag, hurry into my clothes, and make a fast but quiet trip to the bathroom. Once I have myself pulled together, I walk into the kitchen, like I just arrived.

I catch the gleam in Dad's eye when he sees me. Yeah, there's no fooling him.

"Ash, when did you get here?" Zoe jumps from her chair and

hurries to me. I squat down and she throws her arms around me. Clearly, she missed me too.

"That doesn't matter. I'm here now." I don't miss Dad's small chuckle. Jesus, I'm never going to hear the end of this. "What are you doing up so early?"

She rubs her stomach. "I was hungry."

"You didn't want to wake your mom?"

"No, Grandpa makes better pancakes. More lumps."

I laugh at that as Dad stands a little bit straighter and I'm fucking relieved she didn't come running into her mother's room.

"I heard her in the bathroom so I got up with her," Dad tells me. "I thought Gina might like to get a little bit more sleep."

I meet his eyes, and mouth the words, "Thank you."

He hums to himself, obviously completely fucking happy with his matchmaking skills, even though our friends with benefits relationship started long before he got himself involved.

"Great game last night, son."

"Thanks." I toss a coffee pod into the machine, and turn back to find an anxious Zoe staring up at me. That's when I realize she's waiting to hear about her present. "Let me bring this coffee to your mom and when she gets up, I'll give you your presents."

She claps her hands and squeals, and fuck, as much as I should have run the gift by Gina first, it's too late. Not only because Zoe is looking at me with bright-eyed enthusiasm, but also because I don't have another gift if this one is bad.

As soon as the coffee is finished, I add a splash of milk and can't wait to leave the room. Watching my father gloat is not a pretty thing. Speaking of pretty things. Gina stirs as I enter and her soft, sated smile turns to a frown, and worry invades her eyes as Zoe's voice trails down the hall.

"She didn't see me."

She relaxes. "Thank God."

"I thought you could use a cup."

She holds her hands out and gratefully takes the mug. My dick twitches as she presses her lips to the edge and takes a mouthful. "Thank you."

"Zoe's waiting for her gift."

"You could have given it to her."

"Gina, I'm not sure—"

"Come on, sleepy head." I turn at Zoe's voice as she bursts into the room. Man, she wasn't there a second ago and honestly, I'm getting damn tired of sneaking around. I know Gina and I said some important things to each other in the middle of the night and I am hoping things are going to change between us. She called herself an asshole magnet, but she knows I'm not an Ash-hole, like everyone calls me. But if she's not ready, I don't want to pressure her or force the relationship into something else.

"I'm coming. I'm coming." Gina is about to get up, stopping when she realizes she's naked.

"Come on, Zoe. You can help me get the presents out of the bag."

I lead her to the other room, and cast a glance over my shoulder to see Gina. She gives me a grateful smile before I close the door to give her privacy. Back in the kitchen, Dad is making pancakes, and I unzip my big bag. Zoe peers in to see the dark plastic shopping bag that doesn't reveal what's inside.

"What did you get me?"

"Why don't you put the bag on the table? Be careful with it, though."

She crinkles her nose up, perplexed, and it's absolutely adorable, and reminds me so much of Gina. "Can it break?"

"Maybe."

Dad whistles happily as Zoe very carefully pulls the bag out and gingerly sets it on the table. "What's taking Mommy so long?" She pulls out a chair and sits in front of the bag, never taking her eyes off it.

"Oh wait," she bursts out. "I made a picture for you." She dashes down the hall, and into her bedroom. "I did this yesterday after Grandpa and I watched cartoons."

"You had arts and craft time?" I ask, pleased with my father.

"Then we went to Dodge's to work on a Cadillac."

I arch a brow and Dad just laughs. "I'll explain later," he informs me and nods to the picture.

I glance down and see a picture of a young girl holding a leash to what might pass as a stick puppy, and on either side of her is a woman, and a man. Beside the man is a smaller man, who I assume is my dad, and beside him is a box of sorts.

"What's this?" I ask, my heart in my throat. "That's my new baby brother." She spreads her arms. "This is my family."

A sound at the door fills the room and I catch the anguished look in Gina's eyes. Does she think I'm going to be upset by this picture? Or perhaps it's her who's upset. If so, she's really going to hate the gift I got for Zoe.

"Mommy," Zoe bursts out. "We can open presents now."

Gina gingerly walks into the kitchen, her coffee mug in hand, and I take it from her and drop a pod into the machine to refill it. She looks like she could use another stiff one.

Jesus, what am I saying?

"What do we have here?" Gina asks and sits next to Zoe.

"Can I open it now, Ash?"

"You better hurry up. Pancakes with extra lumps are coming right up."

"We have to be careful, Mommy. It could break." Zoe carefully opens the bag and pulls out her present first.

"That one's for you?"

She examines the picture of the colored stones on the blue box, her brows furrowed and I get it. I'm not sure any young girl has ever received a box of stones before. It's probably confusing.

"Open it up," I tell her. She lifts the lid, to find a black velvet bag inside. "Tug on the string."

She does as I ask and pours the stones into her hands. I drop next to her to explain, all the while avoiding Gina's gaze. I really fucking hope she's not mad.

"You see these?" She nods as she examines them. I pick up a stone and run my finger along the white band. I take her little finger and do the same with it. "This is a wishing stone, Zoe. You hold one of these in your hand and you make a wish." She frowns and my heart sinks. She hates her gift. But then, her eyes go wide and she takes the stone from me, holding it on her palm.

"I can use this instead of lump wishes?"

I nod. "Yes."

A wide smile splits her face and she throws her arms around me. "Oh, thank you, Ash. I love these stones." She settles back in her chair and puts her hand on her stomach. "I've been getting tummy aches from all the lumps in my pancakes."

We all burst out laughing, and I let my gaze stray to Gina, who's looking at me with such warmth and gratitude, I know I didn't make a mistake here.

"I thought that might be the case."

"This is the bestest present ever. Grandpa, can I have a pancake without lumps."

"You got it, chicken nugget."

"I'll eat that one, Dad."

"Oh, you wishing for something, son?"

"I don't like food spoilage," I tell him. But that's not the entire truth, because yes, I'm wishing for something too.

GINA

Here it is, Monday again, later in the afternoon. It's been a little over a week since I've been wearing this gorgeous dolphin necklace Ash brought back for me, and I still can't seem to stop playing with it. I also can't seem to stop smiling. Honestly, this was such a thoughtful gift, and those wishing stones...

At first I was mortified that he would give Zoe a gift like that. They felt far more real and maybe even more powerful than wishing lumps in pancakes. However, the fact that Ash got them for her said more than words ever could. He wants for her wishes to come true. Heck, I do too. While Ash and I haven't come right out and said as much, things were said when we made love that night he came home from Florida. Things that lead me to believe we do have a future together.

Of course, Callie tried to come between us, stealing his phone number and calling him incessantly until he finally called her back—because he was worried about me. She's back in California now, and fortunately she's no longer calling him. There's a chance she could have come between us with her antics. The old Gina might not have believed Ash and might have questioned his explanation. That old Gina was hurt and jaded and trusted no one. Ash, however, hasn't done anything to prove he's not trustworthy.

Carla comes into the kitchen from the dining area, just as I pick up the order Andre just finished preparing. "Things are picking up out there."

I nod, pick up the plates and head into the dining area to serve them to a couple of retired regulars. Devon picks up his fork, hunger in his eyes as I set his plate in front of him. Since he always talks about the weather, I'm not surprised when he says, "I hear another storm is on its way."

"I'll be glad when spring comes," his regular lunch partner Webster grumbles.

I glance out onto the sidewalk and note the dark clouds. Nothing, not even the cold wet weather can wipe the smile from my face. But you know what can? The man standing on the sidewalk, staring straight at me. The hairs on the back of my neck tingle, and honest to God, I haven't felt like anyone was watching me since Ash returned home last weekend. Not much has been said on social media since that incident after the game, but that doesn't mean someone isn't looking for dirt. Once again, my gut tells me this is about something else.

I'm about to march right outside and ask the guy what he wants, only to stop when a gorgeous woman, who doesn't look to be that much older than me, and two teenagers who I assume are her sons, step up to him. My steps slow as he turns to them, and they greet him with a smile.

Perhaps he's her husband and this is all clearly my overworked imagination.

I make my way back to the kitchen and pick up my phone to find a message from Ash. He finished up practice a while ago and is helping his dad with a car at Dodge's garage. His second message suggests we all stay at my place tonight because of the bad weather coming in. We've been spending our time together at both places, and I haven't needed Margot to babysit, because Grant insists on being here for Zoe after school, whether I'm working or not. I think that's rather cute.

Zoe hasn't been asking too many questions, but she's been using her wishing stones every morning and every night. I message Ash back to let him know that I can take tomorrow morning off since I've brought in new staff. If the roads are bad enough, school will be closed and the café won't open until late anyway.

With that settled, I pick up the next order and head to the dining room. After I deliver it, I spot the woman and her two teenage sons sitting at a table, the man no longer with them. The woman has her eyes glued to me and once again, the hairs on the back of my neck tingle. Which is crazy. This woman clearly isn't here to get social media dirt. Her sons are both on their phones as I step up to them.

"How are you all doing today?"

She gives me a rather nervous smile. "We're good." She looks around. What or who is she looking for? Is it possible that she's here to see Ash? "How are you?"

"I'm good. Can I start you with coffee?"

"I would love that."

"Boys," she orders in a stern voice. "Put your phones down please."

They do as she asks, and their weary eyes narrow in on me, not with suspicion, but with...anger? What the heck? The bell over the door jingles, and in walks Elias and Tuck. I lift my head and smile at them. They nod back and take a table near the side window.

The older teenager nudges the younger one. "Shit, Josh, that's Elias Ariti and Tucker Delray, the team's captain."

The younger boy, Josh, looks around, his eyes widening. "What, where?"

"Right there, sitting by the window."

Josh's eyes practically bulge out of his head. "Shit."

"Boys, language." The woman gives me an apologetic look. "Sorry. Things have been..." She lets her words fall off.

"Parenting. I get it." I have a girl, not a boy, and I know it can be different, but still, parenting...

Deciding to help the woman out, I lean in. "Tell you what. No more bad words, and I'll introduce you."

"No way," the older boy says.

I give a casual shrug, and gesture for Carla to bring coffee. "Sure."

"You know them?" His eyes narrow in on me, suspicious, but no longer angry.

"Lucas," the mother warns. "Manners, please."

Lucas sits up a bit straighter, and it's odd. There's something familiar in his features. "You really know them?" he asks, in a nicer tone.

"I do. Do you want to say hello, maybe get an autograph?"

"Yes," they both shout in unison, and I laugh.

I glance at the woman. "If it's okay with you?"

She fidgets with her purse straps. "I don't want to bother them."

"They're great guys and they love their fans." She gives me a grateful smile, like my gesture means a lot.

"You're very nice."

I chuckle. "Thanks," I say for lack of anything else. I guess if she's here to find dirt, it will be good dirt.

"Come on, guys." They jump from their chairs so fast, they nearly topple backward. Carla comes to fill the woman's coffee mug as I lead the boys to Elias and Tuck.

"Hi guys, I hope you don't mind." I put my hand on Josh and Lucas' backs to guide them forward. "Two fans who'd love to say hello."

"Hey," Elias greets and holds up his hand for a high five.

The boys are star struck as they clap hands, and I pull my notepad from my pocket so they can get autographs, and then of course the boys need selfies. I glance back at their mom, who is texting something, her brows knit tightly together, and my stomach tightens slightly. What is she nervous about, and why is it making me uneasy?

The door opens again, and a woman who looks to be in her late fifties comes in, glances around and hurries over to sit beside the boys' mom. Judging from the resemblance, I'd say she's the boys' grandmother.

"Okay guys, I think we've taken up enough of the players

time. Let's get you back to your mom." I wink at Elias and Tuck. "Lunch is on the house."

"Well, on that note," Tuck laughs and picks up his menu. "I'm starved."

Chuckling, I take the boys back to their table. "I can't believe you know them." Josh beams up at me. "Do you know any other players?"

"Would you believe me if I said I knew all the players?"

"No way," Lucas says, warming up to me a bit. "Do you know Ash Wheeler?"

My heart jumps at his name. "I know him very well."

"Does he come in here too?"

"He does."

"Mom, Mom," he yells as he slides into his chair. "Ash Wheeler comes in here. We have to come back every day."

"We can't do that, Lucas." She gives me a nervous look and I glance at the woman taking off her coat and scarf. "Coffee?"

Lucas leans back in his seat and folds his arms. "Maybe Boston won't be so bad."

Ah, so they must be moving here, and maybe their anger wasn't directed at me, but at the move itself.

"Love some." She stares at me, like I'm a bug under a microscope and this time instead of calling Carla over, I go get it myself. I fill her up and drop the menus.

"I'll just give you guys a moment."

I come back and take their order, and as I move about the dining area, clearing dishes and filling drinks as I wait on orders,

I notice the woman keeps looking at me. So does her mother. The boys are both on their phones, texting their friends their pictures and blasting all over social media, I suppose.

Andre hits the bell to let me know their meals are up and I walk into the kitchen to get them. I know Ash is busy, but it would have been nice for the boys to meet him. While I don't like all the attention, I do enjoy standing back and seeing him with his fans. He was always good with the kids. It was just my daughter he was afraid of, and that was probably because he had no idea what to do with a small girl. Little did he know how much she'd like going to Dodge's garage. That thought makes me chuckle.

I line my arms with plates and set them down in front of my guests. "Is there anything else I can get you?"

The boys as well as the older woman stare at the mom. They're clearly waiting for her to say something.

She fidgets with her spoon. "Are you here until closing?"

Odd question. I nod. "Yes, for another half hour. Then I have to pick my daughter up at school." I glance out at the gray outdoors. "Hopefully the bad weather will hold off until long after that."

"Okay," is all she says. "We'll see you after we're done. We won't be that long." I wait for a second and when she doesn't say more, I step away and leave them to their meal. I go back to my phone and shoot off a message to Ash. He gets back to me right away, and lets me know he can pick Zoe up for me after school. I'm grateful that I don't have to rush off and I like them having time together. My daughter is falling for the hockey hero every bit as much as I am, and for the first time in my life, I'm not afraid of that.

I head over and chat with Elias and Tuck for a second. "Do you know those boys?" Tuck asks.

"No, first time I've seen them in here." I don't miss the way Tuck is sneaking peeks at their mom. I can't blame him. With her long dark hair, thick lashes and dark eyes, she's rather breathtaking. Her boys both look like her. She's absolutely gorgeous, but not at all Tuck's type. Then again, I'm sure many people would be surprised that Ash is with me. Although my friends weren't. The public, however, that's a different story and one interesting enough to be plastered all over socials that night he held Zoe in his arms.

I head to the kitchen to help Andre clean up, and Carla brings in the dirty dishes. I check the time, noting it's nearly closing time and I'm really hoping Ash gets back before my table of four leave for the day.

The bell over the door jingles, and a bubble of happiness fills me because it's likely Zoe and the guys. I wipe my hands on a dish towel and hurry into the dining room to see them all. The boys both gape when their gazes land on Ash, and I tug Zoe into my arms to give her a hug.

Zoe begins talking a mile a minute, telling me about some new pet guinea pig they have in their classroom, but how she still wants a dog. "Mommy you want a dog too, don't you?"

Strangely enough, after Zoe calls me mommy, Josh and Lucas' attention instantly turns to my daughter, and they stare at her with a mixture of curiosity, unease and apprehension. I thought they'd be all over Ash, but right after they heard Zoe call me mommy, they focused in on her and yes, I find that very odd.

"You're Zoe?" Lucas asks her.

She frowns and looks at both of the boys, her gaze going back and forth like a bobble head, no doubt wondering how they know her name. Hell, I'm wondering the same. I swear if this is about a story...

Their mother looks mortified when she warns, "Josh, Lucas, please don't."

Every nerve in my body jumps, and my muscles tighten. I'm about to ask exactly who they are and what is going on, but Zoe speaks first.

"Who are you?" she asks.

Josh blurts out, "I'm your brother."

Gina pales and takes a wobbly step back. I reach for her, worried that she's about to collapse, and who can blame her after that blunt announcement? As I brace her against my body, Zoe just stands there and stares at the two boys, a completely confused look in her eyes. My gaze jerks to the two women at the table as they begin to shift uncomfortably.

Zoe shakes her head as I stand there and try to understand what's going on. As my brain races to catch up, Zoe blurts out, "I don't have a brother. Wait, did my wishing stones work?" She turns to look at Gina. "Mom?"

"Son," Dad whispers, and gives me a nudge that pulls me from my stupor.

"What is this?" I ask in a deep voice as I hold a trembling Gina tighter.

The younger woman stands on shaky feet and grips the back of her chair for support. "I'm sorry. I didn't mean for it to come out this way." She shakes her head at her son. "Josh."

Josh folds his arms, and even though he gives an unapologetic shrug, it's easy to tell from his eyes that he's as uncomfortable as everyone else. "Well, she is my sister."

Gina studies the boys for a second, her body tight. I'm about to ask if this is some kind of joke, when a little gasp escapes Gina's throat, and that's when I realize she's figured out what's going on here. "Lucian," she whispers. "You're... you're..."

Lucian...her ex. Zoe's father.

"Maybe we should talk in private," I cut in when I clue in to what's happening.

I meet the woman's eyes and she nods in agreement. "I think that would be a good idea."

"Dad, why don't you take Zoe upstairs. Make a snack." He nods and takes her hand, hurrying her up the stairs to give us the privacy we need.

I put my hand on Gina's back and set her into motion, desperate to figure out why this woman showed up out of nowhere, and what she wants. "Let's all go into the kitchen."

"Mom, can you stay here with the boys?" the woman asks.

Her mom gives a curt nod and the boys grumble something to each other as I lead Gina and the woman into the kitchen. Andre and Carla are just finishing the clean-up and as soon as they see us, and read the tension in the room, they take off their aprons and hang them up.

Andre holds the door open for Carla. "We'll see you in the morning, Gina."

"Drive safe," she mumbles and steps away from me, gripping

the counter behind her as she nervously bites her lip and stares at the other woman.

"You're Lucian's wife," she murmurs.

"I'm Maria."

"I didn't know," Gina retorts quickly. Strain lines form under her eyes and I'm guessing she's considering her words carefully. "He...he lied about everything."

Maria waves her hands. "I'm not here about Lucian. Well, in a way I am. I'm not mad at you and I don't blame you is what I'm trying to say."

Gina relaxes a bit. "I'm not a homewrecker. As soon as I found out..."

"You ran, with your unborn child. Lucas and Josh's half-sister."

Gina straightens and everything from the horror in her eyes, to the tightening of her face, tells me she's going into mama bear mode. I'm right there with her.

"How did you find me?"

"I hired a private investigator a few months ago. It wasn't until you were photographed with Ash...." Her gaze strays to me for a second. "Well, he was able to track you down after that."

"Fuck," I curse. This is all my fault. From the way Gina is looking at me, it's easy to tell she thinks so too. "I guess that's who's been following you."

Maria looks horrified. "I hope he didn't scare you."

"What do you want?" I don't even recognize the cold defensiveness in Gina's tone. "I won't let you take—"

"I don't want to take Zoe from you," she cuts in quickly. Her shoulders lift, tightening around her ears. "I just wanted to know her. I wanted the boys to know her. She seems like a lovely little girl. You've done a great job...by yourself," she adds quietly.

Gina folds her arms. "Lucian didn't want anything to do with her."

"I know, and after I found out that he had a child in the world that he'd discarded, I didn't want anything to do with him." Her mouth twists like she'd just eaten something disgusting. "How can a man abandon his own child?" Tears fill her eyes, and Gina softens.

"I'm sorry, Maria. I never wanted to come between you two, and...I never ever meant to hurt you or your children."

"You didn't know. I understand that. I found out about his affairs a few months ago, and believe me, there were many." She shakes her head, glancing at the polished floor, and Gina pushes off the counter, and takes her hand. "I asked around, at the hospital," Maria begins quietly. "There were rumors..." She lifts her head. "About you, and a baby. You'd left abruptly, and when Lucian and I had a big fight, and I pressed him, the truth came out." She sniffs. "I'm so sorry he did that to you. I'm sorry you had to run away like that. If I'd have known..."

"I'm sorry for what he did to us all," Gina responds quietly as tears fill her eyes. I stand there, helpless, not knowing what to say or do. When they hug, and tears fall harder, I grab a box of tissues and hold them out.

"Thank you," Gina whispers and pulls a few from the box to share with Maria. "At least now I know why Lucas was angry when he met me."

"He's going through a lot," Maria explains. "We're leaving California, and he's a teenage boy, with teenage angst and hormones. He's angry at his father, and the entire world, to be honest."

Gina wipes her eyes. "Are you moving to Boston?"

"I don't know. We're in limbo, trying to figure things out. I have my boys and my mom to consider and need to do what's best for all of us."

I take in the dark circles under Maria's eyes. "Did you travel in today?" I ask. She nods. "Where are you staying?"

"I haven't booked anything yet. I came straight here. Our luggage is in the rental car out front."

I catch Gina's eyes and we know each other so well, she can tell what I'm thinking. "You'll stay with me," Gina says.

"How about we all go to my place," I suggest. "There's plenty of room, and the kids can get to know each other in the games room. I think they'd all like that." As Maria glances down thinking about it, I eye Gina. "Gina?"

"I think it's a good plan," she agrees.

Maria dabs at her eyes. "I don't want to be any trouble."

Gina gives her a comforting smile. "It's no trouble at all and I think Lucas and Josh are going to lose their minds if they get to stay at Ash's place."

A small smile turns up the corners of Maria's mouth. "I didn't expect you to be this nice to us."

"You'll stay?"

She nods. "Yes, thank you. Maybe Lucas won't be so angry

with me for dragging him to the east coast if he gets to stay at your place."

"Good, it's settled." I drop the box of tissues. "Let's get out of here before the roads get bad."

Maria nods. "Okay."

With that, I open the door for them to leave the kitchen, and the boys and her mother watch us with curiosity.

"Mom, this is Gina and Ash." Maria glances at us. "This is my mom, Elena, and you've already met Lucas and Josh. Boys, we're going to be staying at Ash's place tonight. What do you think about that?" They high five each other, and instantly start texting. I guess that's a good sign. Elena stands up, her hands linked together as she studies her daughter. "It's okay, Mom. We all talked and I think it's going to be okay." She eyes Gina, looking for support.

"It's going to be okay," Gina assures her. "Come on, let's go up to my place so we can talk to Zoe and get some things packed for a sleepover."

We all head up the stairs, and Dad glances at me as I step into the living room. His worried eyes meet mine and I give a nod to let him know everything is under control. "Hey, Zoe. Want to stay at my place tonight?"

She jumps up. "Yes." She stops jumping when she sees the others coming in behind me. "Are you my brothers?" she asks as she angles her head, completely confused.

Gina waves toward the sofas. "Please, everyone, have a seat."

Maria and Elena sit and the boys perch on the arms of the sofa. I move to the loveseat and Gina drops next to me, calling Zoe over to sit on her lap. "Zoe," she begins. "Lucas and Josh are your half-brothers." Gina swallows. She's having a hard time with this and I don't know how to help.

Zoe slaps her palm to her forehead. "But they're big. I wished for a baby brother."

Gina chuckles nervously as the family of four watch us. "But isn't it awesome to have two big brothers? You can show them Ash's games room and you can play pool and pinball. I bet they'd love that."

"You want to play?" she asks and they nod. "How do I have big brothers?"

Gina brushes Zoe's hair back. "Why don't we save that story for another time, and instead we can all get to know each other."

She sits there for a second. "If I get a daddy, will he be their daddy too?"

"It's complicated," Gina tells her. "Why don't we wait and see if it happens first before we answer more questions."

Satisfied with that, Zoe jumps up. "Do you have a dog? I want a dog." She shows the boys her wishing stones. "I've been wishing for a lot of things, and you can wish for things too. Where do you live? Do you know how to fix a Cadillac?"

"Okay, Zoe." I rustle the hair on the top of her head. "No more questions for now. Let's get going before the snow is bad, and then we can all get to know each other over pizza."

"Pizza, yay?" She starts to jump up and down again, and her resilience still amazes me.

"Not with that fake meat," Dad says and screws up his face.

"Oh, come on, you liked it," Gina counters, her features soft again and maybe there's a part of her that's both relieved and happy about this situation.

"Do you want to follow us in your car?" I ask Maria.

"Yes, that's a good idea." With that, I open the door and they all file outside. The boys run down the stairs, anxious to get to my place, and while I felt helpless through most of this, I can at least help by giving them a place to stay and a safe place to talk.

"Zoe, run and get some clothes packed," Gina tells her.

"I can't believe I have brothers," she mutters as she trots off to get ready and Dad makes his way to the kitchen. I guess he senses that I need to talk to Gina alone.

"Gina," I begin and pull her into my arms. "I'm so sorry. I didn't mean for any of this to happen. The pictures..." I shake my head. "None of this would have happened if I hadn't picked Zoe up that night."

"I think I'm happy it happened. I always knew Zoe had brothers. I never thought she'd ever meet them." She grins. "Our little family is expanding."

"It is."

She shakes her head, her eyes once again filling with tears. "I can't imagine what Maria is going through, though. How horrible for them all. I never wanted to see any of them hurt by what I did."

"It wasn't what you did. It was what her cheating, asshole husband did." I brush her tears. "But she has you now, so that is going to make everything better."

She smiles at me. "Thank you."

"I'm really sorry about the pictures. Keeping a secret was the one thing you asked of me."

"In the beginning, yes. I didn't want to complicate things. Then after a while, it wasn't so much that I was worried about being seen with you, it was that I just...in the back of my mind, I always worried that someday Lucian would change his mind and maybe want to see Zoe or try to take her. It was just a small worry, but a worry, nonetheless. I did tell him I was leaving, and he didn't ask where, so I didn't tell him. I guess I just wanted to keep a low profile."

"You're not worried about being seen with me, about our relationship getting out there?"

"If our relationship is getting out there." She pauses to poke my chest. "I think maybe you and I should first figure out what this relationship is."

I laugh. "You're right. Will you be my girlfriend, Gina?"

GINA

s I roll over in bed and glance at the gorgeous man beside me, I can hardly believe we're nearing the end of April. I can't remember a time when I've been happier, despite the fact that there are numerous pictures of us on social media. I thought it had died down, but when we started going out more, showing Maria, Elena and the boys around town, the interest picked up again.

Not that I really care anymore. I'm living my best life here. Well, except for the fact that I still sneak from Ash's room when we're at his place, which is most nights, and he sneaks from mine when he stays over at my place. I have a little girl to consider, and while I'm in love with Ash, there is certainly no talk of marriage or anything like that. Zoe believes kissing and sleeping together means she's going to get herself a father, and that's just something I don't want her thinking... even though I've been thinking about it myself. A lot.

Moving quietly, not wanting to wake Ash after his late game last night, I check the time. It's early, and everyone is still asleep. Slowly, I push the covers down and pull on my yoga pants and T-shirt. I tiptoe to the bathroom, then head to the kitchen to get the coffee going.

Soon enough there will be three hungry kids looking for food, and I'm just grateful Zoe isn't asking for lumpy pancakes anymore. We were all getting stomach aches.

I toss a pod into the machine and walk to the kitchen window to look out at the quiet neighborhood which I've grown to love. So many of my friends live here in Beacon Hill and while it's a commute to go to work at the café—heck, all I had to do before was walk down the stairs—I don't mind. I have to drive Zoe to school anyway.

Speaking of school, Maria enrolled the boys here. Even though she's in limbo, and has been living in Ash's house as she searches for the right accommodations, she didn't want anything to interfere with their education.

I respect that, and Zoe and the boys have become close. I'm actually happy to have them in my life. I'm sad about the circumstances, of course, but I'm also happy that Maria fell in love with Boston, and has decided to make a life here. We've become good friends and after she drops her boys off at their school, she loves coming to the café to help out. It's all so strange, I know. Somehow it all works, though.

"Morning," Grant says, and I spin.

"You scared me. I'm going to have to put a bell on you."

He chuckles and when the machine beeps, I hand him the cup. He's been staying with us all in this big house too. I still don't think all the bedrooms are full yet. This is what Ash has always wanted—his father living with him so he can take care of him. Although, he'd never tell Grant that.

I do love Ash's protective nature, which he no doubt got from his father, judging by the way he's taken Zoe, Lucas and Josh under his wing, teaching them things, and even bringing them to the garage with him. They all seem to love it, and Grant is getting the grandkids he's always wanted, even though they're not blood. Does that even really matter, though?

He graciously accepts the coffee, takes a big drink and stretches his arms. He seems awfully tired this Thursday morning, but so very happy.

I put another pod in the machine. "Late night?" I ask. He and Elena went to the hockey game, while I stayed home with Maria and the kids and watched from here. I go when I can, and enjoy it a lot, but I was home last night working on making cut out flowers with Zoe. They're decorating the classroom for spring today.

He grins at me. "Elena and I stayed up to watch a movie after we got back. You know, to wind down." He cocks his head a knowing look on his face. "We didn't keep you up, did we?"

"No." That's not the reason I'm suddenly yawning. After Ash came home, and crawled into his bed, I snuck in and we spent the better part of the night making love. It's become a tradition after his games and I love it.

Later tonight, he leaves for a three-day road trip and I'm totally going to miss him. He doesn't always have a lot of time to call or text when away, but we try to sneak a minute in here and there. Although this weekend, that might be hard, because they'll be going non-stop and I might not be in Boston, anyway.

God, I really can't believe what I'm thinking about doing.

"You and Elena have been spending a lot of time together," I point out. "Are Zoe's wishes coming true? She's getting a grandma?" I grin at him over my cup before I take a drink, and he just whistles innocently. I think it's wonderful that they get along so well. If they end up together, married even, and Ash and I do too, what does that even make Elena to me? It's all too complicated to think about and I really don't like complications. That, and of course I'm getting way ahead of myself.

"You tell me," he finally counters as he puts another pod in the machine and places a new cup under it.

"Nothing more to tell." He knows all about Ash and me. The only one we've been keeping it a secret from is Zoe, and while I'd like to tell her, I don't want her to get her hopes up. I haven't really explained to her how Lucas and Josh are her brothers, and she hasn't asked again. One day it will all come out, and it will be when she's older and understands better. I just hope she's not hurt by the truth.

Elena walks into the kitchen, and fixes her hair as she smiles at Grant and on that note, I grab some eggs from the fridge.

"Go on and get ready for work," Grant says. "Elena and I can make breakfast for the kids."

My hand stalls as I reach for a loaf of bread. Honestly, an extra-long shower sounds divine right now. "Are you sure?"

"Positive." My gaze goes back and forth between the two of them and I can't help but think they want me out of the kitchen for their own personal reasons. Alrighty then...

"Okay, thanks. I'll shower and then get the kids up." Leaving the two lovebirds alone, I hurry to the bathroom and take a very long, hot shower. Once done, I sneak back into the bedroom, and with Ash sleeping so soundly, I dress quietly and leave him there, even though I'd like to crawl in with him and wake him up in an intimate way.

Once I'm dressed, I wake Zoe and the boys up, and my good morning greetings are met with grumbles from Lucas. While he loves hanging at Ash's place, he's still out of sorts, and I can't say as I blame him. Both boys are going through a lot, and while Maria wants them to have a relationship with their father, he refuses to talk to him.

I do worry about Lucas. At fourteen, he's at a vulnerable age, and does need strong male influences, and a little bit of firm discipline wouldn't hurt, either. He needs it, and Maria is in such a helpless state, she's giving them everything they ask for to make up for all they've been through. It's not my business, but I'm not sure it's the right strategy. Then again, I'm not a parenting expert by any means, and have made my own mistakes.

We all eventually make our way to the kitchen and Grant has a cup of coffee waiting for me. He's happy and cheery and everything about that seems to get on Lucas' nerves.

"I don't want to go to school today. I want to go to the garage with Grant," Lucas says when Maria enters the kitchen.

She blinks rapidly and since I haven't touched my coffee yet, I hand it to her. She needs it more than I do. She opens and closes her mouth, worry lines tightening on her forehead.

"I'm not going until later," Grant pipes in. "How about I pick you up after school, and take you with me. We've got a nice sports car in I think you're going to love."

"Can I go too?" Josh asks.

"Of course. You can all come."

"Me too?" Zoe asks, her eyes wide and hopeful.

"Of course."

I tap her nose. "We're going shopping, remember? Remember we're in charge of markers for next week's bingo night at school." Bingo. Ohmigod, what would Callie say? Oh, she'd probably ask what a guy like Ash, one of Boston's hottest bachelors, is doing with an old lady mother, who does old lady mother things like bingo.

"Oh right," she murmurs before taking a big drink of juice. "Sorry, Grandpa, I can't come."

He chuckles and rustles her hair. "Next time, chicken nugget." Grant casts me a glance. "Ash not up?"

"Doesn't appear to be. We should let him sleep in after his game last night." I think about leaving him a note, but then breakfast and the chaos of the morning begins and the next thing I know, I'm out the door with Zoe, driving her to school.

After I drop her off, I find myself singing along to the radio as I head to work. I park and practically skip inside, inhaling the delicious scent of cinnamon. "Good morning," I greet Andre, who is pulling a fresh batch of cinnamon buns from the oven.

"Morning," he greets, and I grab my apron from the hook, ready to hit the day running, even though I'm a little sad that I won't be going home to Ash tonight. Maria shows up around a half hour later, and starts taking orders with me. We work nonstop until about eleven, and then take a break before the lunch crowd starts.

The place is still quiet as I sip my coffee in the kitchen, but when I hear the bell over the door jingle and familiar voices filling the café I jump from my stool. In the dining room, I spot Tuck and Theo grabbing a seat, and I look outside to see if Ash is with them. He's not, and while I'm disappointed, I shouldn't be so needy. He's probably spending time with his dad before hitting the road later. Okay, I love being the object of his sole focus, and I can't help it. But I'm an adult and realize others need him too.

"Hey guys. Coffee?"

Tuck glances around the room, and his gaze stays on Maria for a second too long before he answers. "Love some."

"Great. I'll have Maria bring it over. I'll grab your menus." His eyes dart to mine, and I work to keep the grin from my face. Someone has a crush, and I think it's cute. Although I'm sure Maria is not looking to date anyone after her trauma, and she has her boys to focus on. I understand her mental state all too well.

"Hey," Theo greets and tosses me a grin. I know Ash isn't a fan of his. In fact, not a lot of the guys are.

"What's up, Theo?"

"I know what I want."

An icky feeling crawls over my skin as he stares at me, his gaze dropping to the top button on my blouse. I'm almost afraid to ask him what he wants. "Sure." I pull my notepad from my apron. "What would you like?"

He grunts, and Tuck must kick him under the table, because he jumps in his seat and curses. "I'll have the meatloaf," he grumbles as I wave to Maria. He snorts out a laugh as she comes our way with the coffee. "Ash is a lucky man," he blurts out with an almost insidious grin.

"Tuck, do you know what you want?"

"Chicken salad," he tells me, his angry gaze latched on Theo. Jesus, I think steam is about to come out of his ears.

"A really lucky guy," Theo says again, and I just smile. No way am I going to allow him to bait me and I'm pretty sure that's what he's doing.

They both sit back as Maria fills their mugs, and Theo is still smirking at me.

Tuck pushes Theo's mug closer to him. "Drink your coffee and shut your mouth."

Okay, clearly Tuck is worried Theo is going to say more, and everything tells me it's not something I'm going to like.

I'm about to leave, when Theo explains, "I mean, the coach told Ash to be seen with you and your kid because it was a good look for him and his fucked-up reputation, which he was told to clean up after Liza, but now he has Maria and her kids living with him too."

My feet stall, and my gaze flies to Theo's. What the hell did he just say? Coach told Ash to be seen with me?

Theo snorts out a laugh. "All this time, Mountain told us he wasn't banging numerous chicks at the same time and that Liza was simply spreading false rumors." He pumps his fists together, as Tuck's chair scrapes the floor as he pushes to his feet. "Who knew his ex was telling the truth all this time and there were a lot of girls climbing on Mountain. Babe, you should be with a guy like me. I'd never do that to you, and I don't mind Ash's seconds. Liza and I were good together for a while."

Maria pales, and Tuck throws some bills on the table before stepping around me and picking Theo up by his collar. "I'm sorry, Gina. I'll take him out of here."

"Hey, if you don't believe Ash has been using you, go check his hashtags," Theo shouts before Tuck throws him out the door, and follows behind him.

I swallow the lump punching into my throat as Maria's dark eyes widen. She sets the coffee pot down and blinks rapidly. "Are people saying that?"

My God, this poor woman has been through so much. "I don't know. I don't think so. From what I understand, Theo is just a troublemaker." I put my hand on her shoulder. "Don't worry about it, Maria. Anyone who knows Ash, knows the truth and those are the only people who matter."

That might be the case, but what about his Coach? What will he think if he hears about this? He wasn't too happy with him after Liza posted all that trash. How will he see this, and did he really tell Ash to clean up his act?

Wait, is that why Ash is with me? Why he hasn't been out with any bunnies?

My breaths comes a little faster as I try to console Maria, and needing a moment alone, I pick up the untouched coffee mugs and carry them to the kitchen. I drop them into the sink, and hurry to my small office in the back. I pull my phone out, and my heart is in my throat as I pull up insta and type in, #AshWheeler.

The first post I see is from Liza, telling the world how she's not surprised Ash was using me to clean up his reputation. I read a few more posts, and when the room starts closing in on me, I shut down the app and try to wrap my brain around all this.

Just then my phone rings, and it's Ash. Did Tuck call him, fill him in on what just happened? As I stare at it, I think about the first time I ever met Ash, to our sweet lovemaking last night. Voicemail kicks in, and then a second later, my phone starts ringing again. Working to control my breathing, I slide my finger across the screen.

"Ash," I murmur quietly.

"Gina, listen—"

I cut him off. "Is it true?

"Gina—"

"It's a yes or no answer, Ash. Did your coach tell you to be seen out with me? He liked the idea of us because it was good for your reputation and the team's image?"

A long minute of silence, which tells me everything I need to know and then, "Yes, but..." His voice falls off, like he's trying to figure out what he's supposed to say next.

"So, just to clarify, it is true. Your coach wanted you to spend time with me, because it was good for your image, and for the team's?"

"Yes, Gina, but it's not...it's just not what you think. You know me. You know that's not what we're about."

"Why didn't you tell me then?"

"I don't know. I guess, maybe I didn't want you to know."

"Because...you didn't want me to think I was being manipulated."

"Gina, please."

"You shouldn't have kept that a secret, Ash," I say quietly.

"I know. I'm sorry."

I take a fast moment to think about what Theo said, what I read on social media and what Ash just admitted to me, and then I decide right here and now, that yes, I am definitely going to be out of town this weekend. "Listen, I forgot to tell you. Zoe and I are going to be flying to California this weekend."

"What?" His voice is full of shock. "Why?"

I turn on the tap, and put my hand under the water. Once my palm is cold, I press it to my flushed cheeks. "I have some things I need to take care of."

"Gina, what's going on? What kind of things?"

Since I don't really want him to know what I'm up to, and what I'm up to scares me a whole lot, I hedge. "Oh um, well… it's just…ah, some personal things that involve my late grandparents." Not really a lie.

"Can I call you when I'm on the road?"

I'm not good at keeping secrets, especially big ones and I might blurt something out. "I'll probably be too busy."

"Oh, okay."

The alarm on my phone goes off. "I have to go, Ash. Zoe is getting out of school shortly. Kick butt at your games."

A beat and then in a quiet voice he murmurs, "Okay, bye."

"Bye." I hang up, my anxiety at an all-time high, because what I'm about to do is going to change everything between Ash and me, but now that I've made my mind up, nothing is going to stop me.

28

ASH

As I tape up my stick, ready to hit the ice against New York, I try to play it cool, try to pretend that my life might not be imploding. Even though I think it very well could be. Why is Gina running back to California? I mean, it seems so strange, and not to mention it to me all week, and then only mentioning it after that asshole Theo told her about my private conversation with Coach. Motherfucker. I ought to go beat his face in right now.

"Everything okay?" Brady asks. I guess I'm not doing such a great job of hiding my feelings.

"Yeah, just getting mentally prepared." I rip the tape and smooth it over my stick. If we were back home, I might call Melanie or even Brighton to find out if they know anything. But here on the road, I don't want to start anyone panicking, and the guys need me to have my head in the game.

"I talked to Tuck." I don't miss the concern in his voice.

I keep my eye on my stick and answer with, "Yeah." I really

don't want to get into this right now, but I know he's concerned about me.

"That black eye Theo is sporting is from Tuck."

I snort out a laugh. "Good." I glance at Brady as he scrubs his chin and shakes his head like he too wants a piece of Theo. "What the fuck is wrong with that guy?"

"We don't have enough time for that conversation." I stand and stretch out my legs as I shove my tape into my bag.

He looks a bit hesitant when he asks, "You talked to Gina?"

I nod. "As far as I can tell, she believes me."

Then again, maybe she was just pretending to believe me, not wanting to fight over the phone, and maybe she's headed back to California to see if she can patch things up with Zoe's father, now that Maria and the kids are out of the picture.

Dude, come on, you don't believe that?

It's true, I don't. I just don't understand what's left for her in California. The whole bit about her grandparents felt off. They've been gone a long time. What loose ends does she have to tie up and she hesitated when I asked, like she was making it up on the spot.

Her up and leaving felt far too familiar. Far too much like what my mother did.

But Gina isn't like that.

Okay, Ash. Clear your thoughts and get your head in the game.

Brady nudges me. "Let's go."

"I just have to give Dad a quick call." He nods and I pull my phone from the locker and call Dad. Maybe he knows something I don't. I can't come right out and ask. I don't want him worrying about anything either. Dad answers on the first ring.

"Hey, son. I'm in front of the TV with Elena, Maria and the boys. We can't wait to watch you kick butt tonight."

"Thanks, Dad." I go quiet for a second, and unable to help myself I ask, "Have you talked to Gina?"

"At the café she told Maria she had to fly out of town to take care of some personal business."

I grip my helmet tighter as the guys all start filing out. "Yeah, okay. I was just wondering."

"Everything okay?" he asks quietly.

"Oh yeah," I blurt out in a fake happy voice that probably isn't fooling my very astute dad. "I just wanted to make sure you all knew she had to leave."

"Yeah, it's all good, son. Now remember, it doesn't matter if you win or lose, so get out there and win."

I laugh at that and how he says it to me before every game. He even did it when I played in my younger years. "Okay, Dad. Say hi to everyone for me."

"Will do."

With that, we end the call and I stare at my phone for a second, itching to call Gina. Since she doesn't want me to, I shoot off a text. Hey, she didn't say anything about texting. "Hope your flight was good. I look forward to seeing you when I'm back." Okay, yes, that was fishing, but I'm in love with a woman who just found out I kept something pretty important from her, something that could be viewed as me being manipulative. Then she jumped on a plane back to where she used to live.

As my brain spins, I throw everything into my locker, tug on my helmet, and make my way out to the tunnel. Brady is already on the ice warming up and when he sees me, he comes over, taps my helmet and orders, "Head in the game, Mountain."

"You can count on it."

I stretch out, go through my warm-up drills, and prepare to play. If anything, I plan to channel my worry and my anger at Theo into winning this fucking game.

Soon enough the puck is dropped and as a professional, I manage to tune everything out but what is expected of me, and honest to fucking God, I'm pretty sure I'm playing better than I ever have before.

By the time the third period comes around, and we're up two to one, I catch Theo smirking at me. Motherfucker. Is he trying to break us up because he wants Gina for himself? He does seem to like the women I'm with, judging by the way he went after Liza. I really am going to pound him when we get off the ice.

Right now, however, I'm going to channel the anger into the two forwards determined to take me down. I glance to my right and spot Tuck, and he goes after the guy with the puck, forcing him to shoot it and when he does, I intercept and take it behind the net. The next thing I know, I'm hit from behind, and a fight for the puck ensues. I come out victorious and get it to Tuck who sends it to Elias, and they take the play to the other end.

Breathing heavily, I reposition, and glance at the clock. As the play comes back our way, they pull the goalie, and we all prepare. Chaffin, fast motherfucker that he is, works the puck around me, and I chase him. He takes a shot on net, and

Brady stops it with his glove. "Yeah, man," I yell, and a second later, the clock runs out.

We all hug, and after we celebrate, we head off the ice. I go through my normal after-game routine, and after speaking to the media—thank God they were more interested in the game than my personal life—we're bussed back to our hotel.

"Grab a beer?" Noah asks and throws one arm around me.

"I think I'm just going to call it a night. I'm tired and if I have a drink and I'm around Theo, I might just fuck him up."

"Tuck already did that for you."

I grin, loving my hockey family. "Yeah, but I'm going to call it a night." Desperate to be alone, to check my phone, I stab the elevator button as the guys all head to the hotel bar. I hurry to my room, and tug my phone from my pocket. I exhale a big, relieved breath, when I see a message from Gina, telling me I had a great game. I want to ask if I can call, but she made it clear she didn't want that, so I shoot back a message.

Me: Everything going okay with your grandparents' stuff?

Gina: So far so good. I'm just falling asleep with Zoe, so talk soon.

Me: Wait, when are you back?

Gina: Monday, same as you. Bye, Ash.

· · ·

Me: Bye.

With that, I set my phone down. Jesus, that's the second time I said goodbye to Gina on the phone, and the second time it felt far too final. But maybe it's not. She did say talk soon. But what the hell does she want to talk about and why couldn't we do it before she left, or even now? I don't know, but what I do know is by the time the sun comes up, my thoughts are back on Gina and what's really going on.

The next few days and games go by in a blur. I'm not sure how we won, considering I was in a daze for most of it. I finally arrive home Monday evening, and my heart is in my throat, wanting to talk to Gina. As I ease into the driveway, disappointment settles in the pit of my stomach. Her car isn't here. In fact, there are no cars in the driveway. Where the heck is everyone? I head inside and call out, but no one is here. It's after school and the boys should be home by now. I grab my phone and message Dad.

Me: Hey where is everyone?

Dad: I'm at Gina's. I picked Zoe up after school. Maria and Elena are out with the boys but are coming back with pizza. The real kind. Join us.

Dammit, I'm not going to go over there without hearing from Gina. Does she even want to see me? I mean, she's back and she never even bothered to message me. Just then my phone pings again and my heart jumps when I read the message from Gina.

Gina: Can you meet me in the café?

Me: Be right there.

I practically run to my vehicle, back out of the driveway and head straight to the Nook. After parking, I jog down the sidewalk to the café and find the closed sign on the door. I try the knob and it opens.

"Gina," I call out.

"In the kitchen."

I practically run to the kitchen and when I enter, and find her leaning against the counter an uneasy, almost nervous look on her face, my protective instincts kick into high gear.

I take a step toward her. "Are you okay?"

She picks her phone up off the counter, and runs her finger over the screen. "I thought the world should know what you're really like?" She holds her phone out to me, and I recognize one of the social media apps, the one that likes to bash me the most. I shake my head, not wanting to read it.

"Gina, what's going on? Why did you ask me to meet you here?" I pause and glance around her kitchen.

"I wanted to do this here, in the café, where we first..." Her cheeks turn pink. "This is where things started heating up between us, when you...you know, showed up with your tools. One in particular."

I get that she's being cute and cheeky but I'm a hot mess here. "Can you please tell me what's going on?"

She nods. "I need you to read this." She continues to hold her phone out and I reluctantly take it and see that it's her profile. She posted on social media? I really don't know what the hell is going on here. I frown, and make a move to step back when she touches my arm. "Please, just read it." As she gazes at me with warmth and a measure of worry, I nod and glance at the screen.

If you want dirt on Ash, don't read this. But if you want to know who he really is, then continue. Ash Wheeler is the kindest, sweetest man on the planet. I never liked to ask for help and with Ash, I didn't need to. He stepped up when I was shorthanded at the café, and when I needed help with childcare, he was right there.

"What is this, Gina?" I lift my head and find her watching me carefully. Jesus, she's a private person and putting all her personal business on social media couldn't have been easy for her.

"Keep going," she whispers, so I look back down.

Ash is always there for everyone he cares about, even when some are stubborn about that. He has treated my daughter and me with love and care and the utmost respect. He's a great man who protects, nurtures, and loves with his entire heart. He's a jack of all trades, a man of many talents, and not only is he an amazing hockey player, he's an amazing teammate, son, and manny and soon, I hope I can add father and husband to this list."

My heart jumps into my throat. "Gina..." I lift my head and

she has an open ring box in her hand, with a gold band in it. "What…"

"My grandparents left me their rings. They came with very specific instructions." I angle my head as my throat tightens and tears blur my vision. "I am only allowed to put this ring on a man who is honest, truthful, kind, and giving, and is deserving of all the love in the world. You are that man, Ash." She sniffs, as tears fill her eyes. "I know this is unconventional, but nothing about us, or what we've been doing qualifies as conventional, anyway, so here goes. Ash, will you marry me?"

I stand there for one second, completely stunned as her words bounce around in my brain. Is this really happening? Jesus, it is, and I'm the luckiest fucking man in the world. As she stares up at me, nibbling her bottom lip with uncertainty, like maybe this isn't what I want, I pull her to me, and press my lips to hers, kissing the hell out of her as her arms tighten around my back.

"Yes, Gina. Fuck, yes. I will marry you." She's crying as I inch back and I brush the back of my palm over her cheek. "I love you so much." I exhale. "I was so scared, Gina. I didn't know what was going on. I never thought you believed the lies written about me…then after your run-in with Theo, and our conversation, you left for California, and didn't want me to call."

"I'm sorry, Ash. I didn't mean to be all cloak and dagger. I'm just not good with secrets—heck, I told the girls about us when I wasn't supposed to—and I wanted to get these rings and get back to you as quickly as I could. I figured if we talked, I'd spill the beans and tell you exactly what I was up to. I also…" She nibbles her lips again. "I wasn't sure if this was what you wanted, so I was a little terrified."

"It's what I want. Believe me, it's what I want. I think I knew it was what I wanted from the first time I met you. I was scared. Coach told me no more drama, and you had a daughter to protect, and we all know how much she frightened me." That brings a grin to her face. "I never thought I could be a good role model for a little girl. I never had any maternal guidance."

She cups my cheeks. "I know, Ash. I also know that you are amazing with her, and she loves you as much as I do."

I blink, trying to wrap my brain around this, when another thought—a huge thought—hits. "Can I be Zoe's father?"

She laughs. "Yes, if that's what you want."

My heart is pounding so fast, I'm not sure I heard her correctly. "I can adopt her?"

"Of course, you can, Ash."

I hug her again, her warmth and love curling around my heart. "Our family...You, me, Zoe, Dad, Maria, Elena, Lucas and Josh. It's going to be so big."

"It's everything I ever wanted," she says quietly, inching back to cup my cheeks.

"Me too, but I also don't think it's big enough?"

She arches a brow. "No?"

I grin and kiss her again. "I think we could add to it."

"I'd love that, Ash, and I know Zoe will too." She laughs. "Just tell me you'll use the wishing stones and not make us eat lumpy pancakes for months."

"It's why I bought them."

"Should we go tell the others?"

I'm about to say yes, when something else occurs to me. "You need a ring."

She pulls another box from her pocket. "This was Grandma's engagement ring, and again I know it's not conventional, but this is the one I want to wear."

I take it from her, and look at the small diamond, and while I'd like to buy her the biggest one in the store, this one couldn't be more perfect for her. She holds her hand out. "Will you be my wife, Gina?" I ask. "Will you and Zoe move in with me and make me the happiest man in the world?"

"Yes," she answers, and I pick her up and spin her around.

"Now we can go tell the others, and I know just how I want to do it."

"Oh?" She angles her head and I grin at her.

I grab her hand and we head upstairs. We say hello to Dad, who is watching me carefully. I can't seem to keep anything from that man. "Where's Zoe?"

"I'm in here," she calls out, and we walk into the kitchen to find her drawing a picture.

She jumps up and hugs me when I enter the kitchen, and I kiss the top of her head. Before she sits back down, I pull Gina into my arms, and give her a kiss. Zoe's eyes go wide.

"Mommy!" she shrieks. "You're kissing Ash."

Gina breaks the kiss and laughs. "I am, and I think you know what that means."

She shrieks and jumps up and down. "Ash is going to be my daddy!"

I drop down to one knee and take her hand. "Zoe, will you be my little girl?"

"Yes!" I pull her to me and hug her, and she's shaking so hard, unable to contain her excitement, it makes me laugh.

"All my wishes are coming true," she yells and grabs the picture with everyone in it. "This is my family."

Dad comes into the kitchen, a big grin on his face. "Grandpa, my wishes are coming true."

"They sure are," he agrees, and puts his hand on my shoulder. "Congratulations." I hug him and then we pull Gina and Zoe into the embrace.

When we break apart, Zoe picks up her wishing stones, and I take a closer look at her picture, to see that she added Maria, Elena, Lucas and Josh.

"Zoe why do you need your stones? All your wishes have come true. A daddy, a grandpa and brothers. Are you wishing for more brothers?"

"Daddy," she begins, and my heart nearly jumps from my chest. Gina puts her hand on my back, a small noise catching in her throat as my vision once again blurs. "I have enough brothers. Now I want a sister."

"And a dog," Dad pipes in. "Don't forget about the dog."

I laugh. "Thanks, Dad."

"I didn't, Grandpa, it's right here." She points to the dog in her picture then slides her finger to the basket. "This is for my sister. Mommy, you have a ring, and you kissed and now all you have to do is sleep in the same bed...and then—"

Jesus.

"Okay, Zoe," I say and pick her up. When she gets older and realizes what she said, she's going to be mortified. Redirecting, I ask, "How about that dog?"

She cups my cheeks and squeezes. "How about Grandpa and I pick the dog out? You and Mommy need to sleep in the same bed so I can get a sister."

Lord, my daughter is going to be the death of me.

Zoe...my daughter.

Gina...my wife.

My new found family.

How did I ever get so lucky?

The front door opens and voices as well as the smell of pizza fill the house and as Zoe and Dad run to the other room, excited to share in the good news, I pull my fiancée close.

"I love you, Gina."

"I love you, Ash."

I glance around her kitchen, and think about the first time I made love to her. "I don't ever want to stop meeting like this," I tease.

"We never will, Ash. We never will."

EPILOGUE

Gina

S ummer Break

We didn't want to wait to get married, so we tied the knot as soon as the NHL season was over—the Bucks made playoffs but were eliminated after losing to Florida in game six. Zoe, of course was our flower girl while Brady stood for Ash, and Melanie was my maid of honor. We also involved Lucas and Josh, giving them the roles as ushers, and they loved it. Well, Josh loved it. Lucas is still a moody teenager, in need of a male influence.

As the warm Caribbean sun shines down on me, I lift myself up to see my husband swimming to shore. He pulls himself upright and I sigh. I will never get used to the fact that I married such a handsome man. As I look at him now, my fingers itch to touch him, but that will have to wait. He has something secret planned for us, and while we agreed no more secrets, he assured me I was going to enjoy this. What he doesn't know is that I have a little surprise for him too.

He holds his hand out to me when he approaches, and I can't take my eyes off the beads of water sliding down his beautiful, muscular body.

"Hey, babe, you ready?"

"I am." I push up from my seat and go up on my toes to kiss him. He snatches my bag from the sand and tosses it over his shoulder. "I love it here," I murmur. "Maybe one day we can all come back, Zoe, your dad, Maria, Elena and the boys."

"I bet they'd love that, but right now, I want you all to myself."

"I want that too."

We walk down the private beach, and I have to say, I'm happy we don't have to worry about anyone taking our pictures. After my post, the media went crazy, and we were big news, so was our wedding. But the media will grow tired of us, because yeah, when it comes right down to it, I do old lady mother things, and Ash does old man father things, and that just doesn't make for good news.

We walk until we come to a boardwalk, and we step onto it. Ash stops when he comes to a tour boat. "We're going for a boat ride?" I ask.

He grins like a child ready to burst on Christmas morning and I love it. "Yeah."

I sigh again. I still love it when he says that one word in that deep husky tone. It does the strangest things to my body. "What are you up to, Ash?"

He whistles innocently. "Climb on, and let's get into our life jackets."

I do as he asks, and the captain of the boat brings us jackets and introduces himself. "Are you ready to see some marine life?"

I gasp and turn to Ash. "Are we..."

He finishes my sentence with, "Swimming with the dolphins, yes." He grins. "I believe that's the plan. Isn't that right, Captain?"

"That is the plan."

I throw my arms around Ash and hug him. "Thank you. I've always wanted to do this." We break apart and I close my fingers around my dolphin necklace, which means so much to me.

The captain begins, "Okay, before we go, there are rules."

I slip into my life jacket and as we buckle up, the captain tells us the rules. We nod in agreement, not wanting to do anything that would threaten any dolphin's health or their habitat. After our instructions, we settle back for the boat ride and the captain starts the boat, taking us into deeper waters.

I can't seem to stop sighing, and Ash nudges me. "Better than work."

"Better than work," I agree. I'm definitely not worried about the café. Maria, who'd been helping me out, is now manager of the place. She'd been looking for a place to live, and after Ash asked if we could move in with him, they took over my place above the café. It worked out well for all of us, and I have to say, I love having them in my life.

My place was small for a family of four, so when Elena decided she needed her own space, it was rather convenient that Grant just so happened to have a spare room for her. That makes me laugh. If they think we're not on to them, they're wrong. They're not as sneaky as they think they are. Just like we weren't as sneaky with our friends or with Grant. Seriously though, what a big happy family we've become. A huge smile crosses my face.

"Something funny?" Ash asks and tugs on a strand of my hair.

"Just thinking about family and how happy I am."

He kisses the side of my head and I put my hand over my stomach. "Oh no. All this motion."

Panic moves into his eyes. "You're seasick. Should we turn around?" He doesn't wait for me to answer. "I'll talk to the captain." He makes a move to get up, and I tug him back to me.

"No need. I have meds in my bag." I point to the bag on the other side of him. "Can you get them for me?"

"Of course." He reaches into my bag and roots around. He pulls out some antacids and examines the label. "Are these strong enough? I'm not sure they work on seasickness."

I gesture with a nod. "There should be something else in there."

He reaches in again, and when he can't find anything beneath my beach towel, he pulls it out, sets it on the seat and dumps the rest of the contents onto it.

The second his eyes land on the white stick, he stares at it with confusion, like he has no idea what he's looking at. Then his head lifts as understanding dawns. "Did you do a covid test?"

I laugh at that. I guess he's seen lines on covid test kits and just assumed that's what's going on here.

"No. I didn't swab my mouth for this test." I hold his gaze. "I peed on that stick."

As soon as the words leave my mouth, he jumps to his feet, his mouth open but no words forming. The boat turns slightly, and since he doesn't have his sea legs yet, he nearly falls.

"Whoa." I jump up and put my arms around him.

He grips my shoulders, and inches back to meet my gaze. "Gina, babe. We're pregnant."

I nod. "We're pregnant."

"How...when...did you find out?"

I nudge him. "I think you know the how part. For the when part, I found out this morning when you went for a run on the beach. I had a bit of cramping, so I thought I'd give it a try. I was waiting for the right time to tell you." I glance out at the warm waters of the Caribbean surrounding us. "I think this was the right time."

He puts his arms around me and picks me up. "We're having a baby."

"We are."

He stops hugging me and sets me down gently. "Oh, sorry. I didn't hurt the baby, did I?"

I laugh, and it doesn't surprise me that he's going to be that kind of attentive, caring partner during pregnancy, and after.

"The baby is a peanut, Ash."

He frowns. "Maybe you shouldn't swim with the dolphins."

"I'm swimming with the dolphins," I tell him firmly and plant my hand on my hip. "This is a dream come true, and the baby." I point to my tummy. "And the mommy." I point to myself. "Are just fine, so daddy can relax."

"Daddy." He laughs. "I still can't believe my little girl calls me that and I get to call her my daughter."

The love shining in his eyes as he talks about Zoe wraps around my heart and hugs tight. They've grown so close, and she has discovered her love of hockey. So have the boys, naturally. Ash takes the three of them skating every chance he gets. Honest to God, he is the best man I've ever known, and I get to call him husband.

"Speaking of little girls." I cup his cheek. "Will a tiny baby girl scare the hell out of you?"

He grimaces. "Oh, God, yes. She's going to be so tiny and delicate." He looks at his hands. "How will I even hold her without breaking her?"

I chuckle. "You'll be fine, but perhaps you're hoping for a boy."

"Here's the thing." He goes so serious it's amusing. "I've been giving this some thought."

I arch a brow, anxious to hear this. "Oh, you have, have you?"

"Zoe really wants a sister. So, if we have a boy, and I'm okay with a boy or a girl, but if we have a boy, that means we're going to have to keep trying until we have a girl. I kind of like the idea of that."

"Ah, what if we keep having boys?"

"Then we keep trying." He pulls me tight and snakes his hands around my back.

"But...when do we stop?" Just how many children does this man I call husband want? "I mean, just how big do you want this family to grow?"

The playful look on his face is so adorable, and if we were alone on this boat, I'd show him just how much I love him. "Let's just say our house is probably going to be too small."

"It has eight bedrooms," I practically shriek, and he pulls me tighter against him and laughs.

"We don't have to move. Some of the kids can share a room."

I poke his chest. "Ohmigod, I get it. You want to grow your own hockey team."

He shrugs casually, "Maybe, but what I really want is to grow old with you."

"Yeah, with your own hockey team!" I smile up at him. "But seriously, I want to grow old with you too, Ash." As the boat slows, I point down as his erection presses against me. "Now get that thing under control. We're swimming with dolphins, and we don't want them to think that's a squid. Not if you want to make your own hockey team."

He laughs, picks me up and spins me around, and as he kisses me with all the love and happiness inside him, I realize Camryn was right all along. Wishes really can come true.

ALSO BY CATHRYN FOX

Boston Bucks

Stick Move

Sticking Around

Sticking Out

Hook 'em Hard (Written in the Boston Bucks World)

Scotia Storms

Away Game (Rebels)

Warm Up (Rebels)

Crash Course (Rebels)

Home Advantage (Rebels)

Shut Out (Rebels)

Moving Target (Rivals)

Face Off (Rivals)

Scoring Fast (Rivals)

Opposing Teams (Rivals)

Fake Out (Rivals)

Deal Breaker (Rebels)

Hard Burn (Rivals)

End Zone

Fair Play

Enemy Down

Keeping Score

Trading Up

All In

Blue Bay Crew
Demolished
Leveled
Hammered

Single Dad
Single Dad Next Door
Single Dad on Tap
Single Dad Burning Up

Players on Ice
The Playmaker
The Stick Handler
The Body Checker
The Hard Hitter
The Risk Taker
The Wing Man
The Puck Charmer
The Troublemaker
The Rule Breaker
The Rookie
The Sweet Talker
The Heart Breaker

In the Line of Duty
His Obsession Next Door
His Strings to Pull
His Trouble in Talulah

His Taste of Temptation

His Moment to Steal

His Best Friend's Girl

His Reason to Stay

Confessions

Confessions of a Bad Boy Professor

Confessions of a Bad Boy Officer

Confessions of a Bad Boy Fighter

Confessions of a Bad Boy Doctor

Confessions of a Bad Boy Gamer

Confessions of a Bad Boy Millionaire

Confessions of a Bad Boy Santa

Confessions of a Bad Boy CEO

Hands On

Hands On

Body Contact

Full Exposure

Dossier

Private Reserve

House Rules

Under Pressure

Big Catch

Brazilian Fantasy

Improper Proposal

Boys of Beachville

Good at Being Bad

Igniting the Bad Boy

Bad Girl Therapy

Stone Cliff Series:

Crashing Down

Wasted Summer

Love Lessons

Wrapped Up

Eternal Pleasure Series

Instinctive

Impulsive

Indulgent

Sun Stroked Series

Seaside Seduction

Deep Desire

Private Pleasure

Captured and Claimed Series:

Yours to Take

Yours to Teach

Yours to Keep

Firefighter Heat Series

Fever

Siren

Flash Fire

Playing For Keeps Series

Slow Ride

Wild Ride

Sweet Ride

Breaking the Rules:

Hold Me Down Hard

Pin Me Up Proper

Tie Me Down Tight

Stand Alone Title:

Hands on with the CEO

Torn Between Two Brothers

Holiday Spirit

Unleashed

Knocking on Demon's Door

Web of Desire

ABOUT CATHRYN

New York Times and *USA today* Bestselling author, Cathryn is a wife, mom, sister, daughter, and friend. She loves dogs, sunny weather, anything chocolate (she never says no to a brownie) pizza and red wine. She has two teenagers who keep her busy with their never ending activities, and a husband who is convinced he can turn her into a mixed martial arts fan. Cathryn can never find balance in her life, is always trying to find time to go to the gym, can never keep up with emails, Facebook or Twitter and tries to write page-turning books that her readers will love.

Connect with Cathryn:
Newsletter https://app.mailerlite.com/webforms/landing/c1f8n1
Twitter: https://twitter.com/writercatfox
Facebook: https://www.facebook.com/AuthorCathrynFox?ref=hl
Blog: http://cathrynfox.com/blog/
Goodreads: https://www.goodreads.com/author/show/91799.Cathryn_Fox

Pinterest http://www.pinterest.com/catkalen/